Weird

MW00326175

VOL.2, NO. 3   **ISSUE 33**

Fiction

Poetry

Publisher and Executive Editor
John Gregory Betancourt

Editor
Doug Draa

Consulting Editor
W. Paul Ganley

Production Manager
Steve Coupe

A Note from the Editor

Well, here we are. This is our third issue of the revived Weirdbook and so far things have been a roaring success. And what with the "third time being a charm" thingy, I'm hoping that this issue will be just as positively received as the previous two.

This issue is going somewhat against the norm in that there are only 9 pieces of long fiction, a single flash piece, from the esteemed James Aquilone, and our talented rogues' gallery of poets this time around. The nine stories are all of novelette or novella length.

I was tempted to call this our "Super-duper Occult Detective Halloween *Spooktacular*," but feared that that would have been overdoing things a wee bit. To be honest, it's purely coincidental but this issue contains 3 detective pieces. One of them is a new "Nick Nightmare" story from British Fantasy Award winner Adrian Cole, another one is from rising star John R. Fultz, and the third is a tale of shamanistic detection set in *the true north strong and free* by the extremely talented Bruno Lombardi.

This issue also sees the return of two genuine masters to the pages of Weirdbook. A powerful, erotic dark fantasy by Jessica Amanda Salmonson and a wonderfully pulpy adventure from the pen of Franklyn Searight himself.

I hope that you enjoy this issue as much as the readers enjoyed the past two issues. Once again I want to thank everyone who has supported us with goodwill and submissions.

Speaking of submissions, I reopened submission on the 1st of October. I'll be closing the window again on the 31st. This means that Weirdbook is now a going concern and not just a three-issue mini-run. This success is due entirely to those who have appeared in these pages. I know that I'm beginning to sound like the proverbial *broken record* (ask your parents), but a magazine is only as good as its contributors. And thanks to those contributors, Weirdbook has become the premier weird fiction magazine on the market today.

I thank you all from the bottom of my heart.

So enjoy!

And HAPPY HALLOWEEN.

—*Doug Draa*

The River Flows to Nowhere

by John R. Fultz

I hate the city.

I hate the nonstop rain and the blood-salted asphalt slick as snakeskin. I hate the smells of mildew, petrol, and despair. The acrid fogs, the vagrants gathered like clumps of fungi beneath rusting bridges. I hate the eternal night of the city, how the sun never shines there. It's an endless labyrinth of neon canyons, trash heaps, and the husks of dead factories.

It changes you in ways you never thought possible.

I hate the city, but I understand it. That's why I get hired for cases like this. It's the only reason I go back to the streets again, something I swore I'd never do. I've broken that vow many times. Every time the money runs out and the booze runs low. Every time some desperate client with a hefty bank account wanders into my office.

The clients talk, sometimes they cry, and I just listen. Usually it's a remorseful father, the kind who spoils his kid relentlessly and can't figure out why junior ends up hating him. Sometimes it's a lady. A mother or a sister. Out of her mind with worry or guilt.

The last thing anybody wants to do is go into the city. So they show me a picture, write me a check, and one more time I break that promise I made to myself. After an hour or two at the bar I head for the old highway. Far sooner than I'd like, I'm staring at a jagged skyline. The city steams like a technicolor volcano beneath a black shroud of smog. It's always night in the city.

I take a one last look at the setting sun, slip the border guard a sawbuck, and drive into a maze of endless twilight. Walls of rusted iron and rotting stone rise up to swallow my vehicle.

I take a good slug from the flask of Old Kentucky nestled inside my jacket. I'm sweating and nauseous. That's the way it always goes when I come back here. I hate the city.

But I've got a job to do.

* * * *

Her name is Dorothy, if you can believe it. I'll try to keep the Oz jokes to a minimum. Dorothy McIntyre. Nineteen years old. Beautiful girl. Her mother hired me for the usual reason: No other options. Dorothy's story sounded all too familiar. Ms. McIntyre explained it from behind a tear-stained handkerchief. Dorothy's father had been out of the picture for some time. Ms. McIntyre didn't talk about him or what his line of work had been. I could've guessed.

"Dorothy was a good girl until she met that…*boy*," she said. "They call him Roach. A horrible name for a horrible person."

"Any idea his real name?" I asked. She didn't know a thing. They never do.

"First, he got her hooked on drugs…"

"Junk?"

"Yes, I believe that's what they call it."

"Anything else?"

"No," said the mother. "At least I don't think so."

"So Dorothy and this Roach never drank?"

"Oh, yes, there was drinking…I thought you meant—"

"It's all right. Go on, Ms. McIntyre." I offered her a glass of bourbon, the dregs from my last bottle. To my surprise, she drank it down in a single gulp. Momma had done her share of drinking.

"She started staying out all night with him. Coming home a mess. A few days into it I caught him in her room. They were doing drugs. Junk. Dropping it into their eyes. I remember the veins on my daughter's arms pulsing and throbbing. Her eyes rolled back in her head, she barked like a dog… I thought she would die right there. I drove that boy out of the house with this…"

She opened her purse and showed me a handgun. Antique six-shooter. Probably wouldn't have fired at all. But I'm sure "Roach" didn't want to take that chance.

"He came back for her two nights later," the mother said. "Dorothy refused to listen to me, she walked the halls all night long. She couldn't sleep or eat…she was so thin."

"Withdrawal," I said. "Very common in these cases. Nothing to worry about."

Sometimes a good lie is all it takes to make a client feel better.

"He broke through a window and took her. Or she broke the window and climbed down to him. I'm not sure. But I saw them running through the hedges. Him in the black leather jacket with the skull stitched on the back. I'd have known it was him even without that silly jacket."

"What was Dorothy wearing?" I asked. A few more procedural questions followed. She gave me a picture of Dorothy. It was taken a year ago, before Roach came into the picture.

The picture showed sunlight, green grass, and the blossoms of a cherry tree. Dorothy stood beneath the branches in a yellow sundress. Her hair was long and wavy, the color of ripe corn, her eyes black as midnight. She was smiling. The kind of smile that makes you feel good, yet also a little sorry for her. I believed Ms. McIntyre when she said her daughter was a good girl.

Good girls are prime currency in the city.

"Promise me you'll find her," my client said. "Bring her back to me…" A fresh welling of tears ran down her cheeks. Dorothy's mother was a looker too. I could see her beauty beyond the patina of pain and worry that marred its surface.

I knew better than to make a promise I couldn't keep.

"I'll do everything I can," I told her. "I have some experience in these matters. Go home and get some rest. I'll contact you in a few days."

Ms. McIntyre paused at my office door and looked back at me.

"Do you think…do you think he took her…*into the city*?"

I nodded.

She nearly fainted. I grabbed her shoulders and she fell into my arms.

"Don't worry," I told her. "I know the city. Leave it to me."

I cashed her check as soon as she left.

* * * *

The picture of Dorothy lies on the passenger's seat next to me. Neon lights seep through the windshield to glide across its glossy surface, painting her face in shades of hot pink, cherry red, and bruised violet.

Most of the outer streets are lined with the burned-out husks of old cars or service vehicles. You can only drive so far into the city before you have to get out and hoof it. Luckily, I have a good parking connection.

A pack of red-eyed starvelings eyes me as I glide by. A bottle of piss or alcohol smashes across my windshield. I hit the gas and take a few corners fast enough to leave them behind. It's not far to the alley that slopes beneath a crumbling tower. At the bottom of the ramp is a steel door like the kind you used to see in bank vaults. I hit the brakes then lay on the horn.

A couple of armed guards appear from nowhere. I pass them my investigator's license and a pair of neatly folded fifties. They hand me back the license and the vault door opens. I glide through the rows of vehicles, most of them left to rot here years ago. But there are a few clients like me, a few machines left in working order. I pick a spot near the exit, pay the attendent, and get my gear from the trunk. All of this is going on my expense report.

A longcoat hides the hand cannon strapped beneath my right arm. The picture of Dorothy slides into my right pocket, along with my silver flask. The hunting knife slides neatly into my left boot. Sometimes you have to work quietly in the city. That's when a good knife comes in handy.

The door I use to exit the parking vault is hardly visible from the street. I hit the asphalt and head toward the glittering chaos of the inner city. The light rain is steady and warm. Gusts of wind kick up swirls of dirty cellophane. Sheets of hanging moss dance like restless ghosts. Seven blocks later I spot an old woman with a black suitcase walking directly toward me. There's nobody else on the street. I'm in a canyon whose walls are pocked with glassless windows. Firelight flickers through rectangular orficies. The telltale signs of squatters and drug dens.

The woman with the black suitcase is closer now. I see her wrinkled face, the sway of her wide hips. Her hair is long and matted, her eyes hidden by the brim of a moth-eaten hat. She wears a raggedy longcoat over a tattered dress and army boots. She clutches the suitcase to her breast with both hands and walks with a slow limp, like she's never been in any kind of hurry. One of her hands rubs the surface of the case like petting the back of a lizard.

I cross to the other side of the street but she stops, head turning to follow me.

I reach the far sidewalk, step over a junkie who's either sleeping or dead in the gutter, and keep my eyes trained forward. The woman with the black suitcase laughs behind me. It sounds like a death rattle, like her throat's been cut and later healed into a mass of scar tissue.

I turn the corner and leave the horrid laughter behind me.

Up ahead I spot the globe of crimson neon blinking above *Frankie's Utopia*. A crowd of anxious junkies waits outside, quivering like snakes, waiting for their chance to gain admission. I walk to the head of the line, show my ID, and pay off the bouncer. He lets me inside.

Down a set of filthy stairs, through a reinforced iron door, and the pumping bass of the club rattles my bones. The sheer volume makes conversation near impossible. The lights flash and strobe, a mass of half-naked bodies writhes like some great amoebic organism. The room reeks of sweat, cheap perfume, and sex. A dozen clashing colors of smoke rise from the crowd. Overtaxed veins pulse beneath shallow layers of skin. The place is a junkie's paradise. Hence the name.

At the bar Frankie recognizes me. She winks, pours me a shot of bourbon. Her mohawk haircut is covered with glitter, and her contacts sparkle in rainbow hues. Looking at her makes me dizzy.

"How's it hangin', D?" she yells in my ear. "Been awhile…"

I nod and show her the picture of Dorothy McIntyre.

Frankie frowns and looks at me like I just spoiled her evening. She picks up the photo, examines it, then shakes her head.

"Nobody like *that* in the city," she shouts above the assault of the bass.

"At least not anymore, right?" She smiles at my little jest.

I ask if she knows a guy named Roach, wears a skull on his back.

She grins, points across the teeming dance floor. And there he is, Mr. Roach in his skullface jacket, nodding his head, sweating and jerking to the industrial funk. I leave some money on the bar, drink the shot, and make my way through the crowd.

* * * *

"I swear, I don't know where she is!"

It's hard for Roach to talk through his broken teeth and bloody lips, but he manages. He squirms across the puddles of piss and petrol. I grab him up again, slam him against the alley wall. His veins pulse like tiny snakes trying to burst free of his skin.

I drive a knee into his stomach. He pukes. Starting to sober up.

"Tell me another lie and I'll get mad. Dorothy McIntyre. Who'd you sell her to?"

Roach wipes blood and bile from his mouth. He's crying now.

I slap him. "Don't cry. Be a big boy. Who has Dorothy?"

The punk coughs and shivers. "I can't say anything…they'll kill me."

I bring my face real close to his. I let him see the big knife, feel its point on his eyelid. "I'll kill you. After I take your eyes. Tell me now and you'll have a chance to run. Get out of the city. If you don't, it'll kill you anyway. Just a matter of time."

Roach stiffens, too scared to breathe.

"Who has her?" I ask again. Neon glints off the naked blade.

Roach's eyes swivel toward either end of the alleyway. He whispers like he's afraid of his own voice.

"The Man…" he stutters, coughs. "The Man in the White Limousine."

I put the knife away, let him fall back into the mire.

"You stupid waste of skin," I tell him. "Now you better run."

He takes my advice, scurrying like a rat into the shadows and piles of trash.

When I leave the alley there's a boy with a sideways face picking up bottles in the street. He looks at me like I'm a tasty morsel, flashes the fangs lining his vertical mouth. I pull out the hand cannon, let him see the glimmer of its metal. He hisses at me, moves on down the road, disappears among a jumble of rusted-out vehicles.

I stand for a moment in the street, getting my bearings. The White Limousine never comes to this part of town. I've got some walking to do. Maybe I should just go home, forget about Dorothy McIntyre, write her off as another unsolved case. Just another victim of the city.

I take a good shot from the flask and look at her picture. She comes from a world of sunlight. And now she's lost in darkness. The rain picks up, turning from steady drizzle into dedicated downpour. Warm and oily. Like blood.

Damn it.

I shove the picture back into my pocket, turn up my coat's heavy collar, and start walking.

* * * *

On 459th street I pass the Man Who Speaks With Shadows. He's always there, like a phantom shaman who haunts the block. He stands on a pyramid of rusted shopping carts, waving his arms in the rain and muttering gibberish. His face is black with grime and madness, his grey beard a tangled crow's nest. His long robe is a stitched-together quilt of every color that has faded to no color at all. I pass by as far away as possible. I can only reach the River District by going down 459th. All the other streets heading this direction are blocked by toppled skyscrapers, mountains of scrap, or barriers of rubble.

"The River flows to Nowhere!" shouts the old man. He's looking down at me now, bathed in the orange flicker of alley-fires. "To Nowhere!"

I keep walking. He's harmless.

"Give up the skin and you give up the heart!" he bellows. "What are we without hearts? What are *they*? The current carries us all toward oblivion! The River flows to Nowhere!"

Farther down the road I can't hear his ravings anymore. The rain lightens up, but the road is still waterlogged. Steam rises from grates, along with hollow moans of agony. I hear screaming somewhere down below. The city sewers are another world altogether. Couldn't pay me enough to go down there.

This close to the river nature has started to take back the city. Green vines with black leaves crawl up through the pavement to hug the facades of dead towers. Weeds grow waist-high from cracked asphalt, and sheets of purple fungus smother the concrete. Sometimes things like bloated eels crawl out of the sewers and go hunting up here. They feed on each other when they can't find rats or stray junkies.

Now I turn off the main avenue. The snipers up ahead will spot me soon if I keep going that direction. The only way I'm going to get close to the Man in the White Limousine is by navigating the Intestinal, a maze of alleys that leads eventually to the River District. I take out the hand cannon. The weight of it in my hand makes me feel a bit safer in the dark and narrow places. A bit.

Bits of bone and fabric line the alleyway, broken glass, the occasional skull, sometimes a gnawed skeleton. Two-headed rats skitter away at my approach, then reconvene to finish their feast when I pass. I take a right, a left, then two more rights, following tiny signs graven into the brickwork. Anybody else would be totally lost in here. Knowing these kinds of things is why I get paid so well.

Eventually I come to the Alley of Ecstasies. The girls here crawl like serpents across the slimy ground. Forked tongues flicker from their bright red lips, and they whisper filthy secrets. They offer me obscure pleasures as I step carefully between them. Their heads twist to follow me. Their bodies are covered with mud and green-grey scum, but otherwise perfectly proportioned. They're not exactly human, despite their spot-on female anatomies. My stomach turns as they caress my thighs with their long fingers, begging for my favor.

I stop right in the middle of them when I see the man lying at the far end of the alley. Two of the girls crawl across his naked body. His mouth hangs open, head resting on a pile of cast-off clothing. They do unspeakable things with his body, contorting him like a rag doll. He moans and cries out. I turn away, take out the picture of Dorothy and stare at it until the moaning stops. The man stands up, pulls on his clothes, and looks at me with naked embarrassment. He runs from the girls hissing at his feet.

They've given up on me, sensing I'm somehow immune to their charms. They bare yellow fangs, warning me to beat it. I drop a few bucks into the slime and make my way quickly to the alley's end. The maze continues, only now there is a second maze of conjoined fire escapes rising above me. I've reached the part of the Intestinal where the buildings still support life. Hunched figures move and scramble through the network of back iron, like fat spiders in a web. Sometimes garbage drops into the allies from above. I watch my step.

I follow the hidden signs, the ones I learned long ago when I was young and reckless. Back then I saw the city as a challenge, an adventure. I owned nothing back then, and so I had nothing to lose. I spent years in this place before I discovered a way out.

Something to live for besides hustling.

Her name was Carolyn.

* * * *

On my way out of the Intestinal I see the woman with the black suitcase again. She sits on a pile of crumbled stone, cradling the suitcase, watching me pass into the River District.

"Do you know where you're going?" she asks in that rasping, scarred voice.

I pause, for some reason I can't name. Maybe the urgency of her question.

"Yes," I tell her. "I know."

And she laughs at me again. I leave her laughing as I walk into the road beyond the maze.

The streetlights glow white and orange, rising on iron poles from the avenue at regular intervals. The folk here wear dark clothing and heavy cloaks. Their skulls poke through the skin of their faces like fingertips through worn-out pairs of gloves. They shamble about drawing rickshaws or hand carts loaded with cages full of chickens, hairless cats, or snuffling mutant things without names. The people of River District are meat-eaters.

I blend into the crowd along the Street of Succulents, moving between the stalls where hocks of pink meat glisten on hooks. Hooded vendors shout the merits of their products. The smells of animal shit and barbecue smoke fill the gloom. A couple of stands offer tentacled creatures pulled from the river, and a few even display old-fashioned fish with silver scales. Gourmet food.

Several of these places offer fresh human limbs for those with truly discriminating tastes. I might look into these places in my search for Dorothy McIntyre, but I knew better. If the Man in the White Limousine had bought her, she wouldn't end up in someone's stew pot. She'd be in for something far worse than a slaughterhouse death.

The crowd here reminds me of *Frankie's Utopia*, but without the blaring lights and noise. And there's no joy here, not even the simulated kind that junkies are always chasing. No, here the citizens speak in hushed voices, until an argument breaks out and someone gets stabbed or strangled to death. An undercurrent of rage and fear runs through the lives of everyone who lives in the River District. They know who their masters are here, and they're closer to them than anybody else in the city. They have good reason to be afraid.

The Children Without Mouths march through the crowd, which splits immediately to make way for them. I move to the side like everyone else, keeping out of their direct line of sight. They're almost cute, these little enforcers. They might be 5, or 6-year-olds if they were wholly human. But like the girls who crawl the alley, there's not much human left in them.

Fifteen of the little fascists stalk by my position, turning their tiny heads in every direction. Their big, round eyes scan the crowd and the stalls, looking for who-knows-what. Their tiny fists clutch curved knives and barbed whips. They wear dirty rags beneath cloaks of gleaming silver chain mail. Their faces would be adorable if not for the complete lack of lips or mouths, and the raw menace bleeding from their eyes. A smooth layer of waxy flesh covers the lower half of their skulls, beginning just below their tender little noses.

When the last of them passes by, I resume my walk. I hear the cracking of whips behind me, the shouts of alarm. They've found a victim, someone to haul away for whatever mysterious reason drives them. I used to think they worked exclusively for the Limousines, but I learned better. There are other powers in the city. The Children Without Mouths are mercenaries. Like everyone else in the city, they're for sale to the highest bidder.

At the far end of the avenue I reach the riverwalk. Black water stretches away from the shore, and dark shapes swim in its depths. The fogs hang thick above the rippling surface, so dense that the far shore is impossible to see. The big venus flytrap flowers growing along the riverbank yawn wide as I approach. Sometimes they capture a stray pigeon or some other bit of vermin. They'll take your arm off if you get too close.

Here on a platform overlooking the rainswept water, the Women Who Dance with Fire begin their nightly performance. Thirteen of them, naked as savages, swirling lit torches through the air, juggling them back and forth with hands, feet, and knees. Tattooes of ancient fire gods writhe across their backs and breasts. Their smooth skin is marred and scabbed over in places where the fire has caught them over the years. Their faces are invisible behind masks of polished bronze carved into the likeness of leering demons. The demon-masks are vaguely Asian in design, yet the Women Who Dance with Fire are of no specific race or nationality. They come from all over, drawn to the fire like addicts are drawn to the Junk.

I lean against a light pole, watching the cross streets. Waiting for the White Limousine to come by. I know it will be here eventually. Waiting is a part of my job.

The fire-women undulate to the rhythm of drums from hidden speak-ers. The twirling fires mesmerize me, make me less conscious of my surroundings than I should be. I sip from the flask, and the taste of Old Kentucky makes me remember what it should be helping me to forget.

I remember Carolyn. I met her here, twelve years ago, on this same street. We watched the fire-dancers and took a barge along the river. We ended up in her father's penthouse, looking down over the whole rotten, steaming city. I had never been up that high. I knew I didn't belong there, but it was Carolyn who made me feel like I did.

Days later her father found out she was seeing me. He did what any father would do: Forbid his daughter to hang out with a no-good street hustler. Next time I went to meet her I wound up tied to a chair in a burned-out warehouse. Her father and his goons stood over me in their pinstriped suits, looking at me like I was an insect. I was certain they were going to stomp me then. But they just worked me over good, broke my nose and a couple of fingers.

I remember her father's face close to mine. The sour hell of his breath, his crooked nose.

"Do you know who I am?" he asked.

I nodded. My lips were too swollen to speak.

"Stay away from my daughter," he said, "and you'll stay alive."

I nodded again. I would have told him anything to stop the beating.

They threw me in the river, and I barely crawled out of the frigid water before something ropy and hungry could pull me to the bottom. I vomited riverwater and was sick for a week. I promised myself that I'd never see Carolyn again. But eventually I went looking for her.

She wasn't hard to find. She had been waiting for me here, by the fire-dancers. We decided to run away, leave the city and her father be-hind. She stole some money from his safe, bought a used vehicle, and we bribed our way across the border.

We built a life together in the sunshine, made a little home surround-ed by green living things. Had a baby. Best time of my life. I almost forgot about the city.

Six years we were happy together. Safe. Content.

But all of it ended when the White Limousine found us.

* * * *

Before I realize the flask is empty, I'm already half-drunk. The city has that effect on me.

The fire-women are still spinning, and the drums are making my head throb. I think about finding a flophouse to spend the night. I might have to come back here tomorrow and resume my watch.

Before I move away from the light pole, something slips about my neck, pulling me backwards. My skull slams against the pole, and the wire digs deep into my esophagus. A black bulk rises before me, blotting out the flame dancers. Dark glasses reflect twin images of my panicked face. A pair of black-gloved fists on either side of my neck, straining, pulling.

The man before me removes his glasses, and I look into his eyes. But they're not eyes at all, just pulsing orbs of translucent mucous, glistening like toad flesh. He croaks at me, and the last of the air rushes out of my lungs.

Sleep or death comes now. I'm not sure there's much of a difference.

* * * *

I wake up to a splash of icy water in the face. Deja vu strikes me like a fist to the teeth, followed closely by an *actual* fist to the teeth. My head jerks back. I spit blood from swollen lips. The skin of my neck burns and bleeds. There will be a nasty scar there if I survive. A big "if."

Three men with bull-necks stand about me. Their coats are long and black, although one of them has shed his outerwear. His shirt is gleaming silver silk, his well-tailored pants charcoal grey. His fists are covered by black gloves, and the gloves are covered with my blood. His eyes are gleaming toad-flesh.

My arms are locked about something, secured behind my back. A metal chair.

"Hit him again," says a voice from the shadows. It echoes in a way that lets me know this is one of the hollowed-out factories that line the River District.

Thunder rolls into my skull again. A tooth flies from my mouth.

It takes a few seconds for me to come back from this one. My vision is blurred, the ribs of the chair are cold against my naked back. At least they left my pants on. And my boots.

"Die with your boots on," they always say. Makes a kind of weird sense.

The sound of a purring engine fills the dank air. Twin points of light draw near, defining themselves as two headlights. The White Limousine pulls up close, its windows black as tar, revealing nothing of who's inside. But I already know.

The door opens and Carolyn's father steps out. He's every bit as tall and broad as I remember. A granite statue with a few more wrinkles carved into its face. His suit is immaculate. A silver skull pin decorates his lapel, like the kind Nazi SS commanders used to wear. He walks with a cane, fat fingers wrapped around its platinum head.

He comes to stand in front of me, silent as death. I spit more blood and force my head up to meet his eyes. They're cold, like blue ice. Carolyn's eyes were the same color. I bite back the hate and the sickness in my gut. Force a smile across my inflamed lips.

"Son of a bitch," I mumble.

He doesn't smile.

"I warned you, D," he says. His voice is the sliding of a tomb door. The crush of a gravel ton as it grinds your bones. "Told you never to come back here. This is no place for you. Never has been."

"I'm looking for a girl."

Carolyn's father shifts his weight, sighs. Someone brings him a chair. He wipes the seat with a handkerchief from his breast pocket and sits down in front of me. Leans in real close.

"Carolyn's gone, you poor bastard," he says.

"Not her," I tell him. "Dorothy McIntyre. Her mother hired me."

He looks at me like I'm speaking some language he's never heard.

"She wants her runaway daughter back," I say. "Sound familiar?"

He glances at the gloved thug. I take a couple more shots to the jaw before the bruiser backs away. Carolyn's dad leans in close again.

"Do you know who I work for?" he asks. "Do you even begin to understand my business?"

"Flesh trade," I say.

He smiles. It's a terrible, gargoyle smile. Unnnaturally white teeth. He even laughs. Turns to his thugs, who chuckle. I have no idea what's so funny.

"The flesh trade," he repeats my words. "There is that. But there is so much more. The flesh is only the beginning, boy. I work for *The Skinless Ones*. We all must serve somebody, so I serve *them*. The flesh is weak, but limited. There are so many other ways to suffer. So many alternatives to blood and bone. I think you came back here because you want to discover these things for yourself."

I shake my head, wince at the pain it causes.

"I only want the girl. The mother is well-off. I can arrange a ransom."

"It's too late for that, D." He turns around in the chair and motions to one of his goons. Someone brings him a small box of dark mahogony with an emerald clasp. He settles it on his knees. Rings glitter on his big fingers.

"You displeased me when you stole my daughter," he says. "You ruined her. Gave her an illegimate child. You took what was mine. I should have killed you then. But you reminded me of myself...when I was young and stupid. So I gave you a warning instead. Now you leave me no choice."

I flex my calf and feel the knife buried deep in my boot. I have no chance of reaching it. Not with my hands chained behind the chair.

"Unlock these chains," I ask him. "Give me a fighting chance."

Carolyn's dad laughs again. His fingers run across the clasp of the box. He opens the lid, stands, and turns it upside down. A dozen or so black worms fall across my head, shoulders, and lap. Cold and slimy, bristling with short black hairs.

"These are the Worms That Feed On Dreams," he says. "They will feast until there's nothing left of you but an empty shell."

"I loved her." I tell him. "Why did you have to kill her?"

"She was worthless. She disobeyed me. So I gave her to my masters. I'll do the same with you, once you're properly hollowed out."

"What about my baby? Your own grandson…"

"I am not entirely without mercy. I pitied Carolyn's little bastard," he says. "It's out *there* somewhere. On the streets."

I scream long and hard as the worms become tentacles invading my mouth and nostrils. But worse than that, they send fire coursing through my brain, filling my skull with flame. I'm twitching and straining, but the chains hold me tight.

The worms strip away my memories one by one: My mother, who died when I was a boy. I'll never know her face again. My time in the alleys of the city…the gangs, the drugs, the fights…all gone. Carolyn… no, that's the memory I can't bear to lose. It will kill me as surely as a shot to the head.

I feel them tearing at it now…*what was her name?*

Some kind of commotion begins around me. A rush of blurred images. Something quicker than the eye moves between the thugs. Red fountains spray across the concrete floor, across my face. Something rips the worms away from my head, one by one, tossing them into the shadows. I realize then that my screaming has stopped.

For a moment I black out, clinging to the memory of Carolyn's face. *What color were her eyes?*

Then I'm back in the real world, and someone is unlocking the chains on my wrists. Something snuffles and snorts and chews nearby, digging into the spilled guts of the big bruiser. He lies on the concrete, body split apart like an overripe melon. What is the thing devouring him? It's like a canine, but more like spider. Its lucent skin steams and smokes. Bloody light spills from the eight eyes set about its head, most of which is a fanged snout. It squats and feeds, suckles on the goon's viscera, then moves quick as lightning to the next body and continues its feast.

The chains fall away. I hear the squealing of tires and the roaring of an engine. The White Limousine races away, rear fender striking sparks as it leaves the scene of carnage.

A lean figure stands before me, dark face staring from beneath a mildewed hat. Next to her a black suitcase sits open and empty. A strange animal musk fills my nostrils.

"Do you know where you're going?" she rasps at me. When I don't respond, she turns and whistles. The smoking dog-spider-thing scampers into the big suitcase, licking its chops. The old woman leans over and closes it tight. She clicks it shut and turns to face me.

"What is that thing?" I ask, rubbing my wrists and wishing for a shot of Old Kentucky.

The old woman glances at the black suitcase.

"My son," she says.

I try to stand but fall to the cold floor instead.

What was her name?

Carolyn? Dorothy?

Her eyes were…

"Do you know where you're going?" asks the old woman.

"He works for the Skinless Ones…" I mumble. "*He gave her to them…*"

The lights dim. The wet concrete becomes a comfy pillow.

"I know," says the old woman.

She touches my cheek with gentle fingers.

And I'm out again.

* * * *

I wake up fully clothed. My shirt is torn, stained with blood and grime. My face is swollen, my head ringing. My tongue probes a hole in my gums where an incisor used to be. I'm a mass of aching flesh and bones.

Firelight warms my shivering body. I'm lying in an alley somewhere on the edge of town. The woman with the black suitcase sits on the other side of the fire. Mounds of trash and rubble form a crude stockade about us. Rain drizzles across a latex tarp suspended above the flames, drips through tiny holes to sizzle on the embers.

My companion offers me a bottle. I struggle to a sitting position and sniff at the liquid. Old Kentucky. I drink deep, letting the warmth of the booze rush through my limbs, settle in my belly. Always takes the pain away. At least for a little while.

I pass it back. Her eyes are pools of darkness beneath the brim of the broad hat.

The big suitcase sits close to her knee.

"What's in the case?" I ask.

She answers my question with a question.

"Do you know where you are going?"

I blink at her, rub my eyes.

"I'm looking for a girl," I say.

"What is her name?" she asks.

I stare at the heaps of trash about us as if there might be a clue hidden there. I run my hands across my battered body, looking for pockets. Looking for answers. I discover a big knife in my boot and a hand cannon strapped under my arm. In the pocket of my jacket I find a parking stub and a photograph.

The girl is beautiful. Blonde hair, dark eyes, soft skin against a green backdrop. A cherry tree, a sad smile. Right away I know that I loved her. Love her.

"Carolyn," I tell the old woman. "Her name is Carolyn."

She reaches over and takes the picture from my hand.

"That's not Carolyn," she says. "I'm afraid you're too late."

She drops the photo into the flames. I watch it wither and curl and turn to ash. She gives me another slug of the whiskey. I drink it down.

"The River flows to Nowhere," she says, and turns away from me. She caresses the surface of the black suitcase, which seems to throb as if breathing. She might be sobbing. It's hard to tell.

I force myself to stand up. My head spins. The parking stub says there's a vehicle waiting for me somewhere. I stagger away from the woman with the black suitcase, wincing with pain at every step. My belly feels hollow, empty, but I know better than to eat city food. Anyway, the emptiness feels deeper than hunger. I've lost something. The city has taken it from me.

I follow the address on the stub and regain my wheels. I drive away from eternal night and endless rain, putting distance between myself and a thousand secrets.

I swear I'll never go back.

I hate the city.

The Amnesiac's Lament
by Scott R Jones

There's only a few hundred thousand of us left, and only a thousand of us awake at any given time.

That's a rough estimate, obviously. Could be more, could be far less. I'm told there was a period, during the early days, when we knew exactly how many were awake, and how many slept, and of those sleepers how many dreamed, and about what, but record keeping is sketchy now. Too many of the terminals that monitor the Deep Dendo are corroded or burned away or dissolved in a gout of acid from a passing dhole or something worse and besides, it's not like it matters. Knowing exact numbers. Knowing anything. Not any more.

Hell, I don't even know why I'm writing this.

That's a lie. I *know* why. Somewhere in that vast array of sleeping bodies laced together in sticky pits of artificial neural tissue below me, is a dreamer who used to be a writer, or dreams she was one. Less than that, even; some random oneiric spasm is happening in her brain and she's remembered she once spoke to a writer at a party, or fucked someone who said they were a writer. Or he. The dreamer could be a he, though the probability is low. Not many of those left, writers or otherwise. Males tend to burn out quick in the Deep Dendo, or at least their egos do, which is the same thing.

She's dreaming it, producing a phantom scrap of data, a little ghost of information which has as its subject the act of writing. That ghost gets fed into the Deep Dendo, where it merges with all the other ghosts: fragments of old lives, dusty intellectual musings, lacework fantasies, memories of the old world, fears of the new. Horrors and ecstasies. It all enters the Deep Dendo, and the Deep Dendo sifts and flattens and knits and makes connections and when it's done with its esoteric work, the Deep Dendo burst-casts it through the noosphere in rapidly modulated n-waves. Cycle after cycle of randomly generated exo-personality, a churning wash of denatured soul-stuff, which we, the Awakened, pick up with the implants buried in our temples at birth, the super-fine antennas bored into our foreheads like inflamed humming *bindis* before we could take our third gasp of air.

See, that's the writer part talking. "The Awakened". No one calls us that. *We* don't even call ourselves that. Ghosts don't sleep, or wake up. They just *are*, and that's all we are. Shells, treading what's left of the earth on our slow, hopeless missions, camouflaged in the ghosts of our shared past.

I'm not even an "I", not really. My name (such as it is) is a randomly generated designation: this cycle, I'm "Sunset Grey Theremin", and there's a cluster of quicksilver algorithms frantically fucking each other behind the screen of those words, too. Can't be too careful, I guess. There may be something of what I was, who I used to be, buried deep, somewhere deeper than the alien machines of the Deep Dendo can go, but I'll never see it again. Maybe when this mission is over, I might feel like myself for a moment, before I sleep again, and forget.

It's safer this way. Real personalities, real *people,* they don't last out there, outside of the protected caverns, beyond the Voorish Domes. An unshielded human mind, an intact, singular, relatively sane ego-complex? Yeah, outside of the Domes, *that* shines like a beacon, attracting every nightmare thing from miles around. Shines for a little while only, before being blasted to screaming shards, dust in the wind. Sometimes takes a week, sometimes a day. When the Old Ones first returned, it could happen in minutes.

We're a little tougher now, sure, but no one goes topside without a D-D feed at full strength. I don't go outside unless I'm a hundred thousand people at once.

I have to be crazy to go outside.

I woke up yesterday, took a minimal D-D feed to re-orient and debrief, prepare for my mission: Great Western Desert in what used to be Australia, subterranean op, which means a Yithian complex. I'm one-third of a tech recovery team. From here to there, travelling east, it's only three Hoffman-Price jumps to the target. Getting posted to Ajna Ram in the Himalayas is a bitch, but it has its perks: we won't have to get near the Thing in the Pacific at all. When you're outside, it's best to avoid taxing the D-D feed if you can, and those coordinates chew up the camouflage like the tissue paper it is. Nothing escapes the black hole that is the Big C.

Tomorrow I'll go outside, above ground, into their world. It was always their world, of course. We just used it while they napped. My eyes will burn with the things I'll see, and my ears will fill with the screams, and my guts will twist and heave as the reality around me is rendered into paste, into some other reality that's not fit for what we used to be. We're not that thing anymore, though. I don't know what we are, exactly. Survivors, at the least. We survive until we don't, and there's no guarantee I'll come back this time. Not that it matters.

I'll tag this file, leave it open and append it to the mission record. If this Writer fragment is as strong as it feels, it might appreciate the chance to finish.

* * * *

sunnygeesunnygeeohsunnygeethereminareyouintheresunnygee?

There's a heaving mass of flesh and razor-sharp spines over my left shoulder. I can just see it there, floating in the corner of my vision, a Nameless Horror reflected in the dirty faceplates of my companions, and I can tell from the look on *their* faces that the mass is budding fresh foulness into the air, bubbles of bone and hooked teeth in puckering mouths all of which are whispering the same refrain as the parent body...

sunnygeetheremingreyonemanyonesunnygeecomeoutandplay

"You want I should, y'know, zap that thing for ya?" Damocles Muffin Cringe says. Her fingers do a little jig on the hilt of the Yithian lightning-pistol at her belt. "If it's bothering you, I mean."

areyouintheregreyonemanyone? whoisthiswhatfoodisthis?

I check the D-D field output on my HUD. Persona-clusters are sloughing away from the outer layers at a humming pace. If we were staying here, I'd be worried enough to take Dam up on her offer.

"No, I'm good, thanks," I reply as I set up for our third and final jump. "I'm nearly done. Let it gibber."

"Yeah, well, hurry it up," says Livid Ransom Stormcell. "Because it's irritating the living *fhtagn* outta me."

The equipment doesn't always make it through a jump unscathed. Each of us carries a collapsible armature for generating a Hoffman-Price bubble, an armature that's left behind, and if they break, or get fried in transit, well...you don't want to be stranded out here. We've had some luck, though, each jump has been clean. We're in the ruins of some ancient Japanese city, the concrete of a crumbling street beneath us, but our boots are still damp with phosphorescent black sludge from the nameless Sri Lankan swamp we just left.

sunnygeethereminsunnygeeohsunniestofgreysfeeeedusss

The armature is up now, and I plug a key into a slot in the base of the spindly construction. The keys are long ovoid chunks of engraved silver suspended in a grav field casing. In the early days of the jump tech, when the legendary Carter Corp ran the project, one had to master years worth of esoteric knowledge and hyperspatial mathematics to turn the key properly, and it had to be done *by hand*. I shake my head in disbelief as the key twists and rotates on its own, spinning up the correct coordinates in the field. There's a whoofing sound as air is displaced, followed by a high ringing as the armature is engulfed in the Hoffman-Price bubble. It stains the air like an oil spill and I can glimpse sand and aching blue sky through the shimmer.

feeeeedusssunnygreyonemanyonefeedusyouressen—

There's a brief flash of blue light over my shoulder, and the tang of burnt ozone fills my sinuses as the nameless thing squeals and folds itself away into the reality it came from. I look up to see Livid holstering her pistol.

"What? It wanted your essence. And I *said* it was irritating me." She points north up the street, where pustulent sores are breeding in the air, taking on mass. "Besides, it's got friends on the way."

Without another word, we enter the bubble, one after the other.

* * * *

Nameless Horrors are everywhere and nowhere, filtering into the world from the spaces between, and sure, that one "wanted my essence", but Liv didn't *have* to blast it. Nameless Horrors are barely *real* in the first place; their manifestation is almost entirely psychic. They all want our essential Self, want to feed on our sanity, but that's why we have the D-D field camo. And if *I* can't have access to who I really am, there's little chance a Nameless Horror could get to it.

Still. That's Liv. Fiery, temperamental, a bit of a bully, and a crack shot. And Dam? She's gruff, sure. A no-nonsense soldier, but in behind that she's a faithful friend. And me? What's Sunny Grey Theremin like? Well, I'm analytical, observant, the philosopher of the team. And a writer. The Writer.

We're a good, well-seasoned unit with a dozen missions behind us. Together we've seen some awful shit, but we always come through for each oth—…wait. No.

No no no. None of that is true. We're randomly selected. Before today, I've never seen these women. This is our *first* mission. Our first. And whether we're successful or not, our last. Our only mission. I'll never see them again.

The Writer. I'm no more a writer than Dam is a good soldier or Liv a bully. We're not characters in some narrative. We're barely *people.* Shit. This fragment is *strong.* What is going on?

This mission can't be over soon enough.

* * * *

We exit the Hoffman-Price bubble at the right coordinates, unscathed and calm. Well, Dam and Liv are calm, anyway. I have to make a show of it. I'm rattled as I remove the silver key from its lock, trying not to think too hard about how it followed us through to this side. I don't feel right. I don't know *how* I'm supposed to be feeling, but it's not like this.

The heat here is monstrous, more than oppressive. Ever since old Sol was raped by a wandering Carcosan mini-Nebula, her radiation output has been all over the charts, her magnetic field spasming, lashing out at Earth on the daily. We would have crisped beneath her assaults a thousand times already were it not for whatever-it-was that the Old Ones did to the planet when they returned. Yet another proof that this is not our world, not anymore.

Not our world. Not our sun. And this place (*Pnakotus*, they called it) is not our place. It's not our place, to be standing at the lip of a well that will drop us into a library of the Yith. But we're here anyway.

"It was us that did it, y'know," Liv says, and Dam huffs in response.

"You can stow that conspiracy garbage any time, Liv."

"Seriously, though. What were they thinking? *Hey, let's correlate the contents of our knowledge! Let's pull up prehistoric alien death-tech from beneath the sands!*"

"It wasn't *death-tech*," I correct her.

"Oh, yeah?" Liv unholsters her lightning-pistol and wiggles it in the air, laughing.

"Well," I say, feeling sheepish. "Other than those. Which we *need*, as much as we need the D-D field. It was an archive, like this one. A Yithian library."

Liv holsters the pistol and shoulders her pack, checks a reading in her HUD, takes a sip of water from one tube in her helmet, spits it into another.

"Yeah, well, fuck those ancient fungoid mollusc-scholars *and* our own brainiacs *and* anyone else who thought digging here was a good idea. The stars got right double-quick once these wells opened up, fuck knows why."

Dam is fuming now. She anchors a zipline to a chunk of masonry at the edge of the well.

"I said *stow it*, Liv. We've got work here."

"Yeah, yeah. I'm just sayin', y'know, it was us who did it."

It's not true. Or, if it is, then no one knows *why*. We had reached a point where new knowledge piled on new knowledge, and every answer to every question opened up more avenues for discovery. Fresh questions, staggering revelations, addictive novelties, impossible tech. It was said that the Hoffman-Price transport system, with its proprietary Carter Corp SilverKey®™ jump tech, *may* have thinned the barriers between worlds, but we had no real understanding of what those barriers *were* in the first place. Still don't. Some claimed it was the wholesale recreational use of Tillinghast Resonators that tweaked our species to finally *see* what was always already around us. Novel drugs that blazed through all levels of society were blamed: NewJack Lao, the Yellow Powder, Hexstacy.

Many factors were at play. And it could all have been coincidence. Discovery of the Yithian complexes, and the Deep Dendo tech they contained, *did* seem to trigger the Return, though. Not long after the first Voorish Domes were opened (*The Dome is for Dreaming,* went the commercial) "the stars came right". Whatever *that* meant. It certainly had little to do with the position of the actual stars. But *come right* they did, and the Old Ones returned in all their shrieking potency. The First City, the Dreaming City, warped in from elsewhere or rose from the previously vacant deeps of the Pacific or some combination of the two, and the Thing inside it opened its eyes and that? That was it. An abyss, *the* Abyss, yawned wide beneath humanity. We fell in.

The end.

Only it wasn't, was it. There's more yet to be written.

I'm shaking, nervous, and I suddenly realize it's because I'm feeling almost *authentic*. That's not good. I check the strength of my D-D feed and find nothing to worry about, it's at 97%, but I worry anyway. This fragment, this *Writer*…what is it doing to me? It should have passed by now, like the flu, like a cloud before a stiff wind, but it's only getting stronger. Denser. It *feels* like *me,* but I don't recognize it. I breathe deep, try to focus, hope the others don't notice my discomfort.

I attach my zipline to the anchor in the masonry and leap backward, following Dam and Liv into the black.

* * * *

We stay quiet in the library, like you do, but not out of consideration for other guests. It's for survival. Before we were a gleam in the eye of some primeval marsupial ancestor, the Yith prisoned something awful deep in the earth, below their cities. Centuries of war with the whistlers proved they could not be killed, so into the pits they were sent. Locked away. Or so the Yithian records claimed. And like every other monstrosity chained in the deep dark places and dimensional pockets of Earth, these prisoners escaped when the end came, when the walls got thin. There's a flying polyp mega-colony occupying what used to be the Sahara now. Why they chose that desert over this is one mystery out of thousands.

"Whistle if you see anything," Liv snickers.

"Fuck you," I whisper. "Have you not seen the footage? What those things can do to a person?"

The scale of this place intimidates. Another place that's not for us, that never was for us. There's a word for this architecture, and I struggle for a moment trying to recall it before the Writer offers it up to me...

"Cyclopean," I breathe, and the others turn to look at me. By the dim illumination in her helmet, I can see Dam narrowing her eyes.

"What was that, Sunny?"

"It's the word. For this style of build—...for this place. Pnakotus. It's cyclopean."

Liv fidgets with the stock of her pistol while Dam steps to me, toe to toe. There's a scraping hiss that sends a cold shock down my spine as her faceplate contacts mine and slides to one side. Dam's eyes travel all over my face, pupils wide.

"What's going on in there? Checked your feed lately? Where you at?"

"Hundred percent, Dam. Just under, maybe..."

"Hmm." She turns from me, finally. "Liv. Map."

Liv pulls a thin sheet of polymer from her pack, spreads it out on a titanic stone block, and presses a calloused bulb at one corner between her thumb and forefinger. The map rises from the surface of the sheet in an oily glowing mist. Dam darts a finger into the mist, pointing out markers that shine slightly brighter at her touch.

"Last exploratory team got this far. Their feed browned out for maybe ten, fifteen minutes, when some foul thing topside managed to pull a sliver of Azathoth through for shits and giggles. Dropped it right on top of a transmitter."

We survive until we don't. No guarantees.

"Anyway. You two know this already. They found something, before they were ended. Those who sit above in shadow say we need it, and we're on recovery duty, so let's go recover."

Liv takes point, aims a kick at one of the slim metal boxes that used to contain the books of the Yith. The records of a million eras, harvested from across the breadth of time and space by Yithian mind-transfer tech. The molluscs would swap psyches with anyone, only is it really a trade when the target mind doesn't give consent? Psychic assault, more like, and that's just on the level of the individual. They did it to whole species: mass migrations of the Yithian mind-complex into unsuspecting populations of sentients. In the primordial mists of the young Earth, they were multi-limbed molluscs native to the era. In some far future they are here again, as a race of super-intelligent beetle. Or so their records claim.

Liv kicks another box. It careens down the hall, pings loudly off other boxes just as empty. All of us cringe at the sound. We've harvested their harvest, for all the good it did us.

"Weird bastards, weren't they?" Liv whispers. "Hard copies. Y'know?"

"I don't follow," Dam says. "And I don't care. Shut it and keep moving."

I do. I follow her. These halls we walk are decoration. Shelves to proudly showcase the collected knowledge of the Yith. For display only. The back-up is below, in near-bottomless silos bored into the crust of the planet, silos full of tightly laced, indestructible artificial neural tissue, the same stuff the dreaming-matrix of the Deep Dendo was retro-engineered from.

They didn't *need* these records, these boxes full of the frantic scribbling of their captives. Weird bastards. Proud bastards.

"Fucking show-offs," Liv mutters. "*Great Race*, my ass."

But they *were* great, I think. To build all this. To gather so much knowledge. To move their minds wherever they needed to, into fresh bodies on other worlds, in far distant eras. To survive, and keep surviving. Isn't that a mark of greatness?

The hall is silent but for the scuffing of our boots on the softened stone. A ramp branches away to the left, and we descend. Another, and another. A slow spiral into the earth, into a darkness that we know deepens even though our HUDs display everything in faint sheets and traceries of green light. We navigate a ransacked tomb.

Not entirely ransacked, though. Treasure here, still.

The spiral ramp opens up into a vast well in the rock. The dome above us is torturously carved with scenes of incomprehensible battle or migration or sex, each figure blending into the next. Yithian art, best appreciated by Yithian eyes that could see across a wider spectrum of light, and, if the records could be trusted, from a higher dimensional perspective as well. In any case, it's impossible to tell what's going on, or who is who, or the point of it, and it hurts mere human eyes to look at, besides, so I stop looking.

The well is more interesting, as is the structure that squats atop a massive stone pylon rising from its depths: a twisted orrery of translucent tubes coiling between flat planes and arcs of alien metal. Whatever it is, it has been here always. Dormant, still, the upper surfaces coloured the uniform grey of dust laid down over the eons. There is a walkway, a span of rock stretching from the ramp to the pylon, and wide enough for two dozen of us to walk across hand-in-hand with room to spare on either side.

"This is it." Dam doesn't have to say it. She motions for us to follow her. The deep silence of the chamber makes me nervous. No. Not nervous. I feel an anticipation rising in me, like I'm on the edge of re-membering something important. I feel a strange joy.

"Do we...wait," I say. "Wait. Just...hold on. Dam, do we know what this is? What are we...*nnnggh!*" I wince at the sudden, terrible pressure in my temples. Through narrowed eyes I watch as Dam reaches the pylon. She passes the palm of her hand across one of the flat blades of metal, soft plumes of grey rising into the air from her fingertips.

"Yeah, how are we supposed to get this thing back, Dam?" Liv barks. She walks past me and joins Dam at the structure. "It's...I mean, look at the size of it!" Both her hands reach out and begin stroking another plane, clearing it of dust. Then a tube. Another blade shines out from beneath Dam's touch. And another.

"Look at it," Liv whispers. "Look at it look at it oh. Oh it's beautiful."

The pain in my head is exquisite now, and a migraine brightness is filling my vision. I join them by the structure, my own hands dancing automatically across the cool surfaces. On my left is Liv, her face slack, her eyes dimming. On my right, Dam has closed her eyes, and her mouth hangs open at an odd angle, the jaw listing.

Liv hisses something.

"It's freedom," I think I hear.

I note, briefly, that my D-D field is fluctuating wildly. One second it's at a hundred percent, then two percent. Then three hundred percent and change. It's the last thing I notice.

The last thing Sunny Grey Theremin sees.

But then, like her companions who stand at her sides brushing and pawing at the machine, bringing it to life with her at my urging, she was never there to *see*, or experience, anything. She was barely aware in the first place.

Girl could turn a phrase though. *Shells, treading what's left of the earth on our slow, hopeless missions, camouflaged in the ghosts of our shared past.* That? That's beautiful. That wasn't all me. I collaborated with her on that, and even now still pull from her mind a useful if simplistic vocabulary, a collection of grammatical tics, some small stylistic flourishes.

Collaboration, yes. We were simpatico. Like attracts like. I fit inside her shell quite snugly. And I should know from shells.

You who read me, do you know what it is you read? You who read me, do you know what you are and when? Beetle or sentient gas or a child of Yig fresh from a billion years of hibernation? Perhaps some foul avatar of the Crawling Chaos itself, rummaging through the storied wreckage of the world before it is crushed to dust by your masters?

Black One, I am as sure of your amusement at these words as I am unsure of these things about myself, who and what and when I am, and so I ask, knowing I'll never know the answer. I'm being rhetorical.

So much of this existence is rhetorical, after all.

Through the empty minds of these females, and perhaps especially through the mind of she who was (or played at being) Sunny Grey Theremin, I can feel the collective emptiness of the human race, cocooned in their burrows beneath a dozen mountains, sharing a manufactured dream, a larval hive consciousness. There are no individuals left in the species, all souls have been rendered into one. They swim in a weak broth of memories and ideas about identity. They have weaponized their multiple personality disorder, crafted it as shielding against the mad rigours of this world.

I have to be crazy to go outside. Not that, Sunny. Barely sentient, yes. A shell, absolutely. Less than a ghost. All those things, but crazy? No.

I am not without sympathy for their state. How did she put it? *I'm not even an "I", not really.* And this "I" also has a mission. Through her implants, I begin to draw the near-formless consciousness of Man through to the machine, so that it may perform the task we set for it in our final days here.

The whistlers had arisen, then, inscrutable and deadly and tired of their prison perhaps, and we were falling before their winds. We reached out our minds, locating and communing with our next unsuspecting hosts, but one of us (was it I? If it was, I cannot recall) reached further into the future, communing with a member of our own race, already long-embodied in an armoured husk of chitin and strange flesh. And *that* beetle-self related its *own* record, of the machine that had been found, here, in Pnakotus, here in this very well, a machine that had sent the *original* members of the Great Race into the deep past, into the very birth pangs of the Universe, to a black elder orb crawling with inchoate life.

There was no machine, of course. Our confusion was great, our rush to compare the records of the future beetle-Yithian with the elder records of the Yith we were *before* arriving on Earth was…ah, but we were full of questions. We are always questioning. How many times, and on how many worlds, had this self-same scenario played out? Having propagated ourselves through Time and Space, overlaid our psyches onto a thousand different mental templates, who of us could *truly* know what we were? Who we had once been? The original Yith.

The Record multiplies and twists and is far from infallible. We trust the Record, but there are so many accounts, so many stories within it. I'm told it all makes sense from a higher-dimensional perspective, but that is a perspective that is necessarily lost to me as I am now, disembodied, full of doubt and ghosts.

As I am now. A meaningless statement if there ever was one. Yes, I have sympathy for Sunny, and all her kind.

There was no machine, and yet there *had* to be one, since the records indicated this. So, we built it. My mind was set as its keeper, and I was spread thin between its atoms, broadcasting my consciousness over long ages until suitable receivers arose from the muck of this world, to move and strain and make war at my gentle urging. To suffer my influence. To explore, to learn. To draw them to me. To find me here, finally, in the form of these three women, in the perfect conduit of Sunny, in this moment when the stars have come right.

We are never sure. Given enough time, Truth is stretched thin, becomes brittle. I am never sure. I recall things, and can never tell if what I recall is something I experienced, or something I read, or dreamed.

I don't even know why I'm writing this.

That's a lie. I *know* why. I write because the Record must be preserved, even when it is contradictory. I write because I am the Writer.

I gaze back through Sunny's mind. Now a true emptiness yawns there. The Deep Dendo is quiet, the Voorish Domes hold nothing but cooling corpses.

The Great Race. This is what we are called by all who encounter us. But you who read me, hear my confession: *There is nothing great about us.* The stars come round and right in their ancient cycles, and our own hubris catches up with us, or the Masters return, or both, and we flee. We flee. Into the dark, into the night of ignorance. Cowards, subjecting ourselves to a greater amnesia with each migration, with each genocidal rape of another species. And so we write our little stories, hoping they are at least partly True. We keep our sketchy Record, on papyrus and metal and the organic laceworks of living brains. We record. We try to remember.

To remember is to survive, even if the remembering is imperfect.

We survive until we don't.

I'm tired. The machine stills its esoteric action and ceases functioning. Similarly, the three women are brain-dead. I let the bodies of her companions drape over the armatures of the machine like discarded clothing, and in a moment, I will pilot Sunny's shambling meat into the archives above. This is the last file logged in the silent machines of the Deep Dendo, and in our own data-wells below, but I will use her to record the tale by hand in the margins of some overlooked book. We do like our hard copies.

Oh, Sunny. This is the end for you, but there's more yet to be written. *There may be something of what I was, who I used to be, buried deep… but I'll never see it again.* Sunny, I hope you felt a little something of yourself before the end.

My mission is over. There is nothing of myself here. I cannot know myself, know anything, not even for a moment. Not that it matters. There is only sleep now, and forgetfulness.

You who read me, are you awake? Do you dream?

You who read me, do you know what it is you read?

Trance Junkie
by Bruno Lombardi

I hate it when the dead bodies start screaming. It always gives me a headache.

It started, as it always does, with a chick. There was a nasty snow-storm—unusually big one for April—coming in when I got the call to come on over. It was only three blocks to the rooming house but with this snow and wind, it felt like thirty. I called upon the spirit of Coyote with my right hand to guide my feet in the mess and not get lost. I called upon the spirit of Jack Daniels from a bottle with my left hand to not care if I *did* get lost.

Not sure how long it took for me to get there but the 7 ouncer was probably a 5 ouncer by the time I knocked on the door.

Mabel's first words upon opening the door were, "About time you showed up, you lazy bastard."

As you can tell, we used to date.

"Came as fast as I could," I said.

"Oh, the number of times you apologized for *that*," she retorted, as she stepped aside and let me in. She still likes me; I can tell. It's subtle but it's there.

"So, where is she?" I asked, getting straight to business.

"Up here on the right," said Mabel, jerking her thumb in the aforementioned direction as we walked up the stairs. "Nothing's been touched," she continued, as we reached the top of the stairs. She turned to stare at me. "You've got five minutes, and then I call the cops. You got it?" She sounded like even waiting the five minutes was a big deal. Well, I suppose it *is*, technically, but still—you'd think she'll cut me a little slack here?

Wisely I didn't say anything as I walked into the room. Mabel stayed near the stairs. At least she's nice enough to give me a bit of space to do my job, unlike *certain* people I could name.

I sized up the scene as I entered the room. The contents were what you'd expect in your typical grungy but serviceable place in a rooming house; small bed with hand-me-down sheets and pillows, a dresser that was probably already considered second-hand when I was but a vision in mom's eyes, a nightstand with the obligatory cigarette burns and coffee rings, and beige painted walls. Pretty much run of the mill, humdrum stuff.

Well, okay, the dead girl in the bed wasn't run of the mill…

I took a closer look at her.

She was pretty, once. Twenty-something, a bit on the skinny side, long black hair. Almost certainly from one of the rez, probably one of the Stoneys but I heard that there were a big group in from McKay and Big Horn a few months back. Makes no difference I suppose. Her story? Don't need no special powers to figure *that* one out. Eh, like everyone else, came in to Fort McMurray—excuse me, Regional Municipality of Wood Buffalo now—to seek fame and fortune from all the oil jobs. Judging from how skinny she was, the fact that she was rooming in Mabel's place and the rather large collection of scabbed over track marks on her arms and legs, I'm thinking that the whole 'fame and fortune' thing was probably a bust.

I took a step closer in.

She definitely didn't die from no OD. I've seen dead people OD'd before and she didn't look it. Besides, Mabel had many qualities but patience with junkies wasn't one of them. No way she'll allow a junkie to shoot up under her roof. And I was getting a weird vibe from all this…

I practically hit the wall jumping back away from her, that's how bad it hit me. I could practically *smell* it now. Seriously bad mojo here, man.

She didn't die from natural causes. Someone did this magically.

I sighed and sat down and took out my kit; my pipe with my special kinnikinick recipe, my hand drum, a crow feather, soul mirror and a few other odds and ends. To be honest, I don't really need half the stuff in my kit most of the time but, like they say, always be prepared. Knowing I only had a few minutes here, I had to get down to business. I lit up the pipe, leaned back and started up a beat on the drum while saying the prayers under my breath. It took about a minute—thirty seconds longer than usual, which was weird—and then I felt the familiar rush as I became in tune with the spirit world.

And that's when the dead girl started screaming.

Well, okay, I was the only one who could hear her screaming. Still a seriously freaky thing to hear. I was right about one thing though; seriously bad mojo here. Her soul was being tormented here—probably by a Nakani for all I knew—and she was being tormented *bad*.

"What happened?" I yelled. All I got back was more screaming. Damn, I was getting nowhere here. I needed to do something a bit drastic.

So I reached out and opened her chest and flew into her body.

It was quiet in there. Quiet, dark, wet and warm. That's fine if you're having sex, not so fine if you're clawing your way through the soul of some dead murdered chick. Took a few seconds but I got my bearings and started heading for my objective.

Found her in a fetal position, all quiet and dazed and clutching her shadow close to her chest, like a mother holding a thalidomide baby. I sat down next to her and stroked her face, real slow and gentle, to get her out of her daze. I smiled when I saw her eyes flutter a bit and then she opened them. She was, understandably, a bit confused.

"I'm here to help you," I said. Well, okay, not *entirely* a lie; I just left out the 'hopefully' bit, is all. "Who did this?" I asked.

Her eyes just danced around for a while, like she wasn't quite sure what the hell was going on. Which was probably the case, truth be told.

"Who did this?" I repeated.

Her eyes focused—just for a second—and she turned towards me. "Witiko."

Shit.

And, of course, that's when her soul was ripped out and the connection broke and I got booted out of her body...

* * * *

I didn't feel the first slap from Mabel. Or the second, truth be told. Third face slap? Okay, *that* I felt. Fourth slap to the face was just Mabel fucking with me, to be honest, though.

"Wha...what?" was my astoundingly intelligent response.

"Are you done here?" she snarled. "Because I called the cops just now, so you're done."

I was sitting on the floor outside the bedroom, all the stuff in my kit dumped in a pile at my feet. Not entirely sure how I got there. Maybe Mabel carried me outside? Ha—*always* knew she liked me.

Mabel turned and walked down the stairs and I—hesitantly—followed her down. When we got down, she handed me my 7 ouncer. I wordlessly stuck it back in my knapsack with the rest of my stuff. She seemed a bit surprised I didn't take a slug of the booze beforehand. Not sure why she was surprised. I never take booze after one of my trances; it cuts the high I was feeling. She knows that. Boy—she knows that. We would have still been dating if that wasn't the case.

Mabel stuck two cigarettes in her mouth, lit both of them with one practiced flick of a lighter and handed one of them to me. Now cigarettes I smoke; nothing like a little stimulant to keep the buzz going.

"You were right," I said. "Just so you know. Your hunch was right."

"Cops on the way," repeated Mabel. She took a long drag and exhaled, not coincidentally, into my face. "We're even, ok? Last time I do a favour for you, understand?" She scribbled something on the back of a business card and handed it to me. It was a name, address and phone number.

She wordlessly pointed the way to the door, paused and then leaned in and gave me just the briefest of kisses on the forehead. I heard her whisper "Please, take care of yourself."

I nodded my head and turned and walked out of the house. The cold air slamming into my face almost—but not quite—cut the rush I was still feeling. Taking an extra-long drag on the cigarette, I walked out into the night.

* * * *

I suppose I should give a bit of background here. Really not much to tell. Dad was a shaman. And I mean a *real* shaman, like from Siberia, you know, not the bullshit 'shaman' label that you white people keep insisting on putting on *anything* that's 'exotic'. Mom was a Cree and was what they call a nanatawihiwewiyinow, which literally translates as 'a medicine person who uses the good spirit to offset evil spirits'. I was their only child, so with a background like that, you just *know* what the spirits had in mind for me.

Oh yeah sure, you're supposed to be given a 'choice'. You can 're-fuse the call'. Yeah, *sure*. You believe that bullshit, then you probably believe all the bullshit that comes out of Ottawa too, you sad bastard.

Mom and dad bounced around a lot and then when they died, I did the obligatory 'trying to find myself' thing by going from one rez to another. Didn't find myself but I did find myself with what you might call a *very* eclectic education. Hung out with a bunch of, well, I suppose what *you* would call 'shamans'. Picked up all kinds of stuff. Learned all kinds of shit.

Of course if you know nothing about all the tribes, you would think we all have the same practices and beliefs. Trust me; the truth ain't nothing like that. Raven, for example, is a trickster-hero out west and north, is practically a villain out in these parts and is nothing more than an afterthought, if that, once you get past the Prairies.

Still, all that mixing and matching kinda works to my advantage, you know? You've got this big melting pot—or is that mosaic?—thing going in this here fair city of ours and when the weirdness hits the fan and you need an expert, you're not gonna care all that much if the dude you call is Cree or Chipewyan or Dene or even Inuit, you know? Just as long as he gets the job done.

At least that was the plan when I came here four years ago. Like the dead chick—I looked at the business card and saw her name was Kanti Nowak—the whole 'fame and fortune' thing was a big bust.

Mabel—back when we were together—told me that one of the reasons why I didn't achieve this goal (aside from me being 'an asshole', that is) was that I liked the whole 'getting into a trance' thing a bit 'too much'. Hah! Like she knows what the hell she's talking about. I can quit anytime I want to.

Really I can.

Shit, I really need a cigarette…

* * * *

Witiko.

That's what the dead chick– uh, Kanti—said, just before the connection broke.

A Witiko is, well, an evil man-eating spirit. Kinda like the Windigo. The local Cree say that those who commit sins (especially selfishness, gluttony, or cannibalism) are turned into a Witiko as punishment. They end up with all kinds of powers as well, so I'm a bit fuzzy on how that's a 'punishment', but, like, whatever.

So what happened? Kanti sure as hell didn't eat human flesh, so she didn't turn into one. And if fucking up your life was enough to get a Witiko on your ass, then half the people in this here town would have been dead by now.

Did she piss someone off and had a Witiko called upon her as punishment? That *could* happen, I suppose, but you don't wanna mess with a Witiko at all, man; 'controlling' them is basically just pointing them at someone and then, when they're busy eating, run like a fucking rabbit in the other direction before they finish, cause you're going to be next on the menu when they're done.

None of this made sense. Why would you even need a Witiko to mess with some nobody junkie in the first place?

I looked at the card in my hand. I just knew that it was the contact info for Kanti's parents, of which the Mounties have no doubt already called to tell them about her death last night. I'm a detective—sort of, I suppose—so I could do a bit of snooping around and find out what happened. Mounties sure as hell aren't going to devote any time to the case after all; dead junkie found in crappy rooming house with no signs of foul play? Yeah, that's going to be on the top of the 'to do' list. Suuuure…

But—and this here is the important bit—I don't work for free, you know? Man's gotta eat, you dig? Got bills to pay, cigarettes to buy, booze to drink…I need money is the point I'm trying to emphasize here, is what I'm saying. And I don't think that I'm going to get much out of this even if I *do* take the case. And if I gotta mess with a witiko, I'm going to need beaucoup loonies.

But she's just a kid said a voice.

I sighed. Yeah, sure, *now* he shows up…

"Owl," I say out loud, cause Owl is my spirit guide (whenever he deigns to show his face, that is. Three guesses what kind of animal he is. Go ahead, guess). "Don't *you* lay a guilt trip on me, ok."

She's just a kid. And you're a shaman.

"I'm not going to do it for nothing!"

Just a kid…

I fucking hate spirit guides; they're always trying to push you to do stuff you don't wanna do. But I sighed, cause Owl had a fucking point too. This is, well, this is kinda what I do, you know? On the other hand, business is business, you know?

You know what you have to do. Do you want to hear her screams in your dreams for the rest of your life?

Yeah, spirit guides can be real dicks, just so you know.

"Ok! I'll do it!" I shouted, leaning back in my chair. "But I'm going to drop major hints that I'm going to want to be compensated, *comprend?*"

Owl did nothing but smile, cause Owls are good at doing that.

Lighting up one more cigarette and throwing another dollop of whiskey into my morning coffee, I picked up the phone…

* * * *

Long story short, I got the gig. Not much to tell; some bad family blood there, kid drifted away, kid got mixed up in bad shit and bad people, some failed attempts at reconciliation, kid was trying to get her life back together and seeking help, things were kinda/sorta/maybe beginning to work out, she needed a bit of money to get her shit together and get back to the rez, yadda, yadda, you know the drill. Parents knew who I was—I *do* have a bit of a rep, you know—and knew I wasn't screwing with them.

They didn't have any money, of course, but the parents said that they'll scrape up whatever they can. Technically speaking, they're kind of obligated to give me *some* kind of payment, even if it's just a hot meal, but its good manners not to point that out to them. I told them 'that wasn't necessary' (Owl gave me a big thumbs-up for that line) but also told them that whatever they could come up with 'would be greatly appreciated' (thumbs-down from Owl here). Hey man, I *told* you; man's gotta eat, ok?

So, what now?

Well, step one is to check out Kanti's life. Either she did something so spectacularly horrible that the spirits nailed her with a Witiko or she pissed off someone so much that they sent a Witiko after her. Either way, that's impressive.

Now there were two ways I could do this; track down all of her friends and contacts, ask them a billion questions and then slowly piece together all the clues over the course of days or even weeks, looking for that one single clue or thread that ties everything together. Or I could just go straight to the spirits and ask.

Cause I'm a lazy asshole, you can guess which method I used.

* * * *

"You have questions?" said Coyote.

The two of us were sitting across from one another on top of a snow covered mountaintop. Well, not *really* sitting on top of a mountaintop in the snow. Metaphorically. Spiritually. Cosmologically. But in a way, we actually *were*, in a real sense as well. Look, you white people make it really difficult to explain things, you know.

Whatever the nature of the reality, I was also metaphorically, spiritually and cosmologically freezing my nuts off too, cause it was fucking cold and all I had on was my jeans and Nickelback t-shirt (fuck you; they're a good band, ok?).

"Yes. About Kanti Nowak. She tells me that a Witiko was responsible. Is that true?"

Coyote looked up from licking his crotch and yawned. "Yup."

"Why?"

Coyote flopped down on the ground and rested his head on his front paws. "Complicated."

"A bit more detail, please."

Coyote yawned again. "Weird stuff."

As you may have guessed, Coyote isn't what you'll call the 'talkative' sort.

"Please, Great Coyote," I said, using my best pleading voice "I made a promise to her family."

Coyote looked up at me from ground level and there was *something* there in his eyes. Nervousness? Fear? Anger? It was hard to tell.

"Not going to like it."

"Still must know."

"She's a pawn. In a chess game."

Well, okay, now that's…unexpected.

"Pawn of who? And why? And how do I find them?"

Coyote stood up and actually turned around and started walking away. I think one can safely say that we were beginning to come to an end of our scintillating dialogue. Just as Coyote was about to walk out of the clearing, he came to a stop and turned around.

"In answer to your questions, in order: Sorcerer. Power. And they will find *you*."

And having said his exit line, Coyote vanished, along with the mountain and the world.

* * * *

I took a drag on the third cigarette I had in twenty minutes and leaned back in my living room chair.

A sorcerer? Really, now?

But what did Coyote mean by 'power'?

And, more importantly, what did he mean by 'they will find me'?

I sat at the table and shook my head and took another drag on the cigarette, trying to squeeze out as much of the 'trance high' I could. The cigarette felt *good*; the nicotine was sharp and green and tasted like electricity on my tongue while the smoke wafting from the tip was blue diamond dust, with a hint of feathers, and the flame itself was cold red mercury sputtering with the smell of wet musk and humming with the sound of molten copper.

Coming out of a trance tends to do…weird …things to your senses, as you may have noticed.

The sound of my stomach growling reminded me that I haven't had dinner yet, so I went to the fridge to dig around for some leftover pizza.

That's when I heard the floorboards creak behind me. When I turned around, I saw, standing about ten feet away from me, some dude. Well, he *looked* like a dude, sorta. Kinda tall, a bit on the dumpy side, wearing furs and skins. He looked…*unformed*, I suppose is the best word I could use. Like a clay doll that needed a few more minutes of work on him, you know? His face was *weird*, is what I'm saying.

I went for my knife. No, not the KA-BAR I keep on me. That's great against normal people. This? C'mon—I knew right away this was some kind of magical thing. For *these* kinds of things, I use my sacred bone knife. With all the spells and prayers I've put on it, it can handle pretty much anything.

The thing didn't move, though. It just stood there, staring at me. And then its head spun around and I saw that it had a *second* face on the back of its head.

Winyan Nupa! A fucking Winyan Nupa!

And when the thing stared at me, I immediately felt my body become paralyzed. With a rather inelegant thud, I fell on my ass and then on my back. The bone knife in my hand? Yeah, skidded away under the stove, of course. Figures, eh?

So the thing—any guesses why it's nicknamed Double-Face or Two-Face by some groups?—smiled and slowly started walking towards me. I knew I was fucked, cause the misdeeds of Two-Face range from murdering and mutilating people, to cannibalism, to kidnapping or even just frightening misbehaving children. I had a feeling that the last one wasn't on the agenda in this case. It had just reached the point where it was standing over me and smiling down with the most twisted grin I've ever seen on a monster—and trust me, I've seen some twisted monster grins in my time—when I heard a screech.

And that's when Owl came flying in and ripped into its face.

Now Owl has no chance winning a fight against a Double-Face—and he knows it—but that's not what the point here was. The point is that the second face of Double-Face paralyzes you—but *only* as long as it's looking at you.

Kinda difficult to stare at someone with a fucking owl doing its damnedest trying to rip your eyes out. Just sayin'…

Ok, I'm a bit out of shape. I admit that. I should have been able to get my ass off the floor and grab my knife in five, maybe ten, seconds, tops. It took me a good thirty instead—and I just *knew* Owl was going to ride my ass about that for the next two weeks—but, hey, at least I got up, ok?

One bone dagger stab to the heart later and—poof!—old Double-Face vanished in a puff of smoke, forest fire sunset in colour and stinking of red wet mud and feeling like iron dust on my skin and tasting like Snow Moon on my tongue.

Owl fluttered down next to me as I sat down on my ass again. Owl was missing a few feathers here and there and had a couple of ugly scratches that I knew would take a few days to heal, but he was otherwise ok.

"Thanks," I mumbled, knowing that was probably the most lamest thing I could say.

"You look like shit," said Owl. Perceptive spirit guide, ain't he?

"Feel like shit."

Owl shrugged his shoulders, which is a pretty freaky thing to see on an owl, and fluttered his wings. "So, that was, like a clue, right?"

Yeah, you might say that…

So…Two-Face?

Had to admit, that's a bit different. Only seen them two or three times before and this was the first one that tried to pick a fight with me. They're also more of a Sioux and Cheyenne thing than a Cree thing, which made me realize that there was probably a Stoney Band connection here somewhere. That does narrow things down a bit, but only a bit, cause there's three different rez roundabout here where you've got Stoney Band. Which didn't make much sense cause Kanti's family was Samson Cree Nation and lived near Pigeon Lake.

Ok, sure, no reason why there was some 'intermingling' between the two—yours truly is a case in point—but, still; a bit weird.

Also—we've got a Witiko *and* a Two-Face mixed up in this now? Holy fuck, did I get myself in some serious shit.

I needed some more answers…

* * * *

"Where's Coyote?"

Raven shrugged his shoulders and poked his beak at an itch under his wing. We were in a snow covered field this time, one that looked like it went for miles and miles in every direction. The only spot in the whole place that you could sit was a single tree stump which, naturally enough, was occupied by Raven.

"Not here," said Raven.

"I can see that," I replied, trying very hard not to get testy. Getting 'testy' with Raven is never a good idea. "How come?" I asked.

"Two reasons," said Raven, still poking at the itch.

"And those are?"

"Well, reason number one is that he thinks you're an asshole."

"Sadly, not the first time I've been called that by him. Number two?"

Raven stopped poking at the itch and stared at me instead. "He thinks you're a moron too."

"Also, sadly, not the first time either. What did I do *this* time to be called that?"

"I happen to agree with him, just so you know."

"*Thanks*, Raven. Once more; why?"

"You've got a Two-Face after you and you're *still* trying to solve a murder."

"It's what I do, Raven."

"And yet, you haven't figured out who is responsible or why. Hence the reason why we think you're a moron."

"I'm not exactly being overwhelmed with clues here, you know."

Raven actually rolled his eyes.

"You *are* a moron, you know that? The clues are right there but instead of sitting down and, you know, thinking about it, you decide to do yet *another* trance and talk with the spirits for guidance. Despite the fact that you know better than to ask us for advice so often. What's this— third time in twenty four hours you've done this?"

Jeez, you thought *you* had it bad? Imagine being on the receiving end of an Intervention from a freaking nature spirit.

"Look, I'll think about cutting back, ok? Just throw me a bone here, will you?"

Raven looked like he was going to give me attitude again, seemed to reconsider it at the last minute and then shrugged his shoulders. "Fine. Let's do this logically, ok?"

"Ok, shoot."

"Why would someone send a Witiko to kill someone?"

"Trying to figure that one out for a while, you know."

I swear; Raven actually sighed, which is a cool thing to see a three foot high raven do.

"Don't make me peck your eyes out, man."

"Ok, ok!" I said, holding up my hands. "Well, they're man-eaters. And soul eaters too."

"Right. And why would someone need a soul for?"

I remembered what Coyote said, about Kanti and chess games and power.

And then it hit me.

You can do all kinds of shit—really powerful, *forbidden* shit—if you have enough souls in your power. And if you're powerful enough to get a Witiko and a Double-Face under your power, even if it's just for a few minutes, then, oh boy, are we in trouble, cause if you've got *that* kind of power and you're trying to get *more*...

"Finally, the guy uses his brain," said Raven out loud. I blinked. I know I'm a bit a space cadet these days but I was pretty sure I was only *thinking* all that, not saying it out loud. And then I facepalmed myself, cause this is *Raven* we're talking about.

"But wait! How do I find this sorcerer?"

Raven sighed again. "And you were doing *so* well there." Raven tilted his head this way and that way for a minute and remained silent.

Yeah, he wants me to work it out on my own, cause, you know, that's Raven's shtick.

"Ok," I said out loud. "Super powerful sorcerer. Using monsters to collect souls. He knew I was on his case cause he sent a Two-Face after me, which means that he thinks I actually know something. Which means that I actually *do* know something, if I only knew what."

Raven smiled, just for a minute—also a cool thing to see on a three foot high raven, incidentally. "Keep going."

"But I was only on the case for a few hours. All I did was make a few phone calls and do a trance. Which means he knew right away I was on the case. Which means that either he's Kanti's dad or..."

Oh shit.

"Say it," ordered Raven.

I swallowed a lump in my throat, cause I knew where this was all going now. And, of course, I felt like an idiot, cause I should have thought of all this sooner.

"Someone's been watching me from the moment I found the body."

"Did you set off an alarm?"

I shook my head. I may be an asshole and a moron but I'm still good at my job. I would have detected something like that right away. Which meant only one thing...

"I was set up. He wanted me to find that body."

"Which means...?"

Raven, of course, knew what the answer was. And he knew that I knew. But, you know, there's that whole Teacher-Student thing we all gotta follow, so I nodded my head and said what I was thinking out loud.

"He knows me." And then I followed that line of thinking to its next logical step.

"And I know him."

* * * *

I woke up in my bed, naked and sweaty, with the sheets covered in vomit and piss.

Oh, typical Saturday night for you, eh? came Owl's voice from within my head. You know, Owl can be a real asshole sometimes.

The scary thing was I wasn't entirely certain how I ended up in this situation. I checked the clock radio and realized that I was missing about twenty minutes.

When you came out of your trance, you stumbled around like a drunk, collapsed into the bed and then proceeded to puke and pee simultaneously said Owl, in answer to my unspoken questions. *How do you feel?*

My head felt like it was going to explode, my eyes were two pissholes in the snow, the tips of my fingers were buzzing and crackling with green electricity and liquid moonlight, I could see auras on all the bugs and spiders in my room and the pile of dirty clothes in the corner smelled liked pennies on a hot summer day.

"Great," I lied.

Uh huh. Now take a hot shower and get your ass moving. You've got work to do.

"I need a beer."

You don't need a beer. You want a beer. Big difference. What you need is a coffee. Now go take that shower.

"Yes, mom," I mumbled sarcastically, as I got out of bed.

Did you know that the talons of owls can rip a man's eye right out of its socket? said Owl conversationally.

"Sorry, Owl."

Much better. Now move.

As the hot water cleaned the sweat and puke and the rest of the crap off my body, I had a chance to think about what had happened.

Who set me up? That was the big question.

Mabel? Nah; she may think I'm an asshole but she still likes me, well sort of. No, what had happened here was that Kanti got killed to serve two purposes. One was the whole 'soul power' thing. The other was, well, out of all the rooming houses and dives and shithole apartments where some native could get killed, whoever did this picked a rooming house just a few blocks away from me and one run by an ex who knew the kind of business I do and would naturally call me in to investigate.

Which meant…what?

I sure as hell don't know anyone with that kind of power, so it's not like this is some kind of personal vendetta or something.

Or was it?

I thought back through all the little jobs I've done over the years in all the crappy little rez, both here and in the States. I've seen and done a *lot* of weird shit.

But that was years ago. Could someone really have been nursing a grudge all this time? Tracking me down? Building up their power for one big shot at the brass ring and then figuring *'Oh cool; the asshole who broke that sickness spell I cast on that lady five years ago is here as well. Here's my chance to fuck him up'*? Really?

Well, actually, now that I think about it, that's actually *very* likely. We shamans are ornery bastards when we put our minds to something, as you may have noticed.

I got out of the shower and started toweling myself off and thought about this some more.

Ok, never mind the *who*. I'll find that out soon enough. So I thought about what this guy's next move was going to be. If I was planning some big forbidden spell, powered by souls and monsters and shit like that, where would I go?

I'll need something with a lot of connection with the spirits. A lot of connection with nature and the cosmos. Something with a lot of ties with a lot of bands and tribes. Something *old*.

And then I suddenly realized where all this was going to go down.

* * * *

I had to beg Mabel to lend me her car. She wasn't too crazy when I told her that it was probably going to be a good twenty four hours before she got it back. And that it would have a good thousand miles extra on the odometer when it came back as well. "Where the fuck you're going?" she asked. "Calgary?" She wasn't too thrilled when I replied "Kinda. General vicinity, in fact. Seventy kilometres east of it, to be precise."

I think I *totally* pissed her off when I asked for gas money as well…

Before taking off, I sat down and came up with a few contingency plans. And then a few contingency plans for those plans, in case they failed. Then, and only then, did I take off.

Because this is how these things kinda go, I reached my destination just a few minutes before sunrise.

* * * *

Far away, it don't look like much. A big pile of rocks, with a whole bunch of smaller piles of rocks scattered all around it, along with some weird looking lines. Then you get closer and realize that the 'big pile of rocks' is a cairn about thirty feet across and that the 'weird little lines' are 28 spokes that radiate outwards from the cairn and that the 'bunch of smaller piles' is an outer circle.

Majorville Medicine Wheel. Supposedly five thousand years old. Almost a hundred feet across, making it one of the biggest medicine wheels in the world.

Where else would a sorcerer go, eh?

* * * *

I've been to St. Peter's Basilica, believe it or not. The one in Italy. Supposedly it's one of the biggest churches in the world. They *really* make a big deal about its size. About how its five hundred feet across and five hundred feet high. How the dome is a hundred and fifty feet across or something like that.

Now the Medicine Wheel—here in what you white people would call the physical plane—is a decent sized thing but it doesn't hold a candle to St Peter's, right? Well, in what I suppose you would call the spiritual plane (if you could see it there) you'd sing a different tune. The cairn is a dome three hundred feet across. The temple itself?

A *thousand* feet.

There was a big-ass thundersnow going on all around the Wheel. For those lucky bastards who've never seen it before, a thundersnow is a thunderstorm—but with snow instead of rain. Which is actually kinda cool thing to see if you're wearing a winter coat, tuque and gloves. Not so good if all you're wearing is a shitty little jacket like I was.

Sorcerers. *So* melodramatic.

I walked through one of the 'gates' and into the temple—to find the sorcerer waiting for me.

Have to admit; he was playing it cooler than a witch's tit in a brass bra. He had his arms crossed in front of chest and was leaning up against a wall.

"About time you show up. Was thinking I was going to have to actually send you a handwritten letter."

I was sizing him up the whole time I—casually I would hope—walked to the centre of the temple.

"Meh," I said, shrugging my shoulders. "Normally I don't deal with losers like you but my schedule's empty these days."

He wasn't buying my tough guy act for one minute, which was kind of sad cause I practice that a lot in the mirror. "This is the part where you ask who the hell I am," he said, as he started slowly walking towards the centre as well.

"Ok," I said, playing along. "Who the hell are you?"

Dude just smiled. I was close enough to get a closer look at him now. He was kind of old—50's or 60's, with long gray hair. A bit on the pudgy side. Hair thinning a bit on top. Clothes old but useful. Nothing about him really stood out, to be honest. He looked like an overweight old Indian, basically. If you saw him walking down the street you wouldn't look twice.

He did not look familiar at all, though.

Dude kept smiling. I was hoping he was going to introduce himself with his real name but he was probably way too good to fall for that old trick.

"Sick kid in Buffalo River Dene Nation. The Flying Head in Green Bay. The giant spider in Fort Belknap."

"Wow," I said, impressed despite myself. "All those were yours?"

Again with the smile. "And guess who was the asshole who messed all those up?"

"Justin Bieber?"

Dude didn't even crack a smile. Dude had no sense of humour *at all*. C'mon man; that was funny.

"So, I was right. This is just revenge? Cold revenge?"

"Best kind."

"I'm going to kick your ass," I said. Yeah, it's a lame line but what else was I going to say here?

"Oh you sad little pathetic man," said the dude, still smiling. I was *really* starting to hate that smile. "You really have no idea how you've been played, do you?" Again with the smile.

Huh? What was he blathering on about? And then I realized that the gates were all closed.

I was trapped inside with him.

Oh hell; I was going to be the next soul he was going to take. That is, if he kills me.

If.

I let loose with my bone dagger, loaded with all kinds of extra prayers and spells in addition to its usual batch, right at the dude. Dude sidestepped the dagger like he was Neo from *The Matrix*. Then he let loose with a bone dart at me but I was prepared for that and it bounced off my coat and disappeared into the darkness.

Dude decided to go Old School on me at this point and just charged at me, fists whirling. For an old dude he was fast and strong. I blocked the first punch, ducked under the second and sidestepped the third. Unfortunately while I was focusing on his fists, I wasn't paying attention to his feet.

Which was bad, cause that's when he kicked me in the nuts.

I went down on my knees and had just enough vision in my tear-filled eyes to see the dude come at me, the smile on his face growing bigger and bigger and bigger and...

I floated. In warm wet, cold darkness, like a womb. Oddly I felt... comfortable.

I opened my mouth but no sound came out.

Where was I? What the hell happened?

I felt weird. Was I drifting? No, I was swimming! I could feel currents on my skin, coppery and blue and smelling vaguely of almonds and tasting like sea spray. I wasn't sure which end was up. Or down, for that matter.

I wasn't alone in here. I could...well, not see, but feel, others all around me. Lost. Confused. Scared. Off in the distance, just at the very edge of hearing, I could hear a rhythmic pounding sound. *Lub-dup, lub-dup, lub-dup...*

The sound felt *almost* familiar. It was really annoying just how familiar the sound was...and then I blinked, a thousand times I blinked.

You ate me. You god damn son of a bitch. You actually ate *my soul.*

Was that a low rumble of thunder or a chuckle?

"Your soul is mine. And with it and all the others I've taken, I will be unstoppable."

You forget one thing.

A thunderstorm in the mountains, the thunder booming and echoing a thousand times.

"And what's that, little man?"

You forgot that I'm an asshole. And assholes do stupid things. Like set up a contingency plan in case some asshole sorcerer steals his soul. A contingency plan that involves…this.

And that's when I did the equivalent of 'overcharging' my spirit.

And exploded out of the dude's body…

* * * *

I smoked half a pack of cigarettes in a space of 45 minutes as I sat near Mabel's car. The sun was rising just off the horizon, which I thought was a nice harbinger of things to come. I was firmly in the *here and now* and the Wheel—and everything else around me, for that matter—was back to normal.

And I killed a guy, whoever the hell he was…I guess I forgot to ask him, oh well. Sorcerer—or what was left of him—was lying in the Wheel, right next to the cairn. Part of me wondered if I should bury him. Another part of me said *fuck him, leave him for the animals* which I thought was a great idea. Man, the local Mounties were going to have a hard time figuring out *this* case.

As for me…

I felt like shit. Never did that 'overcharging soul' bit before in my life, mainly because you have to be fucking insane to try it, cause only one in a thousand shamans can pull something like that off. I'm an ass-hole, remember? Not insane. Big difference. Well, maybe not anymore.

But hey—it worked. I stopped the bad guy. And I saved the soul of a kid—and a few others, judging from what I could remember from my time inside the sorcerer.

And I killed a guy.

Yeah. Just…yeah.

I picked up the cellphone and called Kanti's parents and told them that I solved the case and that they could send whatever payment they wanted to send. I didn't tell them that once I got back to Fort McMurray, I was going to pack up all my shit and take a bus to a place as far south and warm and quiet as I could.

I was tired of being cold inside.

* * * *

Bad Faith
by Will Blinn

Max opened his eyes as a startled gasp escaped his lips. Sitting up in bed he took stock of his surroundings. Molly was breathing peacefully next to him, sound asleep. Seeing her soft features lit by the gently filtered moonlight put him at ease. It had been a while since the nightmare had invaded his sleep, more than a year he was sure. It was always the same, a very realistic replay of the most horrific moment of his life, which happened to be a car accident he and his girlfriend had been in when he was seventeen years old.

He shivered a bit. More than twenty years had passed and still his subconscious mind wanted to torture him with that one uncompromised, pristinely preserved memory. He felt a dull aching tightness in his stomach. *It's over...just a dream,* he said to himself. He had Molly and the children now and his life was good. Very good compared to the mess it had been before Molly. Those lofty dreams he'd had before that accident hadn't even come close to reality, but youthful notions rarely came to pass for anyone. That was true at least for everyone he knew. He looked at the clock. It was 3:06 AM. He had to piss.

Groggily he trudged down the hallway, past the children's rooms and the tiny office where he kept his guitars. The moonlight was bright enough that he didn't need to turn on the lights in the john. He lifted the toilet seat and steadied himself so as to minimize any errant urine stream trajectory. He got a chill down his spine becoming irritated that his body had now decided to hold off on the evacuation. Out of the corner of his eye he caught movement in the hall-way and cursed to himself for not closing the bathroom door.

He turned to tell whoever it was, Jeremiah maybe, to wait their turn. The urine began to flow. There was no one there. He quaked a bit. But there was *something* there. He strained to see into the darkness. *Something not right...* In the shadows of the hallway a figure stood the outline of a man, but twisted and misshapen. He was urinating on the wall now, mouth agape. Terror welled up in the pit of his stomach. The figure stepped towards him. He could see the grotesque mouth opening, but no sound could be heard.

"No," he whispered into the shocked darkness and it was gone.

Eight months before the car accident all those years ago Max had played guitar in a band. He was the youngest member, but the only one who could write songs or at least the only one willing to let the others hear his tunes. They were practicing one of these, a rocker titled *Bad Faith*, the first time he saw Amber. Tom, the band's singer, had given the band its name, Grin Wild. Amber was Tom's girlfriend and she was everything he had boastfully claimed. Long, slightly curly flame-red locks encircled her rounded face. Her features were slight, yet striking; round pink lips, mesmerizing green eyes, rosy round cheeks and a dazzling white smile that widened as the song went on.

> *Where I go, she won't follow I know*
> *When I cry, her eyes are dry*
> *That's bad faith, girl*
> *Baaaadd Faith…*

"Was I right or was I right," Tom had asked later. Max had to admit he was indeed right. Amber was amazing and became a force that endlessly cavorted through his mind on that day. He couldn't stop thinking about her.

He sat at his desk with Amber's dance moves from that day so long ago playing over and over in his mind. Her head bounced to the beat, hair flying, tight black jeans and slightly over-sized Ramone's t-shirt all gyrating rebelliously. He heard the foreman calling his name from the warehouse, but it seemed far away. The memory held him in that teenage moment for several more seconds then he heard his name again.

"Alright, relax," he shouted, finally pushing his chair back. "I'm on my way."

Jeremiah, four years old, precocious and too cute for his own good greeted Max at the door that evening. "Mommy said you're in trouble," he said, obviously excited by the prospect of someone other than him being in trouble.

"Really now?" Max shot a sly glance at Molly who was helping Jenny with homework at the kitchen table. "What terrible thing did Daddy do?"

Max scooped the boy up and looked over Jenny's shoulder, resting his free hand on the 6 year old girl's head. "You peed all over the bathroom wall," his daughter said, matter-of-factly.

"Ohhhh…" Max sighed guiltily. Molly raised one eyebrow and gave him a smirking glare.

"In my defense I was not even close to being fully awake. In fact I was sleep-walking and in the middle of a horrendous nightmare when this grievous incident took place." He smiled at his lovely wife, a knot twisted in his belly as the memory of the gnarled, shadowy figure flooded his consciousness. "I'm not even kidding. Really…"

"Oh, poor Daddy," Molly said, feigning sympathy. "Next time, can you, maybe…oh, I don't know…clean up afterwards?"

"Are you going to take away his treats, Mommy?" Jeremiah asked innocently.

"Maybe that's what I'll have to do to teach Daddy a lesson." Molly's smirk turned into a gentle giggle.

Several hours later Max ran his fingers over the smooth skin of his wife's belly. The lovemaking had been passionate and Molly had been giving as always. Freshly ravished she looked superbly alluring with her hair tussled, face aglow, still attentive eyes trying vainly to disguise the fact that she was spent.

"I'm so glad you didn't take my treats away, Mommy."

Molly laughed. "Yes, you are a lucky boy. But you wore me out. Must sleep, etcetera, etcetera."

"Ok." He kissed her again and pulled the covers up over them. "I hope no boogey men decide to follow me into the bathroom tonight." He was trying, unsuccessfully, to sound sarcastic.

"It was just a dream or a hypnopompic hallucination," Molly said yawning. "You'll need a better excuse next time."

Max furrowed his brow. "Hypno-what-ic?"

"Hypnopompic hallucination." Molly continued to speak as she closed her eyes. "Sometimes when we first wake up a part of our brain, the frontal lobe, is still partially in a dream state. So… we can hear someone talking when no one's around or see things that aren't there, like your boogey man. Goodnight, hon."

"Goodnight."

He looked at her for a moment. It was easy to forget how intelligent she was sometimes. When they had first met she was working on her still unfinished master's degree. Her future had seemed bright until she met him. Now she was a hair-dresser taking night classes for god's sake. She didn't seem to care or ever look back. Max knew she had saved him from himself, but couldn't help feeling that in the process he had dragged her down.

Max first had sex with Amber in the back seat of her car on her eighteenth birthday. They had parked by the lake and kissed for a long time. Nearby was a tree the band members had all carved their names into earlier in the year. The lake was stormy and beautiful, just like Amber. The touch of her bare skin was hypnotic and instantly addictive. It sent a current through him, ignited a passion that he hadn't known was even possible. Suddenly he understood love. For the first time he could see how two people could truly be connected. It wasn't his first sexual experience, but it was the first time sex had actually meant something to him.

Afterward they had held each other for hours, barely speaking. Her shadowy, moonlit countenance washed over him like a warm ocean current. Max felt very lucky. Amber had broken things off with Tom a few weeks before. They both had some guilt about it and Tom's dejected response didn't help. For now Amber wanted to keep her relationship with Max a secret. He couldn't argue with her logic. He hoped he'd never know what it was like to have to get over her.

So he would show up for band practice, pal around and commiserate with Tom then rendezvous with Amber. At the lake, the park pavilion or, when her parents were away, her bedroom, they would meet up enjoying the simplicity of being together. For Max, always something of loner, it was a revelation. Love was real and worth every secretive, deceptive moment. In a few months it would be over, of course, but he had no way of knowing that then.

Max woke up with a start. Molly's sleeping silhouette greeted him as did the gentle rhythm of her breathing. There was no nightmare stuck in his consciousness and for once he didn't have to piss so why was he awake? Before his eyes could focus on the glowing digits of the digital clock he somehow knew the hour. 3:06 AM, of course.

He sighed and considered waking his lovely wife. Surely she would be able to explain away the spiraling tempest that was growing in his stomach. After a moment he hesitantly got out of bed, though he had no idea why or where he was going. He just knew it would be better to be out of the bedroom. He silently started down the hall for the bathroom, feeling stupid and mildly terrified, each in equal measure.

He stopped at the office for no discernable reason. Scanning the shadowy corners he opted for the window and the fading moonlight that filtered through its curtains. He let his hand rest on the head of the acoustic guitar that stood there on its stand and peeked out at the lifeless street. He had tried to ignore the span of cold air he passed through on his way to the window, but now the hair and his neck stood up and he knew he wasn't alone.

Molly's soothing explanation played out in his mind. Hypnopompic hallucination…it made so much sense, but the knot in his stomach was a dull, deep ache now and the cold on his back was even more pronounced. It was breathing on him, icy cold exhalation falling on his neck. A sickening odor filled his nostrils now. Outside the street was bleak. He wasn't going to turn around. This would all go away in a minute and he could crawl back into his warm bed with Molly.

He could hear the breathing now, a wheezing, frozen rasp. It sounded like gravel being poured into mud. Max groaned solemnly as it whispered to him.

"...been.. here for...soooo...loonng..." The words trailed off. The breathing continued.

An ominous shadow moved in his peripheral vision and Max knew this time that it wouldn't just go away. He had to face it, somehow. Then, maybe, it would vanish as it had the night before. He balled his hands into fists, counted slowly backwards from five. On one he spun and fell back in horror at the sight of the abomination that faced him.

It was surely the same thing that had confronted him the night before, but now it was inches from him, breathing cold foulness into his face. It was as if a man had been partially turned inside out and somehow animated that way. But it was bigger than a man, hulking over Max as he cowered against the window. The head was a swollen mass with half a skull. The brain, swollen and oozing a gooey red discharge, seemed to ripple with each dark breath. The jaw was twisted and disgusting. One eye focused intently on Max while the other, hanging from a fibrous stalk, stared off into the dark. The body was just as gruesome. The arms jutted from the chest and abdomen. The belly was open and each organ was ruptured and dripping with dark decaying matter.

Max felt his stomach give way and vomited directly onto the nightmarish thing. It didn't seem to notice at all. The horrendous smell of the monstrous being mixed with that of the Max's puke and he felt faint. The thing moved closer to him. It was no hallucination. The twisted and gnashed fingers reached for him. The sticky coldness on his skin made him gag again. It was eye to eye with him now. A panicked quake took over Max's body. The cold ick covered fingers touched his throat and everything became darkness.

After a month of sneaking around with Amber the deceit had begun to wear on Max. The morose turn Tom had taken seemed to be waning and he deserved to know the truth. Though he had known Tom for most of high school, Max hadn't really considered him a friend until they had connected in the band. Tom was older and more popular, but also moody, self- centered and not nearly as bright as he believed himself to be. Max hoped he could explain the Amber situation to him without stirring up too much dust.

"What! Unbelievable!" Tom furrowed his eyebrows and began to pace. Max had wisely waited until after practice to spring the news, after their band mates had gone home.

"It wasn't planned, man. It just happened. It seems like a good fit."

"A good fit? Nice choice of words, Max." Tom shook his head. "I just thought she and I had something that was deep, y'know?"

Max sighed, trying hard to find some sympathy. Tom had already dated, in other words screwed, at least three other girls since he and Amber had split. The most recent conquest was now referring to herself as his girlfriend.

"I'm sorry, dude. I just don't want it to come between us. I wanted you to know."

A spectacle of conflicting emotions collided on Tom's face.

"I… appreciate that," he mumbled finally. "I'll see you tomorrow."

For the next week Tom barely spoke to Max. Their interactions were business-like. After practice he would leave before everyone else. Max wanted to talk to him some more, but Amber suggested he let it ride for a bit, so he did. Sure enough Tom eventually came around, slowly at first, but within a couple of weeks things seemed normal again.

Max was elated. His place in the band seemed secure. He could see that the others had really started to respect his playing and songs. It felt good. He also got to keep the beautiful and amazing Amber and that felt spectacular.

"Max!" He woke up startled and confused. Molly stood over him, a look of dread on her face. He was in the office. The acoustic guitar was lying on the floor. Dried and reeking vomit was smeared on his shirt. He tried to hide the gnawing horror that filled him as the memory of his early morning encounter exploded through his barely conscious mind.

"Wh…what the hell, honey," he pulled himself up into the chair. He could still feel the fingers on his throat, smell the breath. "It's the damnedest thing, Molly. Sleep-walking again, I guess. Maybe I'm coming down with something."

"Was it a dream? Do you remember coming in here?"

"No." He paused for moment. She was already in a panic, telling her the truth wouldn't help. Not that he really knew what the truth was. "I can't remember a damn thing."

Soon she had him up and in the shower. She called his boss, explained that he wouldn't be in then made a doctor's appointment for him. Max went along with it. He didn't like seeing her in this state or being the reason for it. He'd go to the doctor, explain that he'd been having some crazy dreams and it would all blow over. To explain the alternative, that the most vile thing imaginable lived among them, but only came out to visit at around three in the morning, wouldn't go over so well. Maybe it was just a dream, he tried to convince himself. He was definitely going to hit the doctor up for some sleeping pills.

The idea that it all had been a figment of the cloudy space between his unconscious and conscious mind made the day easier to face. The doctor did some tests and assured him, and Molly, that he was healthy. He came home, prescription in hand and enjoyed the afternoon off with his family. Of course the dark reality he had somehow fallen into wouldn't easily let go. He tried to stay in the moment but his thoughts kept swirling to his 3AM visitor or, strangely, to the past.

This wasn't the life he had expected. Before Molly had come along he was headed to the gutter, bouncing between jobs and increasingly dire living arrangements. Then, with his beautiful wife, things got better. He had stopped drinking, found gainful employment and become a father. It was what most people aspired to, but in his dark moments he couldn't help but feel that somehow his fate had been twisted far off of its original course.

"*Yous* a good daddy," Jeremiah gurgled adorably, hugging Max as he was carried to bed. It was one of the best things in life, the simple sincerity of his children's love. Max knew he was lucky.

He read a chapter of Jenny's goodnight book to her then watched as Molly tucked her in. They watched television for a while. He tried to not let his thoughts wander, to not think at all. Finally, as they were getting ready for bed, Molly reminded him to take a sleeping pill.

He went to the bathroom, opened the bottle, took out a pill and stared at it in his hand. The fear that was stirring in him, that had kept him checking the time all night, seemed to stare back from its bleak trench. If the horrendous thing was real, whatever it could possibly be and if Max wasn't there to meet it, would it turn to Molly or, worse yet, one of the children? He dropped the pill back into the bottle and secured the cap. He wasn't sure if it was exactly bravery, but the thought of harm possibly coming to his family gave him a strength he knew he wouldn't have otherwise. He would face this thing.

It was a cool September evening when things had turned for Max. He and Amber had been dating for eight months. He had never been happier. She was such a bright light, all of the solace anyone could ever need could be found in her eyes. The band continued to progress as well. That night Grin Wild had played at a local bar. Though more than half the audience was made up of the band members' friends and family the gig still felt like a success.

Max and Amber were driving home when it happened. He was behind the wheel of her car with the lovely young woman sitting next to him gently caressing his shoulder. She had her window down a bit. She liked the cold air on her skin. Max stole a glance as hair was blown gently over her dazzling face. A fraction of a second later, when he turned his attention back to the road, he was blinded by the headlights of a pickup truck speeding directly at them.

Amber screamed as Max frantically turned the wheel to the right just managing to avoid a head on collision. With a crashing sound that was as deafening as it was sudden the pickup struck them just in front of the driver's side door. Both vehicles became air-born and the last thing that Max saw before losing consciousness was the body of the truck's driver, ejected out of its windshield on impact, smashing head first into the hood of Amber's car. Blood and gore seemed to explode everywhere, then blackness.

Max woke before three this time and nervously paced back and forth in his mind for a bit before deciding on a plan. He went to the office and sat in the chair, his back to the wall. A strange calmness and creeping dread battled in his stomach. He would face it this time. He knew it would come and he knew that, despite his best efforts to explain it away, the ghastly thing was real.

At just a little past three A.M. he noticed a distinct chill in the room. He dug his fingers into the arm of the chair. It was right there, just inches from him. Slowly it took form, materializing over him, wretchedly filling the room with its foulness. It appeared in chunks, each twisted and appalling piece joining the previous one from the floor up to the ripped open skull. Max shivered. The thing vented its long raspy breath onto him. Reality seemed to be draining viciously from the universe. Max found himself fighting to keep his mind from shutting down.

"Just tell me what you want," he said through gritted teeth staring directly into its one good eye.

It made a sound. Something oozed out of its mouth and splattered on Max's face. He stifled the scream that was rising in his throat. The grotesque specter reached for his head. He tried to turn away as the fingers touched his face. It pulled him up so they were eye to eye as a distant, haunting voice began to echo through his mind. Max was nauseous to the point of passing out, but he held on.

"Please…" Max stifled the wretch that gurgled in his esophagus. "What do you want from me?"

A gruesome rage crossed the thing's torn features. Max still felt sick, but knew he could hang on this time. He wouldn't pass out. This had to end.

"What do you want?" he asked again through gritted teeth.

The gruesome fingers touching his skin sent violent tremors through Max's body. His eyes began to fail him. A blurry grey-black curtain filled his mind. Slow pain filled visions began to take form.

"See what I see…" The horrible voice was clear in Max's head now.

After the accident Max had been placed in a medically induced coma for over a month. Most of the bones in his left arm and leg were severely broken. He had a collapsed lung. His skull was fractured and his brain was swelling. His doctors feared neurological damage. His family waited helplessly by his bedside. Amber, who had escaped the accident with just a few cuts and bruises, was often there waiting as well, in the beginning. The driver of the truck had of course not survived.

Though the doctors later insisted that dreaming should have been impossible, Max's nightmares started while he was in this comatose state. With few variations it was always the same. The dark dream was simply the accident being played out in vivid slow motion. Max sat next to Amber, the breeze blew her hair across her face so very slowly. Each frame of film that his mind played back for him was stretched until it distorted. The smile on Amber's face, the touch of her hand on his shoulder, all carried out to a torturous denouement. Making the torment even more unbearable was the fact that in the nightmare Max knew what was coming. With each creeping second the anxious terror grew. The truck was coming and there was nothing he could do to stop it.

Then the collision and the poor truck driver's explosive and disgusting demise played out in the same sickeningly slow fashion. Max could see his face as it exploded through the windshield, twisted, horrified and powerless to stop his impending collision with the hood of Amber's car. Frame by frame the horrifically gory conclusion of the hapless driver's life ran through the blood filled gullies of Max's mind. Then Amber's screeching cries followed by blinding, numbing pain pumping into him like a wave overcoming a drowning man.

Amber was gone when Max was finally brought out of the coma. The note she left was full of apologies, and insistence that their relationship had meant so much to her, but no explanation as to why she would abandon him when he needed her most. She had left town early to get settled in college for the spring semester halfway across the country. She left no address and Max soon learned that her cell number had changed. It was months before he found out that Tom had gone away with her.

The loss and betrayal of the girl he loved and the painfully slow recovery process took their toll on Max. It was nearly a year before he could play guitar again. Tom was gone and the other band members moved on. The years that followed grew dark. He tried college a few times, but never graduated due to drinking, drugs, money issues and a quietly simmering self- hatred that had latched on to him. He moved from job to job, leaving home multiple times but always winding up back under his parents roof, humiliated and defeated once again by life.

Then Molly had come along and reminded him of the beauty in the world. She had saved him from himself though the darkness never truly left. It was much easier to bury it in the glow that she carried. Her love was real and true and he was grateful. His soul was no longer hemorrhaging its life-blood into the ether, but the seal that Molly had brought wasn't complete. There were still cracks that let the darkness seep in.

Max sat in the studio plucking at the strings of his old acoustic guitar. He felt better than he had in a very long time. The song he sang into the microphone was one he'd written a few years before, but never played for anyone, not even Molly. It was invigorating to be recording it now, singing it for the world or whoever might want to listen, but mostly singing it for himself.

> *Wishing for air and time to tear*
> *The shadow that you laid on me*
> *Cutting these ropes, burning the ties*
> *All this time was just a long goodbye*
> *Just a long goodbye...*

Tom stood behind the glass in the control room, nodding his head, trying to appear happy to see his old friend. His façade wasn't completely successful. Max wondered what the former singer of that long ago teenage band had thought when his old guitarist had called out of the blue after all these years. Recording the song in Tom's beautiful state of the art studio was just a ruse of course. On some level Max was sure Tom realized that.

Tom hadn't become a famous musician as he had hoped, though he did tour the country in various bands and was still popular in the local scene. He had proven to be a solid business man and producer and had recorded some very successful bands at his studio and other locations. Next to the studio stood Tom's beautiful home, the home he shared with Amber.

"That was great, man," Tom said, beaming just a bit too brightly, when Max was done.

"Thanks." Max watched his long ago band mate. He felt at ease, but deep in his stomach that familiar knot was starting to turn.

Tom adjusted the reverb slightly and started playing the song back. As they listened Max couldn't help wonder about what might have been. Things could have been so different. He loved Molly and the kids and he couldn't imagine life without them, but still the dark emptiness of those years after the accident scratched at his consciousness.

"How is she?" Max asked quietly.

"Huh?" Tom seemed taken aback by the question. "Amber? Oh, she's great man. She's doing really well."

Neither of them had ever reached out to Max in all the in between years. They had moved back to town a few years after college. Max would see them around, holding hands, smiling at each other. Sometimes they would say hello or wave, but neither party showed any interest in having a conversation. No one had the explanation that Max convinced himself he didn't care to hear.

He had swallowed and stuffed his bitterness down deep, but after tonight he could let all of that go.

"Good," he said at length.

He looked at the clock. Nearly 10:30 PM. It was getting late, but was it late enough? How long could he play on Tom's guilt to prolong his visit? Tom stifled what might have been a genuine yawn and Max realized the time had come.

"I have something for you," he said, trying to maintain the calm he had felt earlier.

He opened the inside panel in his guitar case and pulled out a small leather-bound book. It was tattered and marked by a dark green patch of mold on the cover. It was obviously quite old. Max opened it and leafed through the crisp pages each filled with faded hand written passages, mostly in Latin and old French.

Tom gasped and nearly fell out of his chair when he saw the ominous book. Max pretended not to notice the shock that was playing out on his one-time friend's face. He flipped through the pages of the book absently, stopping eventually at a page he had marked earlier.

"I always wondered how you had come up with the name Grin Wild," Max said at last. "I mean now I get it of course, grimoire, grin wild...clever."

"Max," Tom started delicately. "Where? How did you..." His voice trailed off.

"Oh, putting it in the tree was clever too, I suppose. Is that where you stored it when you weren't trying your hand at some dark magic, Tom? Was it there when we all carved our names in it? Was that all part of some spell you were trying to conjure?"

"It was just an old book," Tom's voice was a thin whisper. "I found it in my grandmother's attic. The spells worked. With girls, the band, with..." He turned away staring at the floor.

"With Amber? With me?" Max raised his voice. Twenty years of pain and loss were boiling over in his mind. "You were trying to kill me. For the life of me I would have never believed it. I knew she was important to you, but I didn't think you could do that. You could have had any girl you wanted, especially with your precious grimoire. Bastard!"

An odor had penetrated the room. By now it was familiar to Max. His anger began to wane. All these years, all this time, he thought. Soon things would be different.

"I took Latin in one of my attempts at college," Max said, studying the open book. "Your grasp of the language must have been pretty basic, at best, right Tom? I'm assuming you got lucky with your early spells, deciphered enough to get by. But the curse you laid on me, your friend, your sincere honest friend, I think you didn't quite have a grasp on what you were doing."

Max pointed to the words on the ancient page. "*Mors Obsideo Devoveo*. You thought this curse would kill me, but you didn't have it right. Whatever twisted evil ancient hag it was that came up with this horrid black magic wasn't looking to kill the victim, but leave them to a tormented, miserable life. See it isn't a death curse, Tom, it's a curse that leaves someone haunted and tortured by death, by a dead soul that fuses it's misery onto the poor sucker the curse is directed at. I wished that I had died of course…all the time."

The smell was rancid now and the room had grown so cold that Max could see his breath. Tom sat paralyzed in the chair. His face had turned a sallow grey. In the corner of the room the nightmare bringer was starting to form, bloody flesh and torn, twisted bone, ripped open, dripping organs and finally the split open skull with that one good, hate filled eye. It stood behind Tom, its rancid breath and drool falling on the petrified man's head.

"Do you remember the truck driver, Tom? The one who crashed into me? His name was Mark Donnelly. He was a family man, a good man. The only thing he did wrong was wind up too close to me that night. He has suffered the most unfathomable torture that a soul not trapped in Hell could."

In one sudden, violent flash the thing spun Tom around in his chair, took him by the shoulders and lifted him in the air. Rage flashed blood red in that one eye, but for the first time Max could also see the unbelievable pain the improbable ghoul that had once been Mark Donnelly carried there.

"See what I see," the horrific beast hissed and took Tom to the same ghastly place that it had shown Max a few days before.

Max had seen through Mark Donnelly's eyes as he left his home that night on a quick run to the store for cold medicine for his youngest child. He had kissed his wife goodbye. The smile on her face hung in the hallucinatory memory even as the accident played out, much as it had in

Max's dreams, one excruciating, drawn out frame after another. But now Max felt Donnelly's pain as he was thrown through the windshield and pulverized on the hood of Amber's car. Then, like his life the pain should have stopped, but instead it continued, waves or nauseating blood red agony that never ended, blotting out everything else.

As Donnelly's cursed soul and never ending torture merged with Max's beaten spirit the toll it took on Max's life began to manifest. In the years after the accident the nightmares came every night. The drugs and booze that Max dived into blotted it out a bit at first only to become a part of the ever present curse over time. Max found himself ostracized by his family, abandoned by every woman that came around.

At first Donnelly's afterlife was just the pain and rage that he poured into Max's existence. Then, little by little, fragments of his old life filtered in. Memories of his family and the man he had been took hold. His rage grew and these were Max's darkest years. They were years spent hell bent on drinking or drugging himself to death, lying, stealing and living on the street. Always the inexplicable and impossibly deep blackness was there. It wouldn't be blotted out and the horrific dream was the frame that held it in place.

Eventually something turned. Realization slowly dawned. The anguished spirit saw that Max was equally victimized by the curse. The dead man's soul began to fight the imperious need to inflict its horror on Max. Over time it learned to stifle the pain and Max's life began to improve. By the time Molly entered Max's life the thing that had once been Donnelly had unwound the nefarious and misguided deed that Tom had perpetrated. As his spirit was tied to Max it was also somehow tied to the book that his curse had been born in. He could see it there in the tree by the lake and the man who put it there.

Still tortured at every moment by the replaying misery, Donnelly tried to communicate with Max. The only bridge available was the dream, but it was impossible to turn the nightmare off. It was hard wired into their collective psyche and couldn't be changed. But as it struggled to keep the unfathomable pain at bay a new awareness began to form. The pain, the hatred, the dark intensity of the curse was pure energy. The Donnelly thing could learn to harness it, to take on a physical form.

Years of torpid trial and error led to the consciousness of Donnelly taking on the gruesome physical form that Max now watched pour hellish retribution into Tom's crumbling consciousness. The dead man's will had risen above the curse, strengthened by Max's love for his family and the torturous memory of the life it had once lived. The thing wasn't a ghost in the traditional sense. It was a material manifestation of the crux of the ancient evil curse.

The energy required to enable the gruesome undead entity to cross over into the dimension of the living was immense. It was easier in the early morning hours, particularly around 3AM, the witching hour of folklore. It had stayed in its cocoon of misery for most of the week in preparation for Max's visit with Tom.

At length the Donnelly thing released Tom with a shove, sending him to the floor where he lay in a heap, a dazed, ghostly look on his face. He had vomited several times and the disgustingness of the scene was fitting. The cursed ghoul turned to Max who nodded with a heavy sigh. His life was about to change and Max owed everything to the cursed soul of a good man. The thing seemed to melt away. When there was nothing left to be seen the graven rasp of its breath could still be heard for several moments.

"You know he's still here, right?" Max walked over to the broken man that Tom had become. "He'll be with you now, my gift to you. Once I had the book it wasn't hard to find a spell that would turn your curse back on you."

Tom reached for the book, but fell flat on his face. "Max... I'm, I'm sorry," was all he could say.

"Yeah?" Max replied. "I'm sure you're very sorry. It will take you time to recover from what you just experienced, but you'll never be the same. Your nice life will spiral down the drain. I imagine Amber will leave you and god knows what other shit will rain down on you."

Max stared silently at the now weeping man on the floor. Then he let out a long breath and delicately ripped a single page from the book. He set it on the recording console.

"I'd love to leave you to wallow in your own darkness, but that wouldn't be right. What you did to me was terrible and unforgiveable, but what you did to Mark Donnelly was so much worse. This page will allow you to set him free. God knows he deserves to rest in peace more than anyone else I can think of. You, being the originator of the curse, are the only one that can reverse it. I'm very pleased I could turn it back on you, but it's up to you to set Donnelly free."

He kicked Tom urgently in the leg. "Now! Get up here and do it before I change my mind. There are so many things I could do to you with this book. I'm not like you though. I wouldn't be able to live with myself."

A short time later, sitting in his car and looking at Tom's home in the darkness, he thought about Amber. He didn't know what extent dark magic played in her vacating his life, but he knew it should have been different. Back then things should have come together. Back then Amber was his light and she could have guided him to many beautiful things, but that was gone and letting it all go now was easy.

He drove to the lake and walked to the spot where he had laid out kindling wood earlier in the day. As he tendered and fanned the flames of the small fire he said a quiet prayer for Mark Donnelly. He tore the pages from the book and burned them one at a time being careful not to allow any part of it to escape the flames.

"Be at peace, man."

Later, satisfied that nothing but black ash remained of the grimoire, he drove home to Molly, to his children, to the hope and promise that waited there, to his good life.

Dwelling of the Wolf
by Franklyn Searight

Lois Templer experienced recurring dreams about the place for nearly a month. She wondered why, each morning upon waking, the lovely cottage had such an effect upon her every night after falling asleep. Why it should invade her dreams, she had no idea, but it did, and so frequently that it had become a part of her waking thoughts—troubled feelings that took on a different perspective as the nightly visions continued.

Pink curtains covered the four windows that fronted the small building, fleecy and diaphanous, and even ethereal, so flimsy that those within could see out and those without could see in, if they were close enough and bothered to do so. The square windows, arranged in a symmetrically pleasing pattern, two on the bottom floor, and two on the top, were set in their casements, and peered out to view the forest trail upon which Lois walked in he dream.

Lois couldn't see anyone in any of the windows. From a distance, at least, the hovel appeared to be quite empty.

The young lady, barely having reached her twenty-first birthday, had seen the place in her first dream from some distance away. Exiting the forest, and standing at its edge, she had looked at it in wonder. No one had ever mentioned to her that such a cottage existed deep in the woods, so she was quite certain that it was a place created by the fantasy of her mind, and had no actual presence in reality. In her first dream, she had taken but one step towards it, planning to see it from a closer vantage point, when it suddenly disappeared and she found herself in bed, eyes wide open, a plump sliver of moon peeking through her bedroom window. Each succeeding dream had been rather similar, but during each one she was able to take an additional step or two, allowing her to draw closer to the small house that so fascinated her. And each time she took the steps, she would sense a wavering in the air and feel a shift beginning to take place; the scene would vanish and she would awake in her bed, the little dwelling eerily gone, and she would awake in wonderment. Some night, she thought, if she continued to dream as she had been, she would reach the abode and attempt to learn what was inside, and just whom it was who lived there.

But this would not be the night, she suspected, although this time it *was* a little different. This time she could discern, from the corner of her eye, another shape beginning to emerge. It was an animal that caused her to gasp aloud, but too far away to identify with any certainty, other than that it seemed to belong to the canine family, judging by its long snout. Perhaps a coyote? Maybe a fox? It could even have been a wild dog. Or, and this caused her to slightly shudder, a wolf! This scenario would frighten most young ladies, but as a practitioner of judo, who planned to earn her black belt later in the year, she was unafraid.

She took another step to get an even better perspective and...

...awoke in her bed. She sat up to find the bedclothes were in an untidy heap, no longer covering her, and her skin crawled with what felt like invisible ants and unexpected perspiration, for the night was warm and pleasant.

Oh'm'gosh, she thought to herself. That was awful. Her dream was turning into a nightmare!

Swinging her legs to the floor, she grabbed her yellow robe, lavishly embroidered at the bottom, from a nearby chair; she donned it and stood up. Running fingers through her hair, she found it to more disarrayed than usual, and knew a rigorous combing was needed. But that could wait until morning, which she knew to be several hours away, at least. The golden moon shed enough light into her room to reveal the clock on her nightstand indicating the time to be shortly past three o'clock in the morning.

No point in bothering to get up now, she thought, and removed her robe, placing it on the chair. She sat upon the bed, thoughtfully, and then swung her legs onto the soft mattress and laid her head upon the feathery pillow. She had no problem in returning to sleep, nor did the dreams begin again that night.

* * * *

Lois, for the last three weeks, had been staying at the home of Sue Benson, her college roommate. Actually, the home belonged to Sue's parents who were out of the country touring India, a vacation for which they had long anticipated and tirelessly prepared. They had left Sue to take care of the property, knowing she could be entirely relied upon, and had endorsed the idea of having Lois join her during the summer months while they were away from their dorm room at Westwood College.

Sue had grown up and lived in the rambling house, set at the edge of vast tracks of forested land, ever since her birth. Having Lois as her companion for the two and a half months they would be there was a delightful arrangement they had eagerly agreed to, as both young ladies were of the same age and of the same pleasing temperament, a combination that almost assured them a pleasant time together.

* * * *

Morning dawned with a rosy glow that awakened Lois, but she squinted her eyes, turned over after glancing at the clock, and had no difficulty in falling asleep again. It was nearly nine o'clock when she finally emerged from her bedroom, stepped into the shower for a warm cleansing, and chose and slipped into the outfit she had decided to wear that day. Entering the kitchen, she nodded to Sue, and wished her a good morning. Lois smiled pleasantly, and attempted to appear happy and chipper, but Sue wasn't fooled.

"What's the trouble?" the pretty brunette asked, casually.

"Oh, nothing," Lois returned. "Nothing at all."

"Well, 'nothing' is certainly messing up your face," Sue observed. "If those puffy bags under your eyes were really caused by 'nothing', I'd hate to see what you look like when 'something' *was* troubling you."

"Oh, that." Lois forced a smile and looked at her companion, at the same time moving a box of Cheerios over to her side of the table. "I suppose you're right. Haven't been sleeping at all well, lately."

She bowed her head and stopped talking as she silently attended to her morning prayer of thankfulness. Sue didn't say anything until she raised her head.

"Is that right? That's what happens when you have so many secrets crowded into that perky little head of yours. I suppose most honey-brown-haired people usually have something to worry about."

"Not really." Lois began, pouring cereal into a bowl. She doused it with milk and two pouches of Equal before spooning her first bite. "I just haven't been sleeping well, that's all. Strange dreams—a recurring one, actually, that I've had every night, almost since I've been here."

"I can see it's been troubling you, Lo. Maybe you should take something before you go to sleep—something to relax you and chase those awful dreams away."

Lois smiled again, settling into her meal with her usual gusto. "Maybe I can find some over-the-counter preparation—something non-addictive. But I doubt if it will help."

"*Tell me about it*, Lo." Sue was finishing her breakfast of French Toast swimming in maple syrup. She poured another cup of coffee from the urn on the table. "The dream, I mean."

"Well, as I said, it's a continuously recurring one. It began with me first emerging from a dark forest—might even be the one behind us, for all I know—and seeing a pretty cottage some distance away. I move toward it. The dream doesn't last long before I wake up, or drift into a different dream. In each succeeding dream I'm able take a step or two closer to the little hovel, and then I wake up again. This kept happening until last night, when I found myself closer to the place than ever before. It was a pretty bungalow, painted lovely colors, and it made me think of the cottage that Hansel and Gretel discovered deep in the woods, although there were no candy canes or gingerbread men surrounding it."

"No witch hanging around, either, I suppose. That doesn't sound like a very unpleasant dream to me," Sue observed.

"It was okay until last night. That's when I found myself much closer to the place and learned that I wasn't alone in the dream. Out of the corner of my eye I saw an animal slinking—actually a *beast*—just out of my sight."

"Really? What kind of creature was it?" Sue asked.

"I'm not actually certain. A wolf, maybe. A dog. Something from the canine family, anyway. I didn't have time to become actually scared, because I woke up."

Sue forked the last of her French Toast to her mouth and carried her plate to the sink.

"Now it doesn't sound *at all* pleasant, Lo—not with a wolf hanging around."

"No. Not at all. What do you suppose all of this means, Sue?"

"What it means is that you have to get some medical preparation from the drugstore, one that will help you sleep and prevent these dreams from occurring."

"Do you think they portent danger of some kind?"

"No, not at all. Dreams aren't real, you know. It's just your mind working out problems you've had during the day. In one of my classes I learned that they erase sensory impressions that haven't been completely resolved, and ideas that haven't been fully developed. There's no meaning to them, other than that."

Lois swallowed the last of her coffee. "I certainly hope you're right."

* * * *

Lois's initial observation that the persistent dream was taking on the dimensions of a nightmare proved to be correct. That night, she dosed herself with Nytol, an over-the-counter preparation containing Diphenhydramine, confident it would do the trick and settle her down for a relaxing, dreamless sleep. She squirmed about in the bed, selected a comfortable position, punched up her pillow, and then closed her eyes.

But she was wrong.

She did dream. And the dimensions of the visions that were invoked expanded far beyond that for which she had been prepared. Her stroll through the forest took longer than usual, more territory seemed to be covered, new and somewhat alarming visions appeared before her, such as the sunflower she passed that was unable to control fits of coughing, or the frog she spied on the ground with three legs, that was unable to hop in a straight line. And the noises that she heard were truly alarming: Sounds that might have been innocently made by owls and bats and winged insects, seemed to be magnified and accompanied by strange music that might have been vocalized by a chorus of banshees.

She had just emerged from what she had begun to think of as a magical forest when she saw, directly ahead of her in the distance, what appeared to be a wolf. It was approaching the cottage from a different direction than she was taking, and stood there at the walk leading to the door. It looked about to see if anyone was watching, and turned to the cottage. Swiveling, it placed one back paw before the other and walked on its toe pads up the short walk to the porch on its hind legs. There it looked around once again and, satisfied that it was quite alone, shoved at the door with a forepaw. It swung open, and the wolf entered and pushed the door closed.

Oh'm'gosh, Lois thought, is this all part of the dream? Was that a *real* wolf I saw, or a piece of fancy my imagination projected into my dream?"

Lois was bewildered! What she was witnessing was impossible, of course.

Wolves did not walk on their hind legs!

At least, none that she had ever seen did. Only in one's imagination could such a happening occur.

Wolves did not live in houses!

She rubbed her eyes with both hands, carefully.

* * * *

She just had to find out if what she had seen was real, or a part of her dream, or a portion of some other dream. Walking rapidly, almost skipping, she closed the distance to the little house. She was almost at the place where the one path bisected with the dirt trail she was following, when another figure appeared, near enough to suggest he might have been following the wolf.

The figure appeared to be a woodsman carrying an enormous axe on his shoulder. He didn't seem to notice Lois at all, although he passed so closely that she could have reached out and touched him. The young lady was so stunned by his appearance that she was temporarily speechless, and offered no greeting to the man. She marveled at his attractive good looks, his brown wavy hair that fell almost to his shoulders, and the firm set of his lips. He wore a heavy red-checkered coat and a cap, its earflaps down. He turned at the walk leading to the house, slowed his footsteps, and made his way to the door.

Just as the wolf had shoved the door open and entered, so did the woodsman, closing the panel behind him.

For long moments the young lady was transfixed. But Lois was Lois, and rarely did one encounter a maiden of such bravery and tenacity, combined with such an adventuresome spirit. She started forward, following in the footsteps of the two that had preceded her, her one hope being that she would not awaken yet and find herself in bed, the dream over.

At the door, she stopped and raised her hand to politely knock upon the entryway, then lowered it. Better not to announce her arrival, she decided. Not yet, anyway. Instead, she moved over to the nearest window and looked through the gauzy transparency of the curtain, where she was able to see what was taking place in the room.

A round table was in the center, four chairs drawn up to it, and sitting in one of them was the wolf, its back to the window, studying a landscape picture suspended on the wall above the mantle that framed an old fireplace, empty of kindling.

Behind the wolf stood the woodsman, the large axe he carried raised and obviously in the act of bringing it down upon the head of the creature, which seemed to be much larger than when it had passed her. Why, she asked herself, was the man about to dispatch the animal?

Impulsively, she rapped upon the window, drawing the attention of the two in her direction!

The wolf, seeing the woodsman behind him, scrambled out of its chair and raised itself to its full height to face him. The man spun around to see who had disturbed him in the act of disposing of the wolf.

Lois was surprised to see the man's handsome face twist in rage, reddening by the moment, distress and anguish written over every line. The wolf, in turn, seemed to have more beatific features. Its eyes glimmered in gratitude, a slight smile pulled at the muscles of its snout, and its paws seemed relaxed.

Lois left the window and made her way to the door. She shoved it open and…

…found herself in bed. The moon had risen and was now framed in her bedroom casement.

* * * *

Lois was more than a little distraught as she went down to breakfast the next morning. Sue greeted her, alarmed by the drawn, haggard look on the face of her friend.

"My goodness," she exclaimed. "Another night with no sleep?"

"Oh, I slept, all right," Lois returned, "but it was more of a nightmare than just an ordinary dream."

"Oh, dear!" Sue scurried about, sliding the bacon she been frying onto a plate, and cracking two eggs into the same pan. "You told me you'd be taking some Nytol, so I was hopeful that everything would be fine last night."

"Well, it started out okay," explained Lois. She paused to lower her bowed head in prayer, and then raised it to sip on some orange juice Su had poured for her. "It was the same dream—at least it started out that way. But it…it…"

Lois took another sip and then proceeded to describe the dream she had, in as much detail as she could remember, relating how the woodsman was attempting to kill the animal.

Sue listened patiently, interrupting her friend now and then with what she believed to be helpful questions and comments.

"But I don't know if he killed it or not," Lois concluded, "because it was then that I woke up."

Both were finishing the last dregs of their tea when Sue glanced over to the kitchen clock.

"Oh, oh," she said. "Drink up…and quickly. Don't forget we're going to church early to help Parson arrange the pies and cakes for the bake sale."

"Church? Today is only Saturday!"

"I know that, silly. Did you forget that we volunteered to help set up the display for the church today?"

"Oh'm'gosh!" Lois exclaimed. "I *did* forget! I'll change right away, Sue, and be with you in a jiffy."

Lois did not want to keep Sue waiting, so the change was accomplished without her usual thoughtful consideration. She slipped into a dark pair of slacks and a fetching light blue blouse, the first things that came to hand that were presentable, and ran a comb through her hair a few times while glancing in the mirror. She considered applying a dab of lipstick, and then changed her mind.

As she stood there, debating whether to put on different shoes, she heard Sue call up the stairs, telling her they needed to get moving *now*. "Are you going with me?" she asked, "or are you taking Suzie the Suzuki?"

Lois thought for a moment before responding. "Oh, I guess I'll take Suzie. It needs some pampering."

"I wish you wouldn't call your cycle Suzie, Lo," Sue grumbled, walking to the front door. "I never know when you're talking about your bike or me. Why don't you call it the Silver Screamer or the Silver Bullet, or something like that?"

"I'll think about it, Sue. I think I prefer the Silver Bullet to Suzie the Suzuki."

"See you at the church in a few."

Suzie the Suzuki, now christened the Silver Bullet, was Lois's motorcycle that she had recently acquired. She was still learning the finer techniques of riding the silver-tinted model that sparkled in the sun as she stormed about the countryside.

Sue would be driving her car, and Lois would follow on her motorcycle. Deciding she looked good enough for what they had in mind, she hurried out of her room, down the stairs and outside. It took longer than she thought, Lois considered, seeing that Sue's car was no longer parked in front of the home, and was just barely vanishing down the street. She hurried to the shed where she kept her vehicle, rolled it out, swung onto the seat, put on her helmet, turned the key, and away she went in a burst of speed.

The welcoming purr of the engine was a kind of music to her ears, a sort of riding concerto. She squeezed the throttle, gunning the bike slightly, and followed after her friend. It was another pleasant morning. Lois enjoyed the bracing air as it swept into her face, and the noise of the paved road as the tires caught hold.

Five minutes later she turned into the parking lot at the church and continued to a space near the door. Few cars were there at this time. Lois shut off the engine, removed her helmet and set it on the seat. She waved at Sue who had exited from her car and stood there waiting for her.

"Beat you," Sue said as Lois drew near.

"Big deal. With your heavy foot on the pedal, you beat everyone on the road!"

Sue answered her with a big smile, turned and started for the side entrance.

"Wait," said Lois, stopping suddenly. "That man—standing by the door."

"Nice looking guy," returned Sue. "Hair's a little long, though. You interested?"

"No, it's not that. But I think I've seen him before. Have I?"

She studied him a few moments longer, and then snapped her fingers in remembrance. "Of course, I have! He looks like the woodsman who's been a part of my dreams for the last month."

"He's the man of your dreams?" Sue asked.

"Not the man of my dreams, Sue—the man *in* my dreams."

"You sure about that?"

"Yes, it is—either that, or he's an exact double. Maybe he's a twin."

"But he's not dressed the same," Lois added. "When I saw him, he was dressed as a woodsman: red coat, black high top boots, a bright red hat with earflaps on it. But now he's wearing that snappy blue suit and red tie."

"Well, we'll be passing him in a moment. We can ask him if he likes to hike around in the forest."

"Don't you dare say a word, Sue! I'll handle this myself."

Lois moved ahead of her companion, slowing down when she reached the young man standing by the door. She smiled pleasantly at him, and he nodded his head and held the door open for them. Sue followed behind her, and the two descended to the basement hall where the bake sale was being set up. For the next two hours, the girls spent their time adding decorations to the walls and tables, and bringing out the cakes and cookies and other delicacies that were being dropped off, some even the night before.

"Everything looks so scrumptious," said Sue. "The ladies really went to town for the event."

"They certainly did," Lois agreed. "I want to run my finger over some of that frosting and taste it—just to be sure it's real, and not a fake. Wouldn't want anyone to be disappointed."

Sue giggled, grabbing one of the larger cakes and carrying it to one of the long tables where the baked goods were being displayed.

The morning passed with all of the fun and enjoyment they had expected to have. They stopped to visit with assorted parishioners, who came by to help and chat, and worked with a will to have everything finished and ready for the big festivities to begin later that day.

The young man that had earlier caught the girls' attention stopped by to survey the kitchen crew and spent a few minutes talking with them. He admired their presentation of the baked goods that had been prepared, and introduced himself as Clark Wily. Lois found herself a bit tongue-tied when it came to speaking with him, but he seemed to be so sincere and casual that he soon put her and the others at ease. He explained that he was the church's newly hired accountant, and was there to get an idea of the different activities being offered to the congregation.

After he left to introduce himself to others, Sue asked: "Are you still certain he's the man you saw in your dreams, Lo?"

"Well, no. Oh, I don't know. I *think* so, but Clark didn't show any sign of recognizing me. It must be a simple case of faulty identification."

* * * *

Later, Pastor Durant stopped by to watch them applying the final touches to their arrangement and get ready to begin cleaning up. He smiled pleasantly, thanked them, and let them know what a fine job they were doing for the Lord's work. This pleased Lois so much, an avid volunteer and dedicated churchgoer, that a donut rolled off the plate she was carrying and landed on the floor.

"No harm," said the genial pastor. "Just give it to Irma. No one will notice that one is missing."

Irma was the church kitty, dozing in a corner. Lois didn't know if donuts were on its diet, but took it over anyway and set it next to the dozing, prostrate cat. Irma took no notice of the offering and slept on.

It was nearly lunchtime when the task was finished and everything was ready for the sale to begin in a few hours. Sue and Lois met together and nodded at a job well done.

"What shall we do for lunch?" Lois asked.

"I've been meaning to ask you if you'd give me a ride on the Silver Bullet," Sue said. "Maybe we could go back to the house; you pick me up, and we'll scoot over to McDonalds for a meaty meal."

"Sounds good to me," answered Lois, removing the apron she had been wearing and looking around the room one last time for a final survey. "So, let's go. Race you back to the house."

Sue went to her car and Lois to her cycle. The biker adjusted her helmet and steered her Suzuki out of the parking lot. The air was a bit windy, catching the strands of her blondish hair and forming them into a disarrayed mop as she accelerated onto the highway and began the three-mile journey back to the house. Sue was there, parking her car in the driveway as Lois rode up beside her. Sue wiggled on to the seat behind her friend and held on tightly as Lois scooted back onto the street. Lois sped a little faster than usual, taking the turns a tad more precariously, just to show off a bit and give her friend an added thrill. Soon they arrived at Mickey D's where Lois turned in at the lot, and parked her bike near the entrance.

* * * *

Lois was taking a small bite of the double cheeseburger she held, and sipping from her Coke to wash it down, when she suddenly exclaimed: "Oh'm'gosh! Look who's here?"

"No, don't look around!" Lois cried, but a bit too late. Sue had already turned and was gazing over her shoulder.

"Say, that's Clark, isn't it?" she asked, referring to the young man who had just entered the restaurant.

The man's flowing hair was unmistakable.

Lois nodded. "It's either Clark, or the woodsman I saw in my dream."

"Are you sure, Lo? Really *sure*? I can't imagine how Clark could appear in your dreams. You've never seen him before, not 'till today. How could you dream about him? It must be someone who just looks a lot like him."

Lois didn't answer until she had finished chewing. "I don't know. You're right, of course," she responded reflectively, taking another bite from her sandwich. "There's probably nothing to it at all—just a coincidence. Coincidences do happen, you know. There's a perfectly reasonable explanation for all of this."

"Of course there is."

"So, don't ask me to explain it, Sue. I have no idea. I admit it's strange—extremely strange. Eerily strange, but we shouldn't get carried away.

"Look! He's seen us, and he's coming this way. No, don't look!"

Clark stopped before the ladies, holding a tray with the lunch he had ordered.

"So, you've been following us around, have you?" said Lois teasingly. She fixed him with an elfin grin that seemed to brighten her entire face.

"Not at all," he answered. "I just stopped in for a bite to eat. Do you two eat here often?"

"Only when we're hungry," returned Sue.

"And that's almost all the time," added Lois.

Clark's smile deepened. "May I join you, ladies?"

"Of course, you may," said Lois, pushing her tray aside to give Clark room for his. "Did you finish all your work at the church?"

"Not all. Still lots to do, being the new guy around here. But a fella's gotta eat—keep up his strength."

The girls noted that Clark didn't waste any time consuming his meal. In four large bites, the Big Mac disappeared, as the man masticated quickly, swallowing a gulp of coffee after each bite. A famished tiger might have consumed the meal as quickly.

"Hate to eat and run," he said, blotting his lips with a napkin, "but I've got to be on my way."

"Bit date, huh?" asked Sue.

"No, nothing like that. It's time I bought a new hunting outfit, and I've noticed the sporting goods store down the street. I'm going over there and look around—maybe get a new rifle, too."

"Oh, you're a hunter, are you?" asked Sue.

"Avid," he returned. "Whenever I get the chance."

"I'm done some hunting myself," said Lois, "chasing the dear deer," she quipped. "I even gutted a deer once—love that venison!"

"Me, too. I've eviscerated more than my fair share. Let me know if you have occasion to do one again. I can give you a few tips to make the work easier."

Clark reached for his tray, preparing to leave. "It's been nice, ladies. Thank you for the company."

"Well, have a nice time shopping," Lois wished him.

Clark nodded. "See you two later."

Clark held his tray sturdily as he carried it to the disposal bin, and waved casually at the women as he exited the building.

"Well, what do you think of that?" asked Sue when he was out of sight. "It's a nice friend you've found there, Lo. Appears to be about your age, also—maybe just a little older."

"Stop it, Sue. My interest in him isn't romantic. It's much more than that."

"Is it?"

"Sue, Clark *is* the hunter that I saw in those dreams I've been telling you about." She waited for the laughter to begin, but it didn't.

"You're serious, aren't you? You really mean it?"

"I do. And yet, I don't know *what* to think," answered Lois, taking a small bite from the last half of her burger. "The man is a *hunter*. It's either him or his twin, in my dream. The two of them certainly appear to be the same person."

* * * *

Lois pushed the rocking chair in her bedroom over to the window; she opened it, inviting the slight, cooling breeze to join her inside. The phase of the moon was nearing full, an enormous golden shield, slightly flattened at one side. It rode the sky, as might a monarch in charge of his royal domain. There seemed to be a pattern on the etched surface, but so dim that it defied her ability to interpret any distinct image. The orbiting body seemed to be silently calling to her, attempting to relate to her a narrative of past episodes it had chronicled. She stared at it dreamily, wondering what it would be like to be a fair maiden living on its surface.

That night, Lois's dream returned as though it had never ended.

The pattern was familiar. She found herself wandering through what took on the dimensions of an enchanted wood. Trilling cords of melodic beauty drifted from the treetops, even though it was nighttime and all avian life, except for the owls, should have been asleep. Fawns, their necks decorated with dangling garlands, poked their heads from around gnarled tree trunks, and even smaller creatures made an appearance in an effort to welcome her to their domain. She smiled at each and every one she encountered, and skipped along the path before her.

Reaching the end of the forest, she hesitated before stepping out of the comforting, sylvan surroundings, and then continued upon the path that led straight ahead...ahead to the cottage in the woods that had become so familiar to her.

The place she was beginning to think of as the wolf's house!

The *wolf's* house?

That sounded so strange to her. Wolves didn't live in cottages. They were fortunate if they had a warm den burrowed into the earth in which to live.

Suddenly, from the corner of her eye, she beheld the woodsman coming, and then stop. Was he looking at her? He made no sign that he noticed her at all. There appeared to be something different about him, though, and almost at once she realized what it was. The outfit he was wearing! It was much more of a solid orange, rather than the checkered red, as before. An orange cap, earflaps folded down, was on his head.

But no wolf had walked ahead of him into the house. Was it already inside?

The huntsman turned at the walk leading to the door. On the small porch, he leaned over to look in the window. Apparently satisfied by what he observed, he lowered the axe he carried, lifted his shoulders, and pushed the door opened. He went inside and closed it behind him.

Lois didn't hesitate. She hurried to the walk, up the steps to the window, and peeked through the flimsy, gossamer curtains, just as she had witnessed the woodsman doing.

What she saw brought a cry of surprise to her lips, as she beheld the man who seemed, from this distance, to look so much like Clark. He was standing behind the wolf who apparently had no knowledge yet of his presence, raising his axe in a threatening manner. It appeared to be a continuation of the last dream that had ended so quickly and indecisively.

Lois tapped on the window.

Suddenly, the creature slightly turned, saw the woodsman behind it with the axe raised to strike, and Lois standing outside, watching them.

Everything happened so quickly. Clark, or the woodsman, turned to see where the wolf was looking, and saw Lois watching them through the window. As he did so, the wolf fled to the back door and opened it wide. The noise attracted the woodsman's attention. He turned around, saw the wolf leaving, and hurled the huge axe at it, just as it slipped out of sight.

The wolf was safe, thought Lois, at least for the time being. Whether the man chased after it, caught it and slew it, she did not know because…

…the cottage was gone. She was sitting up in bed, back in the Benson's home, opening her eyes to stare at the earth's golden companion in the window. The moon had advanced considerably, moving from one side of the pane to the other.

What did this all mean, she wondered, relieved to be out of the dream state and functioning once again in the world of reality. She buried her face in her hands, rubbing her eyes, knowing the best thing for her to do would be to go back to sleep and trust that the hallucinations, or dream revelations, did not return.

She hoped she would fall asleep quickly and the midnight hours pass rapidly, until morning came, and she could relate this additional dream piece to Sue.

* * * *

The following day was Sunday. The two ladies dressed in their Sunday best and arrived at the service a bit early, hoping to be seated near the front of the church. Clark was there ahead of them, but had chosen to sit in the back. Sue went ahead to save seats for the two, while Lois stayed back to converse with the young man.

"Yes," said Clark in answer to Lois' question. "I did get a new hunting outfit. A nice one."

"Hope you bought a bright orange coat so the other hunters wouldn't mistake you for a bear or a tiger."

"As a matter of fact, I did. Hat, too. I'm sure I won't be mistaken for a wild animal.

"Didn't find a rifle that I like, though; but I know of another place that sells them, and I'll stop by there tomorrow."

"Good for you," said Lois. "We'll see you after the service."

* * * *

Two nights passed before Lois dreamed again. The same wolf came along and went into the tiny house, followed by the same man who looked so much like Clark, but carrying a rifle this time rather than an axe.

It occurred to Lois: He was no longer a woodsman. He was now a *huntsman*.

As before, the man opened the door when he reached it and followed the wolf into the cottage. Lois, of course, was quick to follow the man and watch the two from her vantage point at the window. What she saw was an animal slaughter about to take place! The thought came to her that she must warn the wolf, so she did, rapping on the pane a few times to get its attention.

Suddenly, the creature slightly turned and pointed its paw at the window, directly at Lois who was standing outside, watching the action that transpired within.

The huntsman lowered his gun and turned to see who had made the noise, and at that moment, the wolf made its move!

With astonishing agility and speed, even for a springing wolf, it lunged at the huntsman. Although smaller, it knocked him off his feet, the rifle flying off to a corner of the room. The element of surprise is always a worthy companion to have during a conflict, thought Lois.

The huntsman attempted to rise, but he was too late. The wolf was on him, its long snout buried in his neck. Clark, if it were actually he, with a loud rattling gasp that could be heard outside by Lois, snatched the knife he carried from its sheath and thrust it into the area of the wolf's heart. It snarled savagely and stepped back, showing long pointed teeth, spitting out a small chunk of flesh and blood that it had ravaged, while from the fatal knife wound in its chest spouted a scarlet fountain to the floor.

The wolf was a goner. But the man, not wounded quite as severely, with only a nasty wound in his neck, just might survive.

And then an extremely curious and unexpected happening occurred. As though it had been a planned transformation, the wolf shifted its position *and turned into a human being*, a large man. The huntsman, at the same time, *slowly evolved into an enormous timber wolf* that glared up at Lois with yellow, sorrowful eyes with a huge nose and ruddy, hirsute face!

Lois cried out, stepping back in awe and horror, unable to move for long moments. Oh'm'gosh, she thought, just what is it that I've seen? The idea came to her of werewolves, beasts that terrorize the evening folk by biting their victims and turning their prey into werewolves, also. The knife used by the huntsman had appeared to be one of silver as it slid into the torso of the wolf. And, according to accepted folklore, perhaps that was all that would be needed to dispatch the beast!

Lois knew, even as she watched, that this was nothing but a dream— but it seemed to be so very, very real—a dream based in some sort of reality, an absurd inner meaning not yet revealed to her. Assembling her courage, she opened the door and began to walk inside, but found herself wide-eyed and looking around her bedroom in the Benson house.

* * * *

Lois could hardly wait for Sunday morning to arrive to inform Sue about her dream. She also intended to mention it to Clark who had said he was planning to attend the eleven o'clock service, and that he would see them there.

However, despite his previous assurances, and the desire he had expressed to see them and the other parishioners again, Clark did not make an appearance. The ladies were a bit disappointed, but not overly so.

They liked him well enough, but neither would have considered him as a serious suitor. His pleasant personality, his rugged good looks, the silky smoothness of his wavy brown hair would have appealed to most young women, but there was something about him, something indefinable that neither one could understand or begin to identify—something that urged both to proceed with caution as they got to know him better. Even so, Lois was wearing her long, yellow-patterned dress that nearly touched the floor, and her new bonnet that she deliberately wore at a rakish angle. Both complemented her honey-blonde hair that was almost covered by her sun-hat.

During a lull in the service, Lois leaned over and said to Sue, in a low undertone, "I'm so sorry Clark didn't make it here today. Maybe he'll show up soon. I'd like to tell him about my wolf dreams."

"Why would you want to tell him about that?" whispered Sue back.

"Why? Because he's a hunter! Perhaps he knows something about wolves. Besides, he coincidentally resembles the hunter in my dream."

"Well, maybe he'll be at next Sunday's service."

"Maybe."

After the processional, the young ladies moved about from one small gathering to another, chatting and exchanging the current news. Pastor Durant was there to greet everyone and ask how they were doing. The only one who was not there appeared to be Clark. No one, including the minister, seemed to know where he could be or what he might be doing instead of being with the group. He had mentioned to others that he planned to be there, so his absence was becoming somewhat of a mystery.

* * * *

It was on their way home from church that Lois, on her bike, followed by Sue, in her car—the two vehicles stirring up clouds of dust—that the unexpected happened.

All would have been well, Lois later realized, if she had not taken her eyes off the highway momentarily, as she approached a fork in the road. It was then that a large animal darted out of the woods directly into her path. Too late, she saw it, applied the brakes and tried to swerve around it. It was like running into a terrific boulder! She bounced nearly a foot from the seat and came down with a jar that seemed to make her teeth rattle. The result was predictable. The animal—a huge wolf—lay near the front wheel of the cycle that had skidded, veered off and fallen near the side of the road. The animal's body was twisted, its long face smeared with blood. It seemed to gasp as its eyes rolled back, and a strange look of contentment relaxed the ferocious lines of its face.

Lois pulled herself off the bike and stood up, shakily.

"Oh'm'gosh," she cried. "What have I done?"

The wolf managed to turn its head, look up at her, and relax with a look of beatitude, as it slowly closed its eyes and expired.

Aghast, her trembling voice saying repeatedly that she was sorry...so very, very sorry...Lois moved away from the bike. The front wheel seemed to be slightly bent and scratched, and she noted a thin stream of blood moving down her right leg from where she had scraped her knee. Other than that, both she and the cycle seemed to be okay.

Lois covered her eyes for a moment. This was something she would never have wanted to happen.

At that moment, Sue's car came to a stop behind her and she emerged to stand beside her friend.

"You have a dislike for wolves, don't you?" Sue noted, looking the situation over, the traces of a slight smile on his face.

"Of course not," Lois said testily, her eyes beginning to brim with tears, showing her obvious annoyance. "This is nothing to jest about!" Her irritation lasted for but a moment, and then she managed a small grin. How could she be annoyed with her best friend, who was trying to calm her down after the accident? "I'm just wondering what to do about this."

Sue examined the bike and announced it to be undamaged, although mildly scratched and possibly in need of minor repair work. "Why don't we just pull that furry brute off the road and pitch it into the woods. That shouldn't be too much trouble."

"Oh, no," exclaimed Lois.

She remembered the time a few years earlier when, accompanying her father on a hunting trip, they had gutted a deer. At first it had been a rather unpleasant, messy job, but as the internal organs of the deer were removed they became acclimated to the task, and began to take pleasure in it.

Why not, thought Lois? Gutting and skinning a wolf can't be that much more difficult than a deer.

"I want the pelt," she decided.

"The pelt?"

"Yes. As long as the brute is already dead, it would be a shame to waste its pelt. I want to skin the wolf and save it in my hope chest."

"You wouldn't!"

"I would. I will.

"Some day, I'll be married and live in a rambling house with two fireplaces. The wolf hide will look so nice on one of the hearths."

"I presume it would," Sue agreed, thinking this was just about the silliest idea she had ever heard, but left that sentiment unspoken. "Suppose we drag it over to my car, then, and put it in the trunk. Your bike appears to be rideable, so I'll follow you home, and then we'll put the beast wherever you want it to go."

"I was thinking of field dressing it first, then laying the remains over the back of my bike—like the olden cowboys did who used to drape a carcass over their horse's rump, to take back to town with them. But I guess gutting it at the house would be best. I'd hate for Pastor Durant to drive by and see me up to my elbows in blood, and my clothes splashed in crimson splotches."

"That's a strange idea, Lois. But I'm glad you agree my plan is best."

"Still—you'll get blood all over your trunk," Lois objected.

"I have an old blanket back there," Sue remembered. "That will soak up any blood. No harm will be done."

"Well, okay then. It's awfully nice of you. You're a real pal. Thanks!"

Sue nodded, knelt down and grabbed the expired animal by one of its front legs. Lois seized the other, and together they dragged the body to the back of the car. Sue opened the hatch and arranged an old blanket on which to lay the remains. They hoisted the carcass in, closed the trunk, and then stepped back.

"That's that," said Lois. "You follow me home, so you'll be near me if I have any trouble with the cycle. It seems to be okay, though, except for a small bend in the frame and a few scrapes."

"Sounds like a winning idea to me, Lo."

Lois stood the bike up and started it again. It roared into action as though nothing had happened to it. Carefully, she pulled back onto the road and continued to the Benson homestead, her eyes sparkling with the notion of how nice the hide of the creature would look, skinned and tanned, and stretched out before her hearth—when she had a hearth, someday.

Sue followed, a couple of car lengths behind her, as Lois scooted down the road, and followed as she pulled into the driveway.

Lois climbed off her bike and turned to find Sue leaving her car, a wide smile on her countenance.

"It runs fine," Lois declared, "but I'll take it into a shop soon and have an expert examine it to be sure everything is okay."

"You still plan to skin that wolf, Lo?"

"I do."

"Oh, Lo, you're such a tomboy at times."

"I know. Isn't it grand! You want to help me?"

"And at other times," Sue continued, "you're such a sweet, demure young lady!

"Well, that's the real me, of course!" She burst out into gleeful laughter.

"But, no, that's not a job that would appeal to me at all," declared Sue. "It's all yours. Have lots of fun with it."

Lois suddenly stopped laughing and turned to face her buddy. "Sorry. Guess I got carried away. I'm not always this giddy, am I, Sue?"

"Often enough," Sue returned.

"Well, help me pull it to the patio in the backyard. I won't be able to get around to it until later today."

Sue went over to the back of the car and opened the trunk. "Be careful not to get any blood on your clothes," she advised.

Lois reached into the compartment and, paying no attention to its weight, grabbed the stiffening wolf by the hind legs, swung it out of the back of the trunk, as though it were a small chipmunk, and onto the pavement. The two women dragged it over to the side of the house and onto a concrete path leading to the back, and then proceeded to haul it to the backyard and lay it on the large patio.

Lois brushed her hands together, as if to cleanse them of any contaminants.

"How about some lunch?" suggested Sue.

"That will be fine," agreed Lois, "afterwards, I'll get started on the wolf."

"Okay with me," said Sue. "Grilled cheese sandwiches sound alright?"

* * * *

Lois was anxious to begin, but nearly an hour passed before the ladies set their dishes in the sink. She excused herself for a while, explaining that she had to consult the Internet for some beginning instruction for the skinning, and tips she might need. More than two hours had passed since their return home before, with Sue's help, she hoisted the wolf up on the clothesline post, where it hung suspended, upside down, its hind paws tied to the cross bar.

"Thank you, Sue. I think I can handle it from here. You can run along, unless you want to stay and watch; but I warn you, this can get quite messy and a bit gruesome."

Sue hurried back into the house.

From Mr. Benson's toolbox in the garage, Lois found a large axe that she used to hack through the clavicle. Holding her filleting knife, which she usually carried in the Suzuki's implement compartment, she carefully made the first incision to gut the wolf. Her dark eyes sparkled happily. It was much like her earlier experience of gutting a deer a few years previously, following her father's instructions. Carefully, as precisely as she could, she bisected the wolf from the top to the bottom, working from the inside to the outside to avoid large accumulations of hair. As she progressed, she noticed a slit in the skin, and was careful at that point not to make the tear even larger. Her next cuts included the skin from the legs and the tailbone, and then she found she could pull much of the hide off, up to the neck, with minimal slicing involved. After that, more cutting was necessary.

Carefully, she carved from the hamstring down the back of the leg where the short hair met the long hair, making the cut all the way from the scrotum to the hamstring. She scrapped out the guts, depositing the sloppy, ghoulish remnants into garbage bags that she had set up for the disposal. As cautiously as possible, she used the filleting knife to remove the skin. It was a difficult and tedious process, time consuming, and the sun had advanced significantly into the west before she was finished. Most of the daylight hours were gone.

With the remaining time that she had, she soaked it in a solution of borax, warm water, some bleach, and commercial iodized salt, which was necessary to preserve the hide. She knew that if she ran out of salt, citric acid could be used just as well. That task completed, she allowed the skin to soak for nearly an hour, occasionally stirring it.

Tired but happy, satisfied that she had done her best, she carried the skin to the old refrigerator in the basement, where Sue said she could keep it until she was finished with it. At this point in the processing, Lois believed the skin weighed in at about twenty-five pounds, or so. She went back upstairs, washed up, and sought the comfort of an easy chair while Sue made noises in the kitchen, preparing an evening meal for the two of them.

Lois sat by her bedroom window that night, looking at the moon as it leisurely journeyed across the sky. She was weary from her work of the past few hours, but sat there contentedly, thinking of the additional tasks to come. By the next afternoon, she knew, the hide might begin to decompose. Before that happened, though, she would salt it again, replacing the old with the new, gently bending and rubbing the skin to keep the fibers pliable.

Lois did not remember any of her dreams that night.

* * * *

It was a grey, overcast morning that greeted her. She breakfasted quickly, retrieved the skin and took it to the patio where she had her processing station set up. She unrolled it, and begin to scrape off what flesh was left on it. She was working industriously at her task, and was going over to the side to spill out some icky water that had accumulated, when she noticed a dull object in the grass.

Lois walked over and looked at it. An amulet? A button? No. She picked it up, turned it over and discovered it was an aluminum dog tag. Printed on its surface, along with other pertinent information about its owner, was the name: Clark Wily.

Oh'm'gosh, she thought, this must be Clark's! Had he been in the service and worn it there? Was it simply an elaborate nametag given to him by an organization to which he belonged? But how had it gotten *here*?

She reflected on this question for sometime before deciding the only way to find out for certain was to ask him. Unless, and this was a laughable notion to which she paid no serious heed, unless it had somehow become entangled on the wolf, and fallen off, unseen, when it was brought to the patio.

A dog tag on a wolf?

Not impossible, but certainly improbable. She closed her eyes for a moment, picturing the savage animal bounding around the forests, wearing around its neck the tag belonging to Clark. Where could the animal have possibly gotten it? Certainly, all of this suggested that Clark knew about the creature. Could it have been a tame wolf that he owned? If it belonged to him she would feel terrible, doing what she was now doing.

* * * *

Using the picnic table in the backyard as a temporary frame, she stretched the skin tightly over its surface, allowing enough air to circulate around it. Carefully, she rubbed more salt onto it and then left it to cure. The next day, she anticipated, she would blow-dry the pelt, and then leave it in the old refrigerator where it would stay for the next couple of days.

And that's all there would be to it, Lois thought—at least as far as the skinning process. She well knew that the task ahead of her was much more demanding than she pretended it would be. But it will be worth all the effort, she thought. I'll have a beautiful pelt to display near my fireplace—when I get a fireplace.

She ran through the procedure once again, committing it to memory, so that everything flowed naturally for her, as though she were an old hand at the task.

* * * *

Lois did not dream that night—or the next—and she wondered why she hadn't. Had the episodes come to an end? She was actually beginning to miss them, but only a very tiny bit, as she expected they would probably return again—soon.

* * * *

The day finally arrived when she had the leisure to renew her work on the pelt. She retrieved it from the basement and carried it out to the picnic table in the back. She found that the hide, now dried, had changed in color from a pale pink to a flaky white, and had softened to a brittle consistency. Muscle tissue left on the skin had dried to a fibrous mush, and was much more difficult to remove than Lois had imagined. Scraping the hide with a two-bladed, metal hand tool, to be sure that any remaining flesh was removed, took the next few days, off and on. She did not allow her time with the wolf to interfere with her enjoyment of the summer days, as they marched inevitably toward the opening day of classes. Carefully, she scraped the hardened white flesh from the skin until she could see the pores of the true skin layer. If she were not careful, the face and belly skin would remain coated with flecks of muscle that wouldn't fully dry, and she would have to pick and scrape it off with her fingers.

It took hours, but by the time most of the flesh had been removed with the scraper, only white material remained around the tail, ears and elbows. She used a tool that fit onto a hand-drill she found in the Benson toolbox to burn away the flesh down to the true skin. She then soaked it in clear water and a small amount of borax for an hour, and then applied a tanning solution before letting it set for a few days, with a small amount of bleach added after that.

After soaking, the skin was removed from the solution, rinsed with clear water, squeezed dry and then laid out, flesh side down. It was soft and slick and the flesh had turned a whitish-grey due to the action of the tanning solution. Now and then, over a period of two days, it was partially blow-dried and gently hand-brushed, then left to dry overnight. After that, a thin layer of commercial hand soap was painted over the flesh side of the skin and left to be absorbed over three days, with the skin hanging upright by its ears. It dried thin and slightly brittle, but bendable. The finishing touch, which she would apply in two more days, would be an application of leather-conditioning oil to soften it.

It had been difficult work, harder than she had expected at the beginning, wearying, hour consuming, and even repetitiously boring at times, and she was beginning to wonder if it was worth all the time she had been putting into it.

* * * *

The following day was Sunday—Picnic Sunday, as it was known. The congregation had brought potluck to share, and Pastor Durant had baskets of fried chicken to pass around. They planned to retire to the park-like setting in back of the church and spend the next couple of hours dining on the goodies they had bought to share, participate in favorite games, and gossip to their hearts content.

It was nearing the time to end the festivities when Pastor Durant stepped up on a makeshift stage and, consternation etched on his face, told his concerns to the congregation. "I simply cannot understand," he began, "what might have happened to Mr. Clark Wily, our new accountant. Many of you have already met him, but no one seems to know where he has gone. Unfortunately, I haven't seen him for sometime now. Nor has anyone else. The man is missing! I'm sure that all of you are surprised and disappointed that he failed to show up today."

A hushed murmur went up around the crowd.

Parson Durant waved them to silence.

"We are befuddled, mystified. I've made extensive calls in an attempt to locate him, with no success. Unfortunately, we can wait no longer, and must find a replacement for him. So, if any of you are aware of a person who is qualified to handle the financial facets of the church, please let me know, and he or she will be considered. In the meantime, I will also go about looking for a new hire to take his place.

"I'm sorry, but we can wait no longer to fill his spot. Where, oh where, can Clark Wily be?" he concluded, stepping off the platform.

Silence stunned the group, but only for a few moments, and then a cacophony of dismay and distress burst out, and swept about the assembly.

Lois was perplexed. She did so want to talk with Clark, return the dog tag to him, and press him with further questions. But it very much appeared as though the young man was gone—possibly for good.

* * * *

That night, swaying back and forth in the rocking chair, Lois cleared her mind and attempted to unravel the weird situation in which she found herself involved. She thought of herself as a detective, perhaps Hercule Poirot, as she attempted to piece together the clues concerning the enigma. It's quite like sewing the patches of a quilt in their proper place, she reflected.

This time she did not discount the strange dreams and unexplained segments of the puzzle. She began with the certainty that the dreams were definitely *not real*, but were in some manner clairvoyant visions of an approaching reality.

Let me see, she began, attempting to put the sequences into their suitable places. Clark had moved to the area to begin duties as the new bookkeeper for the church, and it had been about that same time that her curious dreams had begun. It was in one of those dreams that Lois had glimpsed the wolf, for the first time, acting in some ways as though it were human. It had entered the house, only to be followed by the woodsman who tried to kill it with an axe. Following that, Lois and Sue had seen Clark at McDonald's where he had informed them he was a hunter—further, that he was planning to purchase a new outfit in which to stalk the forest game. In the final revelation, the woodsman appeared as a huntsman, carrying a gun, and followed the wolf into the house to shoot it.

Somehow, the wolf had overpowered the hunter and bit him, and was then killed with the silver-bladed knife. What followed next, the wolf turning into a human, and the hunter changing into a wolf, was the most amazing and unexpected part of the series of events.

Lois stopped, her head spinning. It almost seemed as though there were too many facts—and yet a pattern did seem to be emerging.

Her Suzuki had killed a wolf the following day, but Lois somehow believed that actually had little to do with the paranormal aspects of the situation. That *was* Lois' doing—her negligence— and not part of some mystic revelation. Or was it? Perhaps killing the wolf was the fulfillment of the entire prophetic sequence. Yes, that sounded more likely. But the decision to gut and skin the wolf was Lois' idea, hers alone, and a perfectly natural one, she felt. She had begun skinning it the very same day.

What could all of this possibly mean? One of them must have been a werewolf, she decided, but which? Maybe both?

Lois sat by the window for more than an hour as the moon, now in its full stage, continued its inevitable progress across the night sky.

The only conclusion Lois was able to reach was that, in the dream, Clark had been bitten by a werewolf and had turned into one himself after killing it. The real Clark had not been seen since that dream revelation. Could there be a connection? It was all so exceedingly complicated, but she believed that it must have happened something like that. To her, it all seemed to make some fantastic, weird sense.

She yawned, climbed into bed and closed her eyes, unable yet to answer the biggest question in her mind. If all that she supposed were true, where was the real Clark? Was he lying in some remote dream cottage, severely wounded? She *must* locate him and probe him with all her unanswered questions. She began to drift off to sleep, knowing that she would be up early in the morning to finish processing the hide, turning it into the fine wolf pelt that she had always wanted.

And then, like a jagged finger of lightning flashing out of the darkness, she knew what had happened!

Certain she was right, she closed her eyes again, and enjoyed a relaxing slumber, uninterrupted by mystifying visions.

She did not know it at the time, but she was never again to dream of either hunters or werewolves.

* * * *

It was the following day. Lois and Sue were sitting in the backyard, each in a comfy lounge chair, each enjoying a tall glass of sugary lemonade, enjoying the cooling breeze and the scent of newly mowed grass. Sue was deliberately averting her eyes away from the animal skin, now finished, on the other side of the patio.

"I would have laughed out loud," Lois was saying, "when Parson Durant wondered where Clark was, if I had realized then what had actually happened."

"Why? Do you know?"

"I think I only suspected at that time. I'm pretty sure now that I *do* know, although I can't be certain."

"Tell me more."

"Well, I hope I have everything reasoned out correctly. I sat up last night trying to put the pieces of the conundrum together.

"My dreams, of course, were not real. Dreams never are. But somehow my mind acquired the knowledge that, in his real life, Clark had been bitten by a werewolf, and had become a werewolf himself. The dreams were merely a trick my mind used to present that actuality to me. I've thought for a long time that I might be psychic, and this just might be a proof of it. It was a clairvoyant experience, precognitive visions of an actuality that was happening in real life."

She stopped, waiting for Sue to scoff at her.

But no jeering followed. Sue was listening carefully, not believing, but not disbelieving either.

"As best as I can determine, the reality is that Clark was a man leading two lives, one as an accountant, and the other as an actual werewolf. He was in his human form when bitten—I witnessed it in the dream where I saw him outfitted as a hunter, and he turned into a werewolf. That's why he didn't meet with us at the church. He was romping around the countryside in his wolf form when he ran in front of my cycle and was killed."

Sue was staring at her wide-eyed. "You can't be serious, Lo!"

"Oh, but I am. That explains everything, you see. Remember the dog tag I found? I'm sure he must have been wearing it when the werewolf bit him, and it remained on his neck when he turned into a beast himself. It was still there when he was killed, and it fell off by the patio."

"But are you *sure*?" asked Sue, "Wolfs are hard to kill—especially werewolves. According to legend, only a silver weapon can kill a werewolf. A silver sword, a bullet, a knife…something like that."

Lois was thoughtful for a moment. *"Well, it was killed by a Silver Bullet, you know—my motorcycle!"*

"But did it have to happen that way? Maybe Clark was the first werewolf and infected the second guy—and Clark was searching for him to get rid of the feeding competition."

"I guess it could have happened that way, Sue. But we'll probably never know."

"But *if* Clark was the original wolf, that means he got what was coming to him, and you have no reason to feel sorry for the accident."

"You're right about that. Again, we'll never know. But I'm now pretty sure that the threat of werewolves around here no longer exists."

"But it also means that…that…that Clark is…"

"Yes," agreed Lois, vigorously nodding her head.

"…that Clark is over there on the dissecting table!"

"Exactly," Lois agreed. "I told you I thought I knew where he was, bur I couldn't tell *that* to our parson.

"Won't Clark look wonderful spread out on my hearth?"

The Ruby Palace

by Jessica Amanda Salmonson

"When the nostalgia of red weighs upon me,
I raise my head to the sun,
and there, under its hot stings, with eyes obstinantly closed,
I see under the veil of my lids a red vapor;
I recall my thoughts,
and see once more, for a minute, for a second,
the disquieting fascination,
the unforgotten enchantment."
—Karl-Joris Huÿsmans

"Your name?" I asked the handsome fellow who I thought must be new to the Wind of Sorrows. I had myself been gone so long, and returned so recently, he might well have been a patron for some few months, so that he believed I, rather than he, was the newcomer. Still, by the response of familiar patrons, who eyed him circumspectly with a faint and unconfessed curiosity, I felt I was right in guessing him new to that mysterious and well-famed inn's café, though I did not think him by any means new to Aispont.

He had an unmistakable urbanity about him, and when the first words were out of his mouth, I knew him for that rarest of boulevardiers, a genuine native amidst cosmopolites. He had that hint of the aristocrat's pompous dialect, suggesting birth in the Palace-town, though his accent was muted, I would guess, by living some long while among one or another of Aispont's fashionably decadent quarters, possibly here in the Flauberg itself, though nowhere near the Wind of Sorrows, or I would certainly have made it a point to have known him long since.

"I am Gerard Rebeautou," said he, and bowed slightly from his chair. "Will you join me at my table?"

"I was hoping you would ask," said I, being suddenly conscious of my rawboned, hard appearance contrasted to his youthful beauty. I sat, with my wooden cup of steaming wine, across from him at a window-table overlooking the dark street.

Gerard Rebeautou posed nicely in his chair, wherein he had been settled some while. It did not pass my notice that Herbert Glaes, the obese publican at the Wind of Sorrows, had spoken to him but once, and received no order. These impoverished aristocrats were common enough, yet the patronage of their class was worth something other than the cash they were not apt to have about them. They retained their family connections, to one degree or another, and unless too proud, encouraged any spendthrift to dote on them for favors.

This gentryman, by his costume, which was neatly arranged, well-brushed but several places mended, represented more the fashion of the street's randy coxcombs than the upper classes, although he was rather more subtle, and I gathered he considered himself incognito if not actually convinced he passed for something less than highborn. In this was mystery: the partial disguise of his class standing; the evident poverty coupled with a brave, proud front; the likelihood of having lived in some decadent quarter of the city, by choice rather than necessity would be my guess....Well, let me confess it—I speculated about him so much because his whole posture and appearance was appealing and romantic in the best, most unpretending way. Were he to turn to acting in the city's operas—unthinkable even for a self-exiled aristocrat—he would instantly become an idol, given the fine, solid gaze of his darkly lashed eyes; the soft, sweet sadness of expression; the cultured musicality of his voice; and the excellent physique that could easily win him into the finer artists' institutes as a model.

"And have you a name as well?" he asked, clearing his throat of some congestion as unobtrusively as he could. "But let me guess—a famous swordsman."

My occupation was an easy guess from my attire, a mere speck of dandy's lace at throat and wrist, the tight fitting costume suited for fighting with blades, and the excellent weapon that trailed on the floor as I sat. But I doubted he recognized who I was, though many might, by the unusual appearance of a man with one eye slightly smaller than the other. I said, "While it is true I am well known for my rapier talents, it is also true that here in the Flauberg quarter, of the great city of Aispont, there are an estimated three-thousand professional duelists, many whose deeds echo farther than my own, though some are mere roaring-boys whose exploits are known because they themselves spout them in the chocolate dens and coffeehouses along the boulevards. Still others have become veritable legends because they died uniquely or gloriously, which is not the manner in which I would have my own name of Esben Danesworth widely mentioned."

"I know that name. It is bandied with respect here at the Wind of Sorrows." Again, that pleasant nod that passed for a bow.

"Is it? So you've been here before?"

"Its history impressed me. The inn was founded in this location more than three hundred years ago, when it stood in the suburb of a smaller city than exists today."

"Even so, it is not the city's oldest inn," I remarked.

"Nor, as a rule, is it the haunt of men of your profession," he said, and I might have been insulted by it, though I was not.

"Oh, more of us than you would guess. The better duelists, I should say, are not obvious. The Wind of Sorrows is not a place of fashion, nor yet of braggadocio, for it is too much a home to its established clientele, and the other businesses subleasing segments as storefronts are useful, staid and stolid—the bookman, the printer, the optometrist, an elderly taylor, the seller of swords; no trinketers these—so our street attracts fewer boulevardiers, unless during fairs at the nearby park. But of swordsmen, there are more than a few, melancholy sorts whose names are not often said, unless in whispers. They are fellows who fight fairly but rarely intrude themselves at random and do not arrange their commissions in such a manner that the public must take note."

"You are hard on yourself," said Gerard Rebeautou.

"Not at all; why would you think I describe my own nature? I was of that selfsame breed for a time, though that was years ago, and I have since learned to mix with courtiers, to flirt with coxcombs and ladies— not so much because it suits my nature, but because a duelist who serves in no great house must, perforce, have many acquaintances, so that his name is mentioned foremost whenever the service of one among three thousand is required. Beneath my sociable façade, I may well be the same man that I was when first I came to Aispont so many years ago, kin to those morose and unwilling killers who have no other marketable skill, and who look another fellow in the eye only when it is necessary to stare him down, as is sometimes forced upon them as proof against some bully-hec."

"Morose men are rarely so loquacious," said Gerard, not unpleasantly, though once again, I might have taken it as a criticism.

"Am I bothering you? I am in a good mood, to be certain, and something in your manner attracted me. If I'm intruding on some reverie, I won't think it an insult to be told so."

"It's not that at all. I am uplifted by your chatter. It's just that I was thinking what a cheerful fellow you were, and how much I needed one, but here you are hinting at an inner gloom."

"Ha ha! I've rarely been called cheerful. But for today, perhaps I am. And you say you have spirits in need of lifting? What ails your emotions?"

"Pardon my not sharing my troubles with you just now. If we know each other longer, perhaps."

He interrupted himself with a painful-sounding cough, suppressing it quickly with an evident effort. Then by way of apology he said, "I'm not up to speaking much myself tonight, with this remnant of a cold here in the lungs—" he thumped his chest—"but do speak to me, I beg you."

"Since I'm in the mood, I shall. What would you hear? A story? An adventure?"

"About yourself. You say you mix with coxcombs and damsels as though they were the same?"

"Did I say quite that? You may see me dancing with some damsel at a fête or ball, if she has hired me as bodyguard and consort for a night's safe sojourn in those fashionably disreputable mansions of the Hiereau quarter. When in such employment I will seem to enjoy my duties exceeding well, and, passing a mirror, I might even primp or mistake myself for a courtier or musketeer. It might be said of a man that acts in a fancy manner, that he has become a fancy man. And one who is full of laughter is therefore happy. To some degree, it must be so. When, at times like now, I am minded of the unhappy disposition I once bore with me always, I half think I've changed a bit, while the other half regards the fiercely entertaining and pleasant mask as only that, a mask, hiding an evil and self-destructive temper."

"I can barely imagine you in sore temper."

"Attentive company has softened me this hour. Yet, it may always be that the true duelist has to keep some dark nature always ready, for a more generous or self-preserving attitude would insure a happy unemployment combined with an unhappy impoverishment."

Gerard laughed politely, as though I were a wit, which I am not, but glad of his appreciation.

Outside our window, there came the snuffling, growling sound of piebald pigs, whose coarse fur grows in patches. They were toothy horrid beasts that roamed in packs by night, cleaning the gutters where the toss-pots are emptied and horses' droppings strewn. I paused a moment in my talk to gaze through panes of leaded glass, out into the darkness, catching but a glimpse of the spotted nightmares about their necessary and disgusting business. I turned again to Gerard, and sipped my wine.

"Many of the gentlemen I meet at entertainments," I went on, "are men without that dark element to their disposition, so far as I can see. They have sorrows, no doubt, but have never been crippled by them, have never suspected the abject and lonely darkness that waits beyond the veil. Often enough, their sorrow regards a lost or stolen snuffbox; or an opera, with some foreign amazon in its cast, that has sold out, and spared no box for a come-lately without connections, and he is saddened by his plight. This is not the same as an intrinsically melancholic disposition, which comes from dwelling on the greater and unknown wherefores of our short existence—thoughts that philosophers make into a rhetorical art and which the lonesome, dispirited swain makes into a death-wish. If you cannot understand me, be glad that you do not; and if I cannot make it plainer, I regret only my insufficiency as a poet."

"I understand you well enough, Esben Danesworth, my new friend."

"I thought you might," said I, and felt a strange twinge, part gladness and part apprehension, and his casual yet doomful utterance of friendship. Skipping narry a beat, I continued: "I'm afraid I sound judgmental about such men who would not understand, although, to tell the truth, there are seemingly dimwitted courtiers I should not like to test myself against, their swordskills being match for, or superior to, the above-mentioned three-thousand professionals."

"Yes, there are swordsmen aplenty at court," said my companion, in a tone that suggested how well he knew it. I was silent for a moment, not wishing my chatter to keep him from adding some revealing commentary, but he had apparently exhausted his speech with only that slight hint, and silence fell between us. In a moment, I filled that silence, tailoring an opinion I thought he might favor.

"On the other hand, such polished steelcraft in the hands of cold-blooded courtiers lacks the quality of dark mood I mentioned and think requisite in what I called before the 'true' duelist. Wouldn't you yourself rather feed a well-trained mastiff than a nervous whippet one-tenth its size, if it came to a choice between meat for one or the other, proffered from your naked hand? The whippet has the bluer blood and the smaller teeth, but in many ways the mastiff is less the mongrel and more reliable."

"And the more sincere in his select associations with humanity," Gerard added, approving my simile.

"Here, let me buy you a cup of chocolate—or could you use meat? That cough of yours should be seen to or you'll become consumptive. *Herbert! A meal for my friend! Spiced wine for me, thank you!* He'll bring it in good time—don't worry about the cost. I have recently collected a certain fee and am feeling well off. Just possibly I am also feeling a little more melancholy than I thought, which talking may work out of me.

"I'm often like this after some event. I don't consider myself at all like those roaring-boys who boast, yet my exploits do become known, sometimes because I tell of them myself, although never more than once. Don't feel compelled to listen to me closely, just because I've bought the meal. I can see you're a gentleman and so apt to have the coin yourself; it is mere flattery to me that I'm allowed to take your bill."

He smiled painfully at that, and I realized I had been awkward in protecting his dignity. I let it pass. "Where was I? Ah yes, so I've come to this point in my life, a dancer, a hired companion, little different in my outward manner than some idiot squire who toadies to his betters in hope of eventual title. But my aim is different. You have a foe? A debtor who refuses to your face to make good your loan? I can protect you, or be your dun! How shameful to admit I am good at it.

"Yet, there are no wars just now, unless one speaks Prusk and wants to travel to some god-forsaken land where even mercenaries are more smartly trousered than a backward Duke's standing army. There is at least no war to be found nearby, wherein profits can be cherished. I call 'nearby' anywhere within the King's Good Country, to no farther than Niedkreld or Belique, whose languages I speak and whose soldiers I admire, and their uniforms as well. We are not at odds with any of them, and they are not at odds with anyone else. It could change at any moment. Inevitably, it will. A new policy could send every duelist, fresh or veteran, upon an exodus to succor a beleaguered ally or to pillage the coast of some insulting and obnoxious foe. Who can say, in time of peace, who next will be the foe and who the ally? All of that aside, a man such as I, whose main talent is the fence, must play the gentleman carefully, convincing each acquaintance of my essential readiness and availability in matters requiring steel. I hope that does not make me an assassin. I abide by the gentlemanly rules of combat and have been known to impose some handicap upon myself when asked to bring out some talentless coxcomb of a debtor for a fight.

"Still, at times my tasks feel degrading. It is hard to pose as a gallant and at the same time serve as dun. Then again, I am famous for sparing debtors if they pay quickly, once they've stumbled backward, rapier dashed from hand, and my steel placed on a shoulder as though to knight them and not kill. Or in cases of true villainy, when I am called upon to bring a just vengeance, I do not skulk about, then take the fiend by ambush; I do not challenge when he is least prepared, besotted, or unwilling. Rather, I send a cordial letter, and rely upon my portion of fame to convey my heartfelt wish that said fiend make what restitution he can before retiring to some quiet provincial place, avoiding a duel he is not apt to win.

"Do I sound defensive in all this?"

"Not at all," said Gerard, whose attention was a moment later drawn elsewhere.

The noise of the hogs in the street had suddenly risen to crescendo, accompanied by the shout of a man. In that cry was such distress that I rose instantly from the table, and Gerard Rebeautou soon after. We and two other patrons of the Sorrows were quickly in the street, swords drawn, hurrying through darkness and toward the sound of a grisly feast. Already the man's cries were whimpers. In the faint starlight we could see him tossed and ripped asunder by pigs' tusks. Their shaggy manes were fluffed to huge proportions; their spotted hides danced and prissed about the prey. One of the other men hurrying to give aid stopped suddenly and cried after we three, "Let the pigs have him; he's done for."

It was true. Some pitiful vagrant's blood oozed thick on the cobbles. I kicked a hog's ass and it squealed, turned on me, flashed its tusks like sabers, and I drew back. "Shall we save him for a funeral?" I asked, frankly not wishing to bloody my trousers or my shirt.

"There are too many of the devils. Let them eat him," said the third man. Gerard Rebeautou only stared, I thought rather too intently. The pigs' feast yet moaned, but only from shock's delirium; he would no longer be in pain, though three of his limbs were torn free.

We returned to the café, already shoving the grim spectacle from our minds. Gerard's meal was just then delivered by the deaf giant in Herbert Glaes' employ, along with a fresh cup of hot wine for me. With a nod I thanked the giant as Gerard and I took our places by the window.

"I find myself, due to all the complexities of this life, involved in numerous intrigues," I began anew, taking up more or less where I'd left off in my discussion. "My name is dropped as an idle threat by individuals who have not actually approached me for opinion or with their proposition. And I find myself embroiled in other intrigues partially of my own making, for as I said, I like to make every intention known, so that no unfairness can be implied, and no man need die on my steel without having every clue reach him, every evasive option suggested through subtle and indirect channels.

"To a courtier, such games would be accepted and enjoyed as part of the sport. But to the true duelist, they are as the fires of hell, and as inescapable. So on times I find it essential to withdraw from my beloved Aispont to roam country spaces, or visit other lands, or accept some commission that takes me thither…all to get away from the bustle and dishonesty of this city."

My companion had by now sunken into a quietude that I could not completely interpret, though I pride myself on reading others. He might be engrossed in my opinions, or was dwelling on the pigs' meal as he devoured his own. Perhaps my loquacity finally bored him, though his large bright eyes retained a glint of genuine absorption.

I can't say exactly why I was in such a communicative mood. I'm often charged with being withdrawn into myself, of not sharing my feelings even with friends of many years. I think I had begun flirtatiously and because it pays to have connections with gentry, even those who are poor, since their uncles and cousins may be richer, and because rich merchants also court them. By now, however, I was bleeding on the fellow with honest emotion, and a little bit ashamed to do so, though I could not stop.

I had mesmerized myself with his engaged manner and his beauty—a beauty that was not at all flashy or excessive or obsessed with anything of fashion, but which was no less contented in itself.

"Were I a saner man," I continued, "I would live in a little village. I would aspire to provincial knighthood, or arrange to become sheriff of a restful town, loved by its children, feared by poachers and felons who would therefore live better lives or else ply their criminal trades elsewhere. But sanity is not my finer trait. Aispont draws me ever back. I cannot tell you why. Were I an artist or a man of letters, it would make sense. The garrets overlooking the streets of the Flauberg are full of talented men and women, painting or quilling the classics of tomorrow, although starving in the here and now, much as do most of those duelists who, unlike myself, will not play the proper games in the proper places.

"But I am not an artist. There is no reason for me to come here seeking compatriots or inspiration. Warriors can be found anywhere, supposing I were seeking colleagues. The things of Aispont that I despise are genuinely despicable and my criticisms consistent with reason, whereas my unabated love of the city makes no sense at all. But neither does my love of this spiced wine, when it only makes me dizzy, and loose-tongued, and sillier than I really am."

"I shouldn't worry of silliness," soothed Gerard.

"I was away from Aispont most of last year," I said, "having a number of adventures which were dangerous yet, compared to city life, mainly restful. I obtained a pleasant, temporary commission in a town of good size and sophistication; it's not as though I languished in provincial boredom. I had time enough away from duties to attend operas and cut a swaggering, gentlemanly figure. I was able to appear much more colorful than would be possible in Aispont where such men as myself are a commonplace. I even had a romantic attachment which would pale your brow were I to tell what it entailed, so I will spare all particulars but one: it was a pleasant though peculiar affair and there was no reason for me to end it. These things being so, I should never have thought of returning to Aispont. When my employment expired, I could have lived two years comfortably without further labors—if I avoided the gambling dens, that is—and in all likelihood would have found an even finer and permanent position before funds ran low. But I was out of my employment a mere day, had not had so much as a minor squabble with my lover, and, in spite of all good sense and logic leading me toward another decision, I saddled my friend Elisabeth and rode her home to Aispont."

"Fortunately," said Gerard. "Or we might not have met."

At that I flushed a little, I'm not ashamed to admit. I said, "I had kept my apartment, paid in advance, so my intention was certain even before I left. I realize I shall never be gone from Aispont long at a time, unless I die on some far-away journey, having failed to impress upon someone the importance of returning my bones to this place.

"I am caught, you might say, in a love-hate relationship with Aispont. Perhaps love is not as vital as it can be if there is no dark side to it, just as a courtier with stunning swordskill cannot be what I think of as a true duelist without a dark aspect. For me, at least, such is the case. A faithful lover in a pleasant town, where I could be revered and obtain a respectable position, cannot compare to the enthralling encounters in this jewel of a city, where the mere act of existing is fraught with color and adventure at the highest pitch."

"And fraught with chance encounters," said Gerard Rebeautou, lifting his cup to me, for which flattery I discovered myself ordering refills. I wondered if I were being odious to carry on at such length, but Gerard's whole posture conveyed his eagerness for me to continue. I had meant to court him; but it was now evident he courted me, and while I have no vain ego, I do have a weakness for manly beauty.

"As I said, I am only recently returned, and on my journey home was joined by a man who asked if he could ride some distance with me, for the company. He said to me, 'I am Edgar, known as Sir Falsehood, wandering this world in search of lost souls, whose lives I would set aright, in accordance with the Law of God's Most Gorgeous Angel.' He was beautiful, I give him that. I said to him, 'Your sect is unknown to me, monk-knight; but if my own road has become wayward, then feel free to join me, and save me if you can. In exchange for the good company of a comely man, I will gladly bare your religious intent. But 'ware of me, whose name is Esben, an untitled duelist, but might well be dubbed Sir Corrupting if ever some monarch sets steel upon my shoulder.' Now why did I tell you that? I've lost the thread of my thought. I think I wanted to say how odd it was that he never once mentioned any issue of Faith to me again. And as to who corrupted the other most, before our roads parted, I'm unclear as to that. What do you say of it?"

My friend had delicately cleaned his plate, though I think he would have liked to have wolfed it down if none could have seen him do it. He remained disinclined to speech, but I had put the question to him, so he said, "God's most gorgeous angel is long fallen, so he meant he was the devil, figuratively we must hope."

"Yes, I hope so, especially as he promised we should soon meet again. Afterward, I arrived in Aispont, with my full purse. It was good to be back in my apartment here at the Wind of Sorrows—yes, my rooms are in this very place, beneath the rafters of the uppermost floor; I will take you to them later if you'll let me—and the maids of this most excellent institution had kept the rooms aired for me, so that it felt as though I had left home only yesterday.

"The first thing I wished to do was look at the whole of Aispont, feeling a most romantic attachment after my year away. I was so glad to be back that I entirely forgot the dark side of my nature, which is probably the main point of everything I've told you up to now. Yesterday I could not remember a moment's depression in my whole life! Ah! Aispont! My love! Why did I ever leave you?"

That sounded like a toast, so I ordered wine again, though Gerard changed his half of the order to chocolate.

"It was on this very morning, dawn of my second day at home," I said, becoming more intense, my voice lowering. "The city still slept, at least in these quarters where idle soldiers live, as most of us are not seen abroad until afternoons and evenings. In the early morn, nothing has started up, except a few of the less interesting chocolate dens, but I was eager, and so dressed early. I wanted to see the whole of the city, not merely some favorite spot. So I went to the canals and became a boatman's first customer of the day, and his favorite kind. 'Take me everywhere!' I said gleefully. 'Round and round! Under the bridges and to the Jewish district where I'll pray to the Messiah not to come too quickly, for I so love sin; then to the Catholic district, that I might proposition the Virgin for a miraculous night; then to the Mithraics where I can tell the Sun mind His own business, the night being so much preferred; and also to that little corner of pagan gypsies where I'll buy a lucky amulet. Take me everywhere! You will be well paid!' This, by the way, is the very amulet I bought from a gypsy. Will you accept it as a gift? It's yours."

I had been toying with a thin bracelet of braided metal as I spoke and, unsnapping it, showed it to Gerard. From the bracelet hung a single charm in the form of a serpent's hollow tooth, which doubled as a spoon for coke or snuff. "The bracelet is of greater value than the fang," I said as I snapped the bracelet onto his wrist, hooking head to mouth.

"A serpent of rose gold," he said, fingering the braided metal. "How elegant."

"The rosy sheen, the gypsy claimed, was achieved with serpent's blood in the metallurgical necromancy of its fashioning, the very serpent whose tooth that is. The bracelet is protection against all foes of snakes; the tooth is proof against venom, though I beg you not to test its prowess too eagerly."

Gerard said, "You'll not think me a whore to accept it? A token of friendship, let us say."

"Let's," I agreed, then picked up again the thread of my loose narrative. "So there I reposed in the boat, upon mildewy pillows that to me were sweeter than any courtier's perfume or spiced tobacco. Ah! I can't explain it. Aispont unrolled to right and left: poor families doing laundry at the canal; children catching fish; the brick faces of ethnic architectures passing and changing district after district. What a rich and varied nation this one city is! Nay, what a continent of nations!"

"It does sound pleasant," said my table mate, still admiring the bracelet and its macabre charm. "If you go again, do take me along. What else occurred?"

"Pretty maids and children stood on bridges here and there, shouting at the boats that passed beneath, hawking pastries and sweetmeats. I tossed up coins, and they dropped their desserts. If what they sold was far too alien to my tongue, on account of the strangeness of the neighborhood where it was made, I might well end up feeding it to the fish. But it was worth the coin, for every little thing was an adventure."

"How delightful," said Gerard, and hinted that a dessert would be fine. I shouted to Herbert to have his giant bring us cakes, and refills of wine and chocolate. Then I took up my tale again, completely in the cups by now, robbed by wine of all restraint.

"Throughout my years in Aispont, I had never taken a boat about the city in this manner. I had visited most of the 'internal towns' at one time or another, but they are so much more picturesque from a water-level view, so much more peaceful in the cool morning…as quaint as any provincial town, indeed like a hundred provincial towns from every corner of the King's Good Country, and several foreign lands into the bargain, packed together back to back, so that the canals were like a ribbony ocean and the little gondola a mighty vessel, and I some happy god traveling the whole world in hours instead of months or years.

"My nostalgic state of mind rendered me drowsy, as though I were breathing some rare blend from the tobacconist, Oriental weed mixed in. I felt stalwart and happy.

"One of the longest tunnels of the watery thoroughfares is a narrow one beyond the gypsy district. In that tunnel there is barely room for a second boat passing the other way. When we were halfway through, another boat appeared from the opposite direction. Boatmen have a rule-of-thumb in such cases: Whoever is beyond the halfway point, which is plainly marked, it is the other boat that must back out, if it is not possible to scrape by one another.

"Few of these boatmen have ever been on the high seas, yet they can swear like sailors. The present pair found they could not pass one another, for the second boat was particularly large, and appointed in wealth. The richer vessel felt it should not give way, as it was harder to steer backward and had a more impressive appearance besides. But my boat had first reached the tunnel's halfway mark. A vulgar argument arose between the boatmen, being of a most colorful language and laced with charmingly grotesque threats.

"The other helmsman's key point was that a patently inferior boat should make way for the one that was finer. My man took exception for he had pride in his vessel and had also to protect the rights of his passenger, whom he had transformed into an important dignitary whose time was being wasted. In the darkness of the tunnel, lit by a few stray rays of sunlight poking through the cracks in the roof, my pilot's rival could not see who or what sort of passenger I might really be.

"This argument echoed in the hollow of the tunnel and the two men shook their fists so hard that the boats rocked. The boats' sloshing echoed from walls and ceiling. In the midst of all this, the passenger of the other boat raised herself from pillows, perhaps intending to register her disapproval of the language being used. I had been sitting up this whole while, amused by the pilots' exchanges. But on seeing the woman's beauty, so radiant that the tunnel seemed at once to be lit by her presence, I hissed at my man to be still. He, too, noticed the extraordinary beauty, and must have felt ashamed of himself, only then realizing his vulgar spiel was overheard by a lady. The pilot of the other boat was himself reminded of his ward's tenderness and blustered awkwardly though his speech had been fluent before the lady sat up.

"'We'll go back,' I said, and my pilot began to push his pole against one tunnel wall and then the other, forcing the boat backward. At the mouth of the tunnel, we waited for the larger boat to go by. The lady's hand trailed in the murky water as she lay like some languid animal against the side of the boat. That hand was pale, as was her arm and the bit of flesh exposed at her neck. I was not sure if she used much make-up; there was a little color in her face I thought was artificial and pretty, although the natural alabaster of her skin would have been more magnificent, if slightly pathetic. She was so white that I could only imagine she'd locked herself away in some windowless room for a good many years.

"The look in her pale eyes was likewise pitiable. I was struck to the heart by what must have been, in her life, endless martyrdom and agony. How I understood that inner pain! When she smiled at me, it was by no means a feeble smile, but I was reminded of my own somewhat dandified mask, and I knew what truer feelings her smile strove to hide. My heart caught, and the gaiety of my first two days home came instantly to this moment bleak and tragic, though in such tragedy was a gorgeous splendor.

"I wanted to leap from my boat to hers, take her hand, comfort her, and play the troubadour for the rest of my life! Well you might smile, for I am not as easily drawn to women as to men. Always before that moment I had scoffed whatever iota of the poet reposed within my spirit. But I was suddenly willing to put down this sword forever and compose, thereafter, lyrics to a beautiful and suffering lady, to wallow with her in our mutual self-pities, injuring ourselves with a love that could never be made physical, but must always ache and long, she being of her class and I beneath a scholar.

"In the next moment, however, I recalled that I was a fighter to the core. I desired not to wallow in pity and poetry but to draw forth rapier from hip, or saber from some wall, and slash to bloody ribbons whatever felon was responsible for the beauty's evident misery! His head would tumble onto the floor or his heart would be pierced or he would be blinded with a horizontal stroke across the eyes, to live thereafter in darkness!

"All this went through my mind as her boat passed mine. When she was by, I saw that she had a fan in her hand, trailed in the water, soaking it despite its obvious value. She let go of the fan, and it floated in the wake of her departing boat, her arm retracting and her thin, wan body falling upon pillows and away from my sight.

"I rocked the boat dangerously trying to reach the fan, until my pilot came to the back of the boat and fetched it with his pole, not saying a word about the event. I opened the fan and saw the lady's monogram upon it, and recognized her house as the most illustrious in all Aispont, indeed, in all the King's Good Country.

"I fanned myself until the silk between the ribs of the fan was dry. Then I put the fan in my wallet, already planning some gentle speech for its return to the steward of the very House of Ai!"

Gerard Rebeautou accompanied me to my rooms on the topmost floor of the Wind of Sorrows, the simple elegance of which inescapably impressed him, a fact that reflected on the excellence of the Sorrows rather than upon myself. He inspected with an appreciating eye several of my sentimental treasures, assorted knickknackery and books, until, as soon as I could manage, I showed him to my bed. We spent a wondrous night together although I had been spoiled somewhat upon the road by the monk-knight Sir Falsehood, who was a rare fellow in every respect. Notwithstanding that fabulous encounter, Gerard was someone I could imagine myself being with for some while, if he allowed it, and if he felt himself capable of the degree of exclusivity required for my own well-being; that is to say, I tend to be single-minded in my attachments and exceedingly jealous for the duration of the affair which must be monogamous on both sides. But if the inevitably temporary nature of such obsessions is apt to cast me, in the long run, in the rôle of a villain, merely because I will eventually come to monogamy with another, I would rather be disappointed in the short term and accept rebuff.

Whatever the future would bring as regarded Gerard Rebeautou, our first and for all I yet knew our only night together was exquisite, and only in the late hours of morning did I realize my loquacity in the café had been more on the order of a seduction than I'd formerly admitted to myself. Much as I prize my understanding of others' psychology, I am often slow to understand my own.

The sweet aroma of our lust rose into the tilted rafters of my attic rooms, a musk we savored afterward. The Wind of Sorrows is notorious for its hauntings, its strange noises, its sad moans; but we heard none of them, our own moans were so far from sadness, and dispelled all gloom. I recollected how, at the end of the Legend of St. Julian, the hermit-knight makes love to a leper who transforms himself into the Christ, and off flies the roof of the hermit's hut as in God's lustful embrace the two men fly to heaven!

I liked as well the possibility of a friend, who I felt Gerard might easily become. Lovers come and go but friends are a species most rare, at least of the variety one may rely on through the years. I ache when I recall the intimates I've known, who became, after a while, veritable strangers, neither I nor they having the energy required to service so little as acquaintance. Who could say what Gerard would think of me, or I him, two days from now, or two weeks, or two years. In the flush of a romantic vigor, I felt I should know him forever, whether or not we were lovers very long.

When late morning or early afternoon found us awake—I have no timepieces in my rooms and rarely annoy myself with exact hours—a pale radiance penetrated the smoky gray skylight and illumined our naked bodies. A maid had twice entered, hardly rousing us, and built fires in two rooms, so there was sufficient warmth that we let the counterpane remain cast onto the floor. We lay entangled in one another, limbs wrapped in limbs, sated from the long night of love, pondering the possibility of starting things afresh.

My tough, stringy body is no kind of classic beauty; still, no man has complained of me yet, and I have a stamina and grace in which I take certain pride. I bare my dueling scars proudly as well, on chest and arms, none of which are extraordinary but add to the pleasant creases of passing years. Gerard seemed pale beside me, and, because he was fair and young, there was a girlish quality to his soft skin, a quality that I can usually take or leave but was glad, in his case, to take. Otherwise he was very likely stronger than I, certainly more muscular by comparison to my wiriness, and with no other girlish attributes. Our varied styles of manliness were pleasant to contrast, although a jester might want to call us a beauty and a beast, I being of the less flattering category.

Gerard was opening and closing the fan I had obtained on my previous day's outing. He asked, "Shall we go in search of her today, Esben?"

"Of who?" I asked, hardly recollecting what I may have said the night before under influence of spiced wine.

"The woman you met on the canal was Tristianna Kramerlöf of the House of Ai. The paleness you described has made her famous in that family, although it came about from some disease that nearly killed her. I can probably win an introduction if you'd like for us to see her."

The possessive tone of Gerard's statement did not cause me to alter the kindly thoughts I had nurtured through the night. More startling than his speaking of "us" as regarded a meeting with a princess of Ai was the audacious sentiment that we should meet her at all, or that he of all people could arrange so extraordinary a tryst. I had had in mind merely to return her fan, and even that to a maid in her service, or a Palace steward. If some thank-you letter came to me afterward, I would answer it. If I was eloquent, I might hope to be invited to some gathering in the Hiereau quarter where manners are looser than in the Palace-town and there are jobs aplenty for duelists. Even this may have been a great deal to expect. My wine- and nostalgia-induced romance, as regarded the pale lady, was ultimately a selfish desire for the chance of advertising my skills to people who paid highly.

Gerard was suggesting an impossibility, a meeting with a woman of royal caste. I thought him simply mad, a trait that always wins my fondness, so I laughed.

"I might as well tell you," he said, "the Rebeautou clan is well-connected at court, as hereditary retainers to the House of Ai. You may not have detected it from my speech, but I was raised veritably in the corridors of the Palace, my father and uncles among the royal guard to the King and his late Queen. I was even dandled on Tristianna Kramerlöf's knee when I was small, though she had not yet turned so pure a white when I had my childhood crush on her."

"Now that I shan't believe, Gerard. You could never have been dandled on her knee. You're young, but she is younger."

"Did you think so? But you saw her in a dark tunnel."

"And then in broad light of morning."

"Nay the less, she is several years my senior. I was removed from the Ruby Palace at an early age, to attend a school that trains exclusively the boys of the Rebeautou clan. I was saved from all that later, by a nervous disorder. I was prone to fainting spells and fits, but grew out of them some while after. As I look back, I think I faked them, as I didn't want to be a Palace retainer. It means putting on displays of martial skills to titillate whoever demands it. It means running messages back and forth between factions in complex games of intrigue, cruelties, insidious betrayal. It means rutting on command with anyone of any appearance who's in the mood and has authority over you, while your own mood counts for naught. If I had no perversions of my own, I might have adapted. But my dreams were of the Flauberg and of men like you. Does that surprise you? You can't imagine the insufferable mannerliness of men devoured by ambition and consumed by Palace etiquette."

"I can imagine it perfectly. I have never been to the Palace, but a few who reside there have been known to take their pleasures in the Hiereau, or even here in the Flauberg, though less commonly. Still, I'm surprised that *you...*"

"I've lost all trace of Palace dialect, or you might have guessed."

"Not quite *all* trace. I knew you were an aristocrat of some kind. I presumed you were disinherited gentry."

"A son of a Palace retainer is not quite aristocratic. Glorified soldiers really. But after so many generations, I suppose it's the same thing. Not all Rebeautous learn to fight any longer, or if they do, it's more dance than battle skill. Be that as it may, I do retain privileges there, or relatives rather, and they're fond of me, though they disapprove of my living outside the Palace-town, for a Rebeautou in Hiereau or Flauberg is practically unheard of. I also understand, far more than you seem to do, that if a Kramerlöf leaves her fan for a soldier to retrieve, it is his duty to return it to her in her boudoir. Your boatman represented you as a sight-seeing dignitary? She likely saw through that ruse, but there's no denying your appealing attributes. I should have told you of this last night, as already she'll be insulted, but I wished you for myself."

"A moment ago," I said, "you were boasting that you could arrange a meeting with her. Now you suggest the meeting was arranged the instant she dropped that fan!"

"You've seen through me. I shan't let you go without me, and I dare say she wouldn't mind the pair of us. I've heard she has, among other desires, the passion of a voyeur. I've not seen Tristianna since my childhood, but I know her reputation as the milk-white succubus of Ai. She's very perverse, wonderfully so. She always takes blood. But her form of vampirism is not catching; it's said to be worth the experience."

"And if I'm not interested?"

"But you are! Last night, you told me as much."

"Last night was last night. It is more interesting to have poetic fancies than to service royal vampires. I had imagined her the ultimate victim, so sad did she appear, but you insinuate she is spoiled and demanding, a blood-letter into the bargain. Your information destroys my interest, Gerard, supposing it was ever more than idle."

"I'm afraid you have no choice, dear Esben."

"Of course I have a choice."

"The fan is the same as a royal command."

"Perhaps so. But she doesn't know who I am or where I am."

"Your unusual face makes you easily described. What other duelist has one eye smaller than the other? It makes you especially charming; and considering the good mood you said you were in, you must have gleamed like polished bronze when she saw you. No wonder she dropped her fan for you to find! Oh, she's already annoyed that you ignored her summons, be sure of it. As you say many aristocrats know you and have even hired you on occasion, and if even half her reputation is correct, she'll already have tracked you down, and will know of me as well."

"You're a raving paranoid, Gerard. I've only known you these few hours. This Tristianna Kramerlöf knows of neither of us as yet."

But at that moment the door from the hallway opened into an adjoining room. The usually unobtrusive maid flung herself through my apartment in a dither.

"What's this ruckus, Liddy?" I asked, sitting up in bed with one hand upon Gerard. Liddy stood wringing her hands at the doorway of the bedroom.

"Oh sir, forgive me, but you'll need your pants! Royal guardsmen have come to see you! Mr. Glaes convinced them to wait in the café, though their preference was to barge upstairs at once!"

"Rebeautou clansmen, no doubt," said Gerard, and with a manly giggle added, "Don't worry, Esben. I'll protect you."

* * * *

A grizzled clansman in full regalia of light armor stood between two soldiers. He unrolled an official looking document and read several charges to my discredit: that I had posed as a royal dignitary; that I had slandered with all manner of vile language a princess of the House of

Ai; that I had stolen property belonging to that very lady, namely, an ivory-ribbed fan.

I listened to the account of my sundry ridiculous crimes, squinting at the three men with one eye, and my blood was raised. "Sirs, I love this city and would not like to start anything that would result in my exile. Nay the less, I shall not stand for silly charges, and from panderers no less. Tristianna Kramerlöf gave me her fan under no false pretenses and I, having small comprehension of the manners of court, only learned this morning what it meant. If you insist in this charade, I shall kill the three of you, and make a petition to the court pleading it a matter of honor."

The Rebeautou clansman turned red in the face but did not change his expression. The other two men glowered and moved their hands toward the hilts of their swords. The clansman made a gravelly sound deep in his throat and we held each other eye to eye. I raised my chin.

In strode Gerard, who had dressed more slowly and more decoratively than I. He said, "Esben, Esben! This is an uncle of mine; I beg thee spare him."

"Gerard," said the clansman. "You, here? I shouldn't be surprised. Don't insult me by begging for my life. I could have my two men quarter him at once, or cut him down myself."

"Uncle, uncle, this is my dear friend Esben Danesworth, I beg thee spare him for my sake."

The clansman rumbled anew. I said, "You well know your lady's tastes, so I ask as one gentleman to another that you drop these other matters. If I must attend to Lady Kramerlöf, I will arrive this afternoon, at my own choice of hour, and if she is then indisposed, I'll not mind."

The clansman looked left and right and said to his two men, "Leave."

They stepped outside at once, but stared through the panes into the Sorrows' café, mistrusting what I might do. He said, "As you may guess, I am commissioned to bring you at once. If you will not come, I shall be flailed. As you have made it a matter of gentlemanliness, and as my commission forced me into an insulting behavior of which I am ashamed, I will submit to a flailing at my lady's displeasure, unless you will consent to see her now."

"I'll not consent."

"Esben, don't be cruel," Gerard interjected. "Do you know how seldom a Rebeautou apologises to anyone?"

"If it is true, Gerard, then I admire your uncle for setting honor above pride. I'll admire him more after he is flailed."

The clansman waited no longer. He bowed slightly—a motion reminiscent of the way Gerard had bowed to me—and turned with a rustle of mail toward the door. Gerard called after him, "Uncle! Tell Tristianna your very pretty nephew wants to attend the meeting also, and for that reason Esben is delayed."

Not turning to face Gerard, the Palace veteran said, "I'll tell her no such thing, especially if it is intended to save my back from bruises. The two of you do as you please, and be damned for all I care."

When he was gone, Gerard said, "Secretly he's fond of me."

"It nearly shows," I said.

"Really, you should go to the Palace at once. My uncle is strong but not young; a flailing will do him no good. And really, it's quite an opportunity for you, you must admit. The number of Flaubergians who've entered in the Ruby Palace is not great."

"I prefer royalty outside their turf, where they're less sure of themselves and not as deadly. I am not glad of this invitation, and I won't attend to their whims quickly, least of all to save your uncle a well-deserved thrashing. I'd leave Aispont for a few weeks until this foolishness blows over, except that I only just returned and am not eager to be away so soon. I'll make the best of the encounter; and you're right, it may help in my career. I long ago discovered, however, that the respect of royal brats is not gained by fearing them, and in fact they are leery of shoving a duelist too much, whatever they might do to harm someone unarmed. You would not suggest I hurry to the call if you had heard the charges your uncle read aloud! Had there been customers of Herbert's about, I would have had to fight your uncle for such asinine lies."

"I did hear the charges; I was listening from the hall. I thought them amusing."

"As I might have found them, had they been leveled against you."

Gerard laughed, then stifled that cough that worried me about him. "Your real problem," he said, "is that you are bitter."

"About what?"

"You had imagined Tristianna Kramerlöf a faint, frail, tragic creature. A moon-eyed fool's romance invaded your head. Now you've discovered she's a monster. It annoys you. For myself, the strong ones appeal most. I prefer her as she is."

"Perhaps you have me at that. I'm usually good at judging character, and alarmed to have read her so incorrectly at first glance."

"A good judge of character, are you? And how do you judge me?"

"I think well of you, be certain."

"Prepare yourself for more than one disillusion, therefore," he said, scoffing my sentiment. "For the moment, my dear Esben, I beg you feed us. My family has severed me from funds, in order to force me back into the protective bosom of the Palace-town. Instead, I place myself in your hands."

He played the sponge with combined sarcasm and bathos, but I thought he did so out of affection, as though to warn me against delusions of his perfection. I liked him the more for that, and did not at the time think myself blind. The night before, he had been so mysterious, so quiet, but had actually played to my vanity and ego, and was less submissive to my opinions today. I had no reason to mind, no reason to interpret his behavior as especially manipulative; and I felt, indeed, that he would as soon be my protector than I his, were our finances reversed.

We seated ourselves, the café's only customers for the moment, and I gazed appreciatively at my new companion. I called out, "Herbert! Coffee and rum, and a hearty breakfast for two." To Gerard I said, "It promises to be another interesting day, in the Chinese sense. Aispont! So full of surprises."

* * * *

The Ruby Palace is thought by many to be the city's centerpiece, although it by no means rises from the center.

There is a hillside overlooking a quay that in olden days, when ships were smaller, was the hub of the nation's trade. Today a deeper harbor is required and is located nearer the mouth of River Ai, while the antique quay has become part of an extensive waterfront park where sports-fishing is good although only the privileged class may go there. Pleasure craft are moored at numerous docks. Landless gentry, supported by their more successful relatives, are crowded into handsome little communities of floating homes where they—incredibly!—lament their ill fortune.

On the hillside upward from the quay is a forest, enchanted some will tell you, where the same privileged few hunt deer, quail, and hare; and above that is a rough, wide clearing where ladies ride with hooded falcons, intent on killing doves. At the very top of that hill, overlooking the forest and fields, and visible to all Aispont to the rear, is the Ruby Palace in faded shades of crimson.

The view from those towers, we may suppose, looking toward the river and the sea, is magnificent, though it is not for such eyes as ours to see. The view in the opposite direction may strike the Palace inhabitants as less charming. Due to the fact that Aispont is surrounded on three sides by bodies of water—lake, river, sea—the swelling metropolis has been unable to spread outward and away from the Hill of the Ruby Palace. Rather, it encroaches, century by century, up the hill, unto the rearmost door of an opiated elite's fabulous home. The Palace-town provides something of a buffer against those of us who are utter plebeians in their regard, inhabited as that town is by people of the blood, with or without Palace connections, and by their retainers and the relatives of their retainers. Yet, within the Palace-town, there can be found every level of prosperity and failure, so that it is not a place much different in aspect from many common districts. Undoubtedly the mighty few of the Palace look from their west windows, toward the Palace-town and across all of Aispont spread below, and experience a degree of trepidation; for intrigues within their own walls can result in a once-favored courtier, prince, or musician unexpectedly eased out that rear exit, and not let back in.

As to the architecture of the Palace, it is of ancient vintage, derived from an alien culture, distant in both time and place, the influence of invaders little remembered even to the memory of scholars, though the House of Ai believes itself descended from those conquerors whose names they revere as gods. Such strangely convoluted architecture defies gravity and hints of madness and is to be found nowhere else in the city. Prohibitions against plebeian imitations are strictly enforced. Therefore strangers and pilgrims may think the Ruby Palace something other than a part of Aispont, though to her citizens it is the symbol of our hearts. Even those of us who are apt to speak ill of the decaying aristocracy find, in the mad architecture of the Ruby Palace, a hint of every man's, and every woman's, twisted passions and desires, in which we take such pride.

Realities and symbols are often far at odds. Our King is in theory an autocrat and his word is God's word; his cruelties go unquestioned even by cynical observers who malign his minions but not his self. The reality is that His Majesty, and those others of his blood, have little author-ity that need be construed as absolute. They of high birth fritter away their remnants of power and of wealth on snuff and lace and the pursuit of deviant pleasures. Many of them sit in coffeehouses lamenting their dwindling sway, or complaining of the locked back door of the Palace. The truth is that merchants rule the city and control the monarchy be means of ceaseless loans and the periodic forgiveness thereof.

We all enjoy the existence of our gentry and aristocrats, useless though their lives may be. Our enjoyment may stem from awe of their blood, or more likely from the manner by which they lend to us an ironic sense of superiority over them. We observe what lowlifes they are that resort to snobbery, who use costly perfumes thinking no one will then de-tect their failure to bathe. And they are pretty, some of them, as much so as the alien architecture of the Palace: elegant, perverse, self-consumed. They provide the models for our own vices.

It is all too obvious why the Palace is called Ruby, for its windows are tinted the shade of pigeon's blood, while many of the towers are conglomerated prisms of rosy quartz held together by their own weight and artful fitting. When the sun goes down, a dazzling crimson gleams through the translucent towers and across the river and the sea. It is an awesome sight to passing or incoming ships, though we of the city nights rarely condescend to notice those visions of a failing day.

The city's finest are its unconventional plebs, with many of the same depravities as manifest themselves at higher levels of society, but lacking the pompous delusions of a withering aristocracy and the tasteless money-grubbing of the mercantile class. As regards intemperance and debauchery, all castes are equals; but the vogue of abnormality and artifice achieves its most subtle refinements at street level, among indigent æsthetes, although we cannot presume to exceed in sublimity the sweet cruelties and furtive assassinations practiced among Palace decadents. That we are a people of the black, black night is understandable when even our dawns find us in the red shadows of the Ruby Palace.

Where precisely I may fit into Aispont's modes and fashions I cannot specify. If ever I set a fashion, it must have been among a half-dozen impressionable and unimaginative young duelists who admired the way my rapier dangled when sheathed. There are a myriad illusive roads to æsthete favor. Gambling is one, costume another. There is personal comeliness or the ability to convey illusions of the beaux ideal. Artistry with pen or brush or on the stage is especially to be regarded. Dueling is my own means, and that too is popular. But if I think much concerning trends, it is chiefly because I am an appreciative observer, neither leading nor, to my knowledge, obeying what comes and passes. I know only that I am comforted by the revulsionary glamours of my era and I feel free to be nothing other than myself amidst a beautifully iniquitous company.

Although I would have liked to have kept him with me, Gerard pleaded other engagements, and we agreed to meet in a certain chocolate den later in the day, there to plan the last leg of our journey to the Palace. After he parted from me, I played chess for a while, with an elderly champion, resident of the Sorrows, who I've yet to defeat but from whom I've learned much of value in defeating others. Then I went into the streets of the Flauberg to pass the hours, but soon discovered I was weary. It was my third day with scant rest, so excited had I been about one thing then another. I hailed a brougham, told the driver where I wished to go, climbed within, and nearly fell asleep on the way.

I came earlier than arranged to the chocolate den where I was to meet Gerard. The den was situated outside the fringes of the Palace-town and patronized by rowdy sorts of men, petty vassals mostly, who liked to step out of their district to trouble other classes. Several toughs took my measure, then let me be. I took my drink outside where there were a few tables and chairs pressed up against the wall between pots of dried up bushes. As it was windy, no one else sat there, and I was glad to be alone.

Here was a view of Aispont I rarely experienced. For one thing, it was still daylight, rare enough for me; and the chocolate den was halfway up the Hill of the Ruby Palace, so that I could look down upon my own preferred haunts as though into a valley.

Aispont is hilly and strangely laid out, an unplanned patchwork, having grown in stages along the centuries. I gazed across the roofs of that splendid chaos below, then upward at the bizarrely tilting towers of the hilltop Palace. Both sights were dizzying to my sleepy brain.

A few people passed where I was sitting. They were dim shadows of the Flauberg boulevardiers, though they thought themselves impressive. The gaudily scabbarded swords of lesser vassals in the service of various highborn but not necessarily well-off families seemed to me to be nothing but tin spoons and bread knives excessively adorned. I could not help but look down on these young soldiers whose lives were set for them before their births and who could not even make the best of that.

I was not surprised, therefore, when a group of cudgel-players appeared at one end of the street, their barker pounding on a drum and calling for a crowd. Cudgeling is crude sport and only satirists would attempt such a display in the Flauberg, where duels are engaged with steel and sincerity and artistic flare, whether announced beforehand or erupting spontaneously, afterward to be critiqued. The survivor is not always decided to have been the winner, based not upon the final thrust, but upon the overall dramaturgy and number of dazzling moves.

The cudgel-players' barker offered an insubstantial prize to challengers, not half as much as would be required to attract men with a modicum of talent and a chance of success. But there are many retainers who serve their houses only by hereditary presumption; they receive no income from those families that have fallen, for vassals tumble or rise with whoever owns them. Hence a small prize can make them risk their lives.

There were multiple offers of acceptance of the challenge. The barker selected from among them a man who was homely, huge, but with awkward gait, and undoubtedly the safest opponent for their little troupe of three.

The cudgel-players put their best man, such as he was, against the awkward fellow. The crowd that gathered was not large, so I was able to keep a clear view of most of the goings-on from my table outside the den.

The challenger was allowed to select a wooden club from among many and predictably he chose something large and awkward like himself. The cudgel-player hefted two small, hardwood sticks which he twirled and juggled whimsically, filling time while the barker and a second cudgel-player gathered bets. The gamblers preferred the larger man, thinking the smaller nothing but a clown.

At last the cudgelers—professional player against amateur—squatted several paces apart and, at the drop of a glove, leapt at one another, cudgels swinging. The crack of wood against wood echoed and reechoed. That it wasn't finished quickly was only to prolong the entertainment. The crowd encouraged the bigger man, on whom their money rested. Spectators moved about a bit, following the action, but while the battle was in my view, the big man never landed the lightest blow upon his adversary. The professional tried to make it look as though it might go either way, but the inevitable outcome was to me only too obvious.

The first blow taken by the bigger man was in the side. Even from my seat some distance off, I heard ribs break. The fellow should have quit then, but proved himself to be as stubborn as he was dull. He bellowed and swung wildly with the idiotic club, a menacing performance that at least gave the lithe cudgeler a moment's look of worry. Still, the pathetic bull could not land a blow and, out of frustration, he took an unexpected swipe at the barker who was doubling as referee.

The barker's arm was struck hard enough to injure bone. He tumbled badly and whacked his head on the street. The crazed challenger moved to the kill, but the lithe cudgeler stopped him with a swift pair of blows, one from each stick to either temple. The big man's skull was broken.

The fallen bull was lifted by several men and carried off, I presume to a physician. If he lived, he couldn't have been made much stupider by the crushing of his head. With him went a miniscule losers' prize, inadequate to cover either doctoring or burial. The little troupe of players kept all bets and only the barker was worse for wear.

Then they moved on, to ply their artless gaming on some other street of half-wits.

Some short while later, the chill of dusk drove me back into the den's stuffy interior. To my amaze, there stood a familiar fellow, although he had not been there when first I came, and I had not seen him enter by the street. "Sir Falsehood," said I in a whisper, approaching the monk-knight Edgar. "How have you come to this unfashionable location?"

"Seeking you," he said, his expression as wild as a drunkard's, though his pose was more steady.

"I'm flattered. I thought you were headed elsewhere, for when we parted on the road…"

"Whist!" he warned, silencing me, pulling me into an unlit corner away from prying ears and eyes. He said, "I came to bring you warning."

"Gerard sends you?" I asked, for no one else could have known where I would be.

"I am sent by Another," said Edgar, mysteriously. "By the Author of Debauchery and Transgression. By God's Most Beautiful Angel."

How charming I found madness! I leaned toward Sir Falsehood and matched the earnestness of his comedy. "And what news does Satan send to me, sweet monk?"

"The Black Doctor protects his own, and his eye is on the Palace. It does not serve the Undivine Plan if Lust should die, so I'm to tell you you must visit Tristianna Kramerlöf alone. Take no one with you! You need fear nothing if you leave this den at once."

His hand still clutched my arm and now began to hurt. I looked at that hand, fair and small for a man, with burgundy lace showing from the sleeve of his black jacket. That hand did not appear to grip unduly; yet it felt as though icy talons pierced my flesh.

At that moment someone called, "Esben," and I turned to see Gerard had arrived. When I saw him, the sharp pain left my arm. I said, "Gerard, let me introduce you to Sir Falsehood who I told you of before."

"Where is he?" asked Gerard, casting a jealous glance about the room.

"Why, here," I said, but Edgar was no longer with me and I could not spot him elsewhere in the den.

"Never mind," said Gerard. "Are we ready?"

Then together we entered the Palace-town, the estates of which are wooded, the avenues winding and uncrowded. Gerard led onward, upward, and toward the Ruby Palace.

* * * *

Imagination alone could prepare no one for the sanguineous halls of the Ruby Palace. The ancestral gods of the House of Ai, carved from great blocks of precious rubellite and jasper, stood at every doorway and bend, frightful guardians with upraised swords of jet, their ruddy visages variously angelically placid and menacingly grotesque. Along the broad halls in cases and on narrow tables sat row atop row of candles encased in crimson chimneys, a thousand fulgid fires, while red-robed children, as innocent in their appearance as the altar boys of a cathedral, and surely as corrupted, went from place to place, replenishing these lights.

The walls were flocked in phosphorescent velvet of reds on gold, the whirling patterns thereon suggesting sinister, poisonous roses. Those convolutional symbols, coupled with the weird angles of the interior architecture, wrought havoc on my sense of balance, though Gerard was unaffected. He and I strode in a rutilant haze, as in a violet dream, through a world of jaded appetites, glittering hatreds, treacherous loves. Before us went a turbaned servant, a gorgeous black giant naked from the waist and with appealing swagger, carrying a large bronze tray on which reposed the fan I was gloriously returning.

"Remember," said Gerard, "speak not unless addressed. Seem not to notice anything or anyone but Tristianna Kramerlöf, even if her maids become forward with you or me. In every other regard, abandon yourself to bizarre caprice; make of these events a pleasure."

Ordinarily such advice would annoy me, who am versed in sundry arts of love and things that pass for love. I doubted the Lady Kramerlöf could surprise me, or that I, however jaded she might be, could prove wholly unsatisfactory. Yet the Palace itself had me undone with awe. The furious rubicundity drew my emotions in opposing directions, as though I were tied to tails of horses and pulled in two. Everything inspired ennui, much as a battlefield, strewn with fresh slaughter, numbs the souls of the survivors, destroying pity and sorrow. At the same time, the virulent shades inspired rage and lust, as though the slaughter were in full sway, and I the hero of God's most frightful opera.

At every open door there came from darkened rooms spiraling ribbons of golden smoke, the familiar sweetness of opium, though not quite like that which I had previously encountered. Gerard, I noted, breathed deeply of these odors.

We were brought at last to an enormous parlor, where our absent hostess's maids-in-waiting poured us glasses of dark port from pitchers of red crystal. We reposed on silk pillows of fine embroidery. Gauzy pink curtains divided the room in luxurious waves of golden shadow and rufescent light from garnet chandeliers.

Gerard saw that I was dazzled. He said, "A resplendent whorehouse, would you say? Not more than that," and brought me closer to the earth, while at the same time he pocketed a ruby goblet and toyed with a lamp's red prisms. On the table before us sat the bronze platter, the fan upon it, folded. Around us tittered women with lips and eyelids dyed with insect cochineal, hair like streams of fire wound with purple ribbon. One sat at a harpsichord of cherry wood, striking gothic cords, her voice as highly pitched as a violin's, lending greatly to my sense of having slipped into the phantasmal world of sleep.

These women were supple, insinuating creatures, by turns demanding and submissive. Yet I'd been warned to ignore them. Another man could not have succeeded, but I was able to distract myself by the presence of Gerard.

"Where is she?" I asked, annoyance rising in me. "It's been hours!"

"Scant minutes have we been here," said Gerard, and waved his nimble fingers through the trails of smoke around us. He laughed and told me, "The opium of His Majesty's house is known nowhere in the world but here. It is grown in the quartz towers overhead, a potent hybrid that would not survive outside the protection of herbariums. It is harvested by magicians who commingle it with sandalwood and myrrh. This is kept always burning throughout the Palace, as holy incense to their ancestors, and because the denizens of this place believe such heady smoke lengthens their lives."

I was too sedated to add to his discussion. My brain amused itself with unanswerable riddles and childlike jests. One of the maids-in-waiting tickled me with a peacock feather and I began to laugh quite loudly. I could not stop, for every time one of those teasing women moved toward me, for what ever purpose, I fancied she was going to tickle me again. Such hearty laughter was never heard in the Ruby Palace, so that the waiting-maids drew away in horror, uncertain what it was that I was doing. For Gerard, however, my laughter was infectious and he leapt on me in a subduing manner, and said sweetly, "Whatever happens, Esben, I love you now."

In the midst of our embrace, Tristianna Kramerlöf entered from another room. Her waiting-maids fell into the bows of swan-lake ballerinas. Red crinoline whispered to the floor.

"Do not stop," said Gerard. "Do not look at Tristianna yet."

She drew near the stack of pillows, a mystic blaze of white fire amidst red embers. She was a ghost. She was Death. White gown and veil fell away from her so slowly they might never have struck the floor. There was revealed the unnatural glory of her snow white flesh, made more extraordinary by its contrast with glistening hair, black as jet, surrounding her like velvet night.

Gerard undressed me, slowly and with care. It took a hundred years. I removed his garments as well, careful not to betray the several stolen items in seams and secret pockets. Momentarily he wore nothing but the gypsy bracelet, and I only my scars.

Tristianna Kramerlöf had lain down above us, on higher pillows, and stroked our manes, and other places. I could barely feel her touch, as though she were not really there, as though she were illusion. Nor did she make a sound. I was almost afraid, of what I did not know, but lost my fears with Gerard's lips to mine.

The ballerinas had joined arms and were swaying, humming, and fondling one another. My eyes opened a little. At the corner of my vision I saw Tristianna's knife, lamplight gleaming redly on its edge. She touched the knife first to my neck, traced white scratches down my arm, then along my thigh.

Then she pierced me.

I clung harder to Gerard. Or was it he that held me fast? If I tried to escape, would he release me? Was I in the clutches of them both?

A fiery distrust arose within my heart. I was suddenly brought round to the mystery of my having met Gerard at all, on the same day I'd first seen Tristianna Kramerlöf! There was some conspiracy here, this I divined even before I felt my own warm blood against my thigh.

Before I could act on my sense of danger, Gerard threw me off, took Tristianna's wrist, and with one deft motion, broke it. I was aghast. The white beauty, whose face personified sadness, did not cry out, and by that shocking stoicism I knew she was no monster after all, regardless of her fondness for the knife. I grabbed Gerard's neck in the crook of my arm and tried to draw him from the woman, but both his elbows slammed my ribs and winded me. He growled, "Don't be a fool, Esben! Stop her maids!"

Then he snatched Tristianna's knife from the pillow where it had fallen.

The world moved in slow motion, due, I realized, to the opium. Yet I believed that on some level my senses were not dulled; I felt that I might move with supernatural swiftness through the fumes and blushing curtains, for it was the world outside myself, and not I, that had lost all speed.

The waiting-maids were leaping toward Gerard, floating in mid-air, their hands outspread like talons, their faces twisted into demoniacal masks. Their transformation was so utter and horrible, I could not believe them human and not Furies. My arm reached for my weapon and, as I'd envisioned, I was able to move as swiftly as a serpent strikes, and instantly had my rapier to hand. One waiting-maid fell upon the red tiles which turned liquid underneath her. The others fled, wailing like Harpies.

I was still lost between my fondness for Gerard and my distrust of our coincidental meeting. Was he the fiend, or was Tristianna? The answer was simple: neither one was a monster, unless all people of this world are demons of some sort. I watched as Gerard sank the blade into Tristianna's heart over and over, ripping her perfect flesh and bosom. Blood sprayed everywhere like a stormy rain. And as he struck her again and again, he screamed insanely with that so-musical voice broken twice by a harsh cough: "How patient I have been, awaiting this moment of revenge for my dead mother! Die, Tristianna! Die!"

I stood there lost of hope. There would be no escape for me from the Ruby Palace. I had been Gerard's pawn in a vengeance pursued, no doubt, since his very childhood. And I was as trapped and doomed as he!

He might never have stopped stabbing but that an epileptic seizure threw him backwards to the floor, foaming through his teeth and kicking his limbs with a terrible spasmodic force injurious to himself.

And then as though the cosmos had set out to prove to me that no height of horror was the most that could be achieved, Tristianna Kramer-löf rose to her knees, although her heart had been well carved. I stood over her, naked but for my sword, standing in her blood, and gazed down into her eyes. That martyred look by stages eased away from her expression, and I was so moved by concerned emotion that I dropped my rapier and knelt before her. She said to me, serenity upon her angelic visage, the single word, "Finally."

With that, she leaned forward in my arms and was dead.

The Screams at the Keyhole
by Garrett Cook

She was tall, Elena Saavedra, long as Winter, half as gentle. Though the patrons of the bar were motley, gilled, scaled, a bugeyed, veiny lot, she was the one who seemed strange here; swarthy, darkeyed, skin tanned even browner by hours upon hours on the decks of ship after ship, dressed in trousers, boots and a hooded black cloak, Elena Saavedra was a curious sight indeed. She walked to the bar with purpose, with strength and determination, her gaze only wavering from its objective to take note of the curves of the slave girl who served bread and wine to a shirtless silver scaled brute, a creature a head taller even than she. But that was only momentarily.

"Rum," she declared, putting a coin on the bar.

Webbed fingers trembling, he poured her a shot, which disappeared much faster than it came. She set down a few more coins spoke a name, a name that was not to be spoken here, which was why she had come here to speak it.

"Never heard of her," said the bartender, grateful that his eyes were on the side of his head so they wouldn't shift and dart about the room.

"He's lying," said the woman who walked beside her, cloaked as well, but wearing flowing blue robes underneath instead of the garb of a pirate. Her name was Ril and she knew men's hearts.

Elena fingered the hilt of the cutlass sheathed at her side.

"I assume you heard me. I speak clearly and I don't mumble. Ten men gave their miserable lives so I could get the name of this tavern and the location of this island. Hard men. The sort of men who pay tributes to rumpfed scum like you. Are you calling the last of ten dead men a liar?"

"This man is lying," said the veiled woman. Her name was Ril. She knew men's hearts.

The barroom shook as a hillock of a man covered head to toe in silver scales stood up, a trident in his hand.

"I think you should leave now," he said.

Webfingered, gilled, longfaced, toadish, suckermouthed, more of the bar's patrons stood up with him, arming with knives, cleavers and clubs. There looked to be about seven of them, unburdened by mercy, empathy or any of the qualities that made human foes hesitate. The two women did not back away from the bar, did not turn tail and run. They had come to this place expecting such a thing. Instead, the taller woman drew the main gauche at her left side, pairing it with the cutlass.

With a strong kick, she knocked the nearest table to the floor, sending plates and tankards and cutlery clattering down. With a second kick she rolled the table forward and it flew into two of the icthyean things, knocking them down and pinning them underneath it. The shirtless hulk advanced on her, trident in hand and with long strides he closed in quickly. He expected her to back off, to give him space to keep her a spear length away, but he was used to fighting barbrutes and not skilled fencers. She stepped forward, claiming space, hooking a leg between his, a consummate dancer. Though protected by thick scales, the creature's nose still made a loud crunch as her left elbow made contact with it.

Ril reached into the folds of her cloak. pulling out a curved and perfectly balanced throwing knife. A graceful twirl, a step forward. It wasn't just a single knife, instead a cascade of blades, three knives thrown circus deft. Bleeding, croaking, clutching their throats, almost in unison, three of the gilled horrors stumbled back, gurgled red and hit the barroom floor, dead. A mortified bartender caught sight of this and started to flee out the back.

Elena in the meantime used the commotion to gain momentum, hooking a leg between the great scaled ogre's, she came in too close for him to make effective use of his trident, too close for him to back away from her cutlass, which quickly proved the scales upon his body were little protection against a practiced swordsman. In. Out. A spray of blood, of viscera and he was gutted like the fish he was. The barroom shook with the impact of the brute's fall, enough so that the fleeing bartender hit the floor as well.

"Now," said Elena, pressing the sword to the bartender's back, "you will tell us of the witch and where to find her."

"I can't tell you about her," he said, "anything I say would mean an end to me. Just leave, please, before you bring down more trouble!"

The big woman laughed.

"You think because I am a woman that I will be tender and merciful?"

"You know very little of women," said the veiled one.

The bartender hanged his hideous head.

"She has been here. She will come back someday to recruit for the Deep One crew she sails with. That is certain. But I can tell you nothing of her plans. She will know. She always knows."

"Then you should hope we find the witch," said the bigger woman, "so that she won't come back for you."

"And if you face her and you fail?"

"Then we won't need to worry about anyone," said the veiled one, "we'll be dead, won't we?"

"What makes you so damned foolish, why do you do this?"

The tall woman grabbed him by the throat, lifting him in the air.

"She gave me love, hope, a ship and a crew and taught me to sail. She gave me the freedom of the seas. And then she took it all back. I would take every hand that used me wrong at the brothel she plucked me from again to find her and hear her curse my name on her last moldy, fetid breath. I will kill her and I will write the names of every woman I sailed with who died from her betrayal. I will splatter the earth with fish guts, kill every stinking, scaly, croaking miserable inbred webfingered monstrosity that lives until I do."

"She is looking for something," the bartender wheezed out, "a tablet. It opens the way for something. This is all I know, I swear to you."

The veiled woman nodded.

"The monster tells the truth. Leave him."

And at that, the two left the bar to head for the docks. The veiled one heaved a great sigh.

"Monstrosities," she said, voice heavy with despair.

The taller woman pulled up the shorter one's veil.

"It is no one's fault who their father was. Especially not under your circumstances. I am always ready to show you that you are from monstrous."

The tall, dark lady leaned in to kiss cold blue lips. She lingered for long on those lips, knowing it would be awhile before they could find passage off this island anyway. It had been hard enough to get there in the first place. They shared a long embrace, comfort, gratitude. Without her ship and crew she still had the ocean in the cool blue of Ril's skin and the stormy grey mystery of her eyes.

The two were interrupted by the sudden appearance of a figure in hooded violet robes embroidered with the image of open mouths. From the lack of features inside the robe and from the symbols on them, it was clear to Ril who had some experience with beings like these that this was a wizard's messenger. And that snapped them to attention.

"I am Ril," she said, "priestblooded, marked by Dagon. Who do you serve?"

"I have come from Slen the Unmade," said the messenger, the messenger who was the message, "he asks that I bring you to him. He has news of the witch."

Before Ril could speak or make another inquiry, Elena interrupted.

"We accept. We will come with you."

And as it was said, it was done.

* * * *

The chamber they appeared in when the word was spoken was more dust and neglect and mold then wizardly resplendence. The books stacked upon the floor rose to the ceiling, jars of laboratory equipment gathered cobwebs and trinkets and medallions lay in discarded heaps with plates, bowls, cups and saucers as if these objects differed not in their importance or their place in the hearts of their owners. Sitting in a wicker rocking chair was something that could not possibly be Slen the unmade.

The creature appeared to be made of sticks hewn together with twine. There were shoes nailed to the bottom of these sticks to create the illusion of feet and a bucket with a face drawn upon it as if to mock the very concept of a head. This creature surely couldn't be Slen the Unmade, though it wore a wooden placard around its neck that proclaimed it was. Someone or something had scratched the word "SLEN" into it.

"I am pleased that you've come," said the creature, "though I must tell you that I am not Slen the Unmade."

"I don't know who Slen the Unmade is," said Ril, "but whoever he is, I would not have believed you if you told me you were him, so your honesty is, I suppose, refreshing."

"I must also tell you that I am Slen the Unmade. Or, more accurately, his replacement, since he was Unmade."

"Who unmade him?" asked Elena, "Is that what this is about?" "It is not," said Slen's replacement, "Slen unmade himself. He cast a spell of such potency that he could no longer exist to cast it. It is important that he did though. So this is about Slen's unmaking."

"We were told you know about the witch," said Elena.

"Yes," said Slen's replacement, "she is Slen's business and I know only Slen's business though I am not Slen."

"Can you tell me where to find her?"

"Yes," said Slen's replacement, "it is Slen's business that you do the favor I ask of you so it is my business that I have the information to trade for it."

"Then tell us about this favor."

"One of Slen's books was stolen by The Somnambulant Brothers. Slen needs you to retrieve it. They have taken it to a temple far away and plan to use it to unmake the spell that unmade Slen. The book must be retrieved, lest the spell be unmade and Slen is unmade for nothing."

"What book?" asked Ril. She knew of the Somnambulant Brothers, a cult that lived and went about their business in their sleep, half in and half out of dreaming. There was more or less only one book they'd be interested in and if the book in question was stolen, then there would be trouble.

"It is called the Clavis. The Silver Key."

Which was exactly what Ril was afraid of.

"That does not bode well."

"How typical of wizards," said Elena, folding her arms severely, "leaving out dangerous things so they might be taken. What is this book?"

"It is a key, a key that opens the way to the Dreamlands," said Ril, "and the way to the king of dreams."

"The king of dreams? That doesn't sound that awful."

"How long's it been since you've had pleasant dreams?" Ril shot back.

Elena swallowed hard.

"I can lead you to your witch if you go to the place where the Somnambulant Brothers will open the gate to the Dreamlands. It is Slen's interests for you to do so and I represent Slen's interests."

Elena nodded.

"If you bring us there, then we can get your book back."

The substitute Slen handed Ril a scroll.

"There is a ship at the docks. It will take you where you need to go."

With a nod, Ril accepted the scroll.

"We'll take our leave then."

They left the tower and walked out to the dock.

* * * *

The ship docked outside was to say the least a derelict, long abandoned. The warped and rotted decks of the ship were vacant, cobwebbed, dusty. Rotten, fleshless heaps that were once men were the closest thing to signs of life the ship had known for what might have been decades. The dead men's mouths were open, contorted in eternal agony. Strips of timeshredded cloth clung to what was left of them. Elena folded her arms about her chest and heaved a sigh.

"Accursed wizards and their stupid poppets! Send us to this damnable island and give us a ship with carcasses stacked on the deck!"

Ril smiled beneath her veil. She pulled out the scroll the substitute Slen had provided. Bone, sinew and rag and body began to knit together. Neglected skeletons stood up, took the wheel, set the sail, took to oars. Elena unsheathed her blade, surveyed the decks, preparing to take arms if this was some sorcerous trap. Elena had little trust for those who worked magick, with the exception of her darling Ril. But the skeletons attended to their task, not even so much as acknowledging the women.

Though hollowfaced and decayed almost do dust, the crew knew its purpose and worked with speed, strength and precision that would do any living sailor proud.

"You needn't concern yourself with them," said Ril, "they are here to do Slen's business and Slen's business will take us to the Somnambulant Brothers. We needn't worry."

Salt and sun touched Elena Saavedra's face again as the skeletons launched the ship. She took in cool sea breeze and spray, doing her best to ignore the stench of longdead sailors. She never quite felt at home on land, so it was a pleasure to sail again, even if she could do nothing command these men. Ril sensed that her lover's satisfaction to sail again was tinged with discontent, wrapped her arms about Elena's waist.

"We should rest."

The two lay together below decks on a ship of dead men. Elena staring at rotted ceiling, Ril rested her moist, clammy face on Elena's bosom. They took comfort in the warmth of each other's bodies, the closeness that was all that they had left, though Elena's softhard features were worn by melancholy. She stroked Ril's back though her heart was heart was not quite in it. It was more perhaps to make sure someone was there than to express her love for the woman right beside her.

"I sail with the dead again," said Elena, "and there is nothing I can do to guide this ship."

Ril planted a kiss on Elena's cheek.

"It will be over soon. Slen will lead us to her. We will find her, we will kill her and then we will find you a new crew to sail with."

"She gave me that ship," said Elena, "she took me from where I was and she gave me that ship and I learned to sail and I learned to fight under her. I learned to love and trust. And she took it away again. She sold me out when she found what she'd needed for the Deep Ones."

Ril knew this. She had witnessed this betrayal and even if she hadn't, it consumed Elena utterly. She felt sometimes like she lay with half a woman and the other half was in the past, dwelling in that hateful love that treacherous love.

"You will have your ship again, my love."

In fitful sleep, Ril dreamed of a great black palace, overlooking plains where howling, cackling doglike things feasted on the dead. She dreamed of an Earth flooded by the god who lurked in the blood that flowed through her. She dreamed of the floundereyes and tentacle hands of the worst of her kind and of the old gods and the consequence of their coming. She dreamed of degradation, of the sea, of the Dreamlands of the predatory nature of the divinities from before time. She saw the condescending obsidian face of the king of the land beyond sleep.

"Come forth," he said, "stop me if you will. It is inconsequential. There is no order beyond me. No truth but change. In the end, I will always triumph. There is only failure."

Ril awakened screaming. She was relieved to be in Elena's arms but still despair weighed heavily on her. Elena caressed her seagreen hair, clutched her to her very heart, soaking up the tears that came forth.

A silent skeleton came below docks, motioning to them to come to the deck. Up on the deck, they saw up ahead an island surrounded by fog. All jungle, all swamp, all primeval poison. There were distant fires burning and in the air a terrible hum. The skeletons docked the ship and Elena and Ril disembarked, breathing the suffering and venoms of this long neglected place.

The two slogged together through swamp and jungle, cutting vines, splashing in muck and mud. Stinging serpents hanging from branches up ahead lunged at them only to have Elena take their heads. They sliced, slogged, sloshed through until they came at last to the light of balefire in the swamp, where a group of men in dark robes adorned with sigils and eyes were gathered, chanting. The cult 's magus held a great silver book in his hands, a book he could read to conjure forth its energies even in his sleepwalking state.

The Somnabulant Brothers blew on skullshaped whistles, which burst out into screams, some thirteen screams. The air seemed to vibrate and tremble with the noise, with the sound and the clarion call of disaster, the shriek of disaster. Elena felt the hands of the witch upon her again, felt the kiss and the promise, the potential, the tomorrows on her body. She felt the tickle of hair, upon her thighs, strands that danced like marionettes with the magic that resonated from the witch's body. Strands that sometimes reached out to stroke and give secret kisses. And the eyes that said "mine" and "forever" stared into hers again.

She wanted to cry out "no", she wanted to scream so loud it put the skulls to shame but she wouldn't betray their position, she wouldn't betray their position. She wouldn't betray….she wouldn't betray…

Her shipmates bound again, her shipmates suffering lash after lash from whips in the hands of those brineblooded devils. Beaten, used ill, tortured and finally tossed overboard, abused for days before their captain's eyes. The eyes that the witch had stared into and said "forever", the eyes that would now play back this treason forever.

Ril's hand was on her shoulder, Ril's voice in her mind. Ril had to rouse her companion from this fog if they were to survive. The world was rippling, sleepers tossed and turned and shrieked and suffered. Reading with his eyes closed, the priest continued and simian beasts with sloping brows, flying on filthy grey feathers came into being, not born not sent but simply manifesting. They let out a triumphant screech, like the those of the skeletal whistles.

Ril Priestblood shook the lover, the pirate, the adroit and perilous swordlady beside her, begging her to stand and fight.

"Elena! We'll die here! They're coming! It's coming! Draw your sword."

Elena's hand shot out at her beloved, grabbing her by the throat, her eyes, tearful but halfmad and aglow with rage met hers. They blinked quickly, thousands of times, hunger and aversion all at once.

"Draw steel on what? What's happened already has been. We walk wounded, good as corpses, we bleed deep. And you who'd have me love you, you're worst of all. Will everything be calm when the witch is dead at our feet? What happens if another kills the witch? There is witchcraft, there is always witchcraft and there's no need for witches to make it."

She squeezed tight. Though Ril breathed through gills, the grip on her throat was still tight, the pain of betrayal and anger was still tight. She struggled, though it would have been much wiser to go limp.

"Elena…"

"It is coming, Ril, it comes now!"

Then suddenly, the night sky went silver, then shifted into more colors than nature could ever render. And from those colors, there came forth a batlike shape.

It flew in on wings dark as tombs, dragging behind it serpentthick tails, pulsing, writhing, quivering, seemingly outside the control of their master. A terrible humming noise that set the hair on the back of the very planet's neck on end emanated from each of these tendrils. All along them were eyes that blinked open and shut constantly, as if to take in and shut out the life around it . In homes around the world, children were beaten, husbands took wives by force, despondent young men and women tied nooses to take their lives. It flew on wings of woe and woe was its nature, disaster its legacy and chaos, its primal name, given shape, given fearsome cartouche as "Nyarlathotep."

The ape creatures descended, Ril still struggling in Elena's grasp and Elena still struggling the grips of treason, the grips of fear, the grips of loveless and gone, the grips of sea unsailed and voices that would never be heard again. Though Ril was held fast, she could not let the flying beasts or the great black bat take Elena as this would mean certain death. She gestured with her one free hand, struggling to gather her fleeting will and petition the one whose power lurked in her blood.

In blood. In the sea of red in every being's veins, all things are water. Dagon slept in their veins as well as the planet's seas. Ril's petition bubbled blood free from its veins, the flying apes careened, crying tears of blood, turned upon each other and their changing hearts, flew at each other with ferocious claws and howls of incoherent, shapeless fury. Ril's own heart was beating fast, Ril's own soul and lifeforce, Ril's own throat, much in danger of being crushed. The red streaked flying apes, fought on among themselves, with blood caked eyes and bubbling cuts bursting open. She had hated herself for her priestblood but the power of cut and clot was buying her a moment's respite.

Elena's grip loosened.

"We're going to die here today," said the pirate captain, "all things we know die here today. What happens now?"

"If you don't draw steel, then nothing. Nothing good might ever happen again."

Elena Saavedra let go and steel was drawn to meet this devil. It descended, screeching miscarriage, screeching genocide, screeching children abandoned in the woods by their kin. The great black bat howled poverty, lovelorn and incest into men's hearts and Elena Saavedra, ready as she was to fall upon the sword in her hand, ready as she'd been to murder her love to spare her another moment's suffering stood ready, leaping and slicing as she reached out for one of the rogue tentacles that hung low from the chiropteran fiend, moving of its own volition. As it dove, she leapt and she did indeed catch hold of it.

The bleeding, blinded apes still rolled about in combat, as the Somnabulant brothers chanted and played, oblivious. Ril, now disengaged let fly her knives, striking three of the hooded magi in heart or throat, as they gurgled and staggered and then fell silent to the ground. She was shocked to see one of these chanting zealots draw a dagger from his belt and charge at her, soon joined by another. Though their eyes were still closed and they still lurked half in and half out of dreaming, they came at her. She had proven herself a threat to the pharaoh's will and that could not be tolerated.

Ril again focused, channeling water, the connection to Dagon, the power of the priestblood , sole gift of the Deep One rape that made her. The muck and mire of the swamp rose up, forming a great hand, which began to slap away her attackers, pushing three more of them backwards. Given extra space, Ril let three more of the blades from in the folds of her cloak fly to kill another two of the Somnambulant Brothers. The great hand clutched a fourth one of them in the animated fist of muck and twigs, squeezing the brother until bones began to snap and organs squish.

Elena in the meantime held tight to the creature's tentacle and starting to shimmy up the monstrous bat's body, slashing and slicing out inky blood as she climbed. It shook attempting to buck her off and drop her to the ground. Elena was a prodigious climber , quick and capable from her time spent in the rigging. It did not take long before she was up on the monster's back. Though the dreams clattered around her mind, though the Earth shook in fitful waking dreams and hateful imaginings, she maintained her ground on the god's back.

She held aloft the cutlass, the witch's hands all over her body in waking nightmare, betrayal still in her eyes, the agony wracking her. Through fear and pain and hopelessness, she struck, plunging the weapon into Nyarlathotep's back, then again , then again, then again. As it bled and suffered, the nightmares blinked out of the world's minds, people saw again glimmers of potential and purpose. Bleeding, blinded apes flew toward her, some of the grabbed by shaking, ambulatory appendages that dragged them to its mouth to swallow whole. Nyarlathotep had no more regard for its followers than it did for any other living being.

Withdrawing a knife from the corpse of a nearby cultist, Ril took aim at the Somnabulant Brother that had been reading from the Clavis. The knife flew just past shy of the cultist. The magus of the cult kept hold of the grimoire and even in his sleeping state, managed to point a judgmental finger at her and though blinded by blood in their eyes and rage toward one another, the swarm of winged apes descended at her. The fist of murk and grime and muck and twigs dispatched the last of the magus' brothers but the monsters from the sky were diving at her, coming for her.

The priestess had no choice but to reach for the rapier at her side and charge the magus. Ril was not the fencer Elena was, generally preferring to step back, invoking her magicks and throwing knives but times had gotten desperate. There were flying apes trying to break up the ruckus between them so that might fall upon her and tear her to shreds to honor the dark god that had rewarded their devotion by devouring them. As she closed in, the magus reached for a long, curved obsidian blade at his side to defend himself and the Clavis or just keep her busy long enough for the misshapen, shrieking monsters to devour her.

The magus and the priestess traded strike for strike, steel clanging against obsidian as above them, Elena held onto the god of chaos for dear life, hacking and slicing the monster for what felt to be forever. Her despair had become rage, at dysfunction, at defeat, at loss and futility and the knowledge that the witch's death wouldn't bring back the lost, the loss of love and the loss of life alike. What was once defeat was now just red red red , a poem played out through the only art she knew, which was the sword.

Again, the thing screeched, again the thing careened, again the thing dragged winged apes into the eternal black furnace of its belly. Stabbing, punching, screaming, Elena Saavedra beat at being beaten as Ril below clanged steel against steel, taking on the sleeping magus. Sidestepping swipe after swipe, she hooked her leg between his, pressing close as she had seen Elena do so often, pulled back and with a quick, adroit stab, drove the rapier into the magus' gut. He bled out quick but she stabbed him thrice more to make sure before lifting up the Clavis from the ground.

The shimmering silver grimoire now in her hand, she opened it up, taking in all of its mad words, rantings, flavors, colors, letters no longer letters, images of unlikely beasts, men with hands where their head s should be, fish that walked on stilted human legs, reptile priests, dogs with insectoid faces, perversions of sense and anatomy, androgynous figures of such unearthly beauty that they brought tears to her eye. But she read on and the grimoire, the Silver Key, once turned was now being turned again.

When Ril read from the Clavis, it vanished from her hands and fitful dreams that plague mankind were gone and the air around the island grew dense, colorful again and in a tornado of these most unusual colors, the apes and the bodies of each dead Somnambulant brother were drawn up and the batwinged thing was drawn up, dropping Elena quickly, her life spared only by reaching out to grab the limb of a tree. But the island itself soon began to float, to rise out of the sea, above the Earth and into the multicolored skies.

And the shifting skies grew hungry and the night it grew eternal and the gates, the gates were opened, and the gates they drew them in. The world they knew had vanished, the island and all on it exiled with the god that they had saved this world from. And though the island was gone to them and the pharaoh was gone from the world, Elena and Ril swallowed heart, hearts heavy. It was going to be harder than they thought to track down the witch. The trees, they were inconstant and the wind full of scents and sounds the likes of which the two had never heard before, and the wilderness extended unto what seemed infinity, at the end of which lay the great black palace of the king of dreaming.

Diary of an Illness
by C.M. Muller

Brent gazed through the window of his fourth story apartment, wondering how he had not noticed, until that morning, the construction across the way. Had he really been oblivious to it these past few weeks— or, judging by the scope of the renovation, had it been months? He'd be the first to admit that the majority of his attention prior to yesterday had centered upon his now defunct day job, but still, not noticing this change in cityscape left him ill at ease.

The previous structure had housed some sort of museum, but it took embarrassingly long for Brent to recall the old place. A memory resurfaced of him wandering its musty, ill-lit halls as a child, terrified not only by its skeletal wonders but by the strange artifacts set behind murky glass. This was years before he and Samantha had moved into the city. Now, no visible remnant of the structure remained, all having been engulfed by a modern shell. Colossal frameless windows encircled the first and second floors, and from there a cascade of stainless steel spilled into the sky.

Brent speculated as to the building's new purpose, and if, once complete, he might find employment within. The aesthetics of the place appealed to him and the commute would certainly be agreeable. He planned to look into it later that day, but for now he was desperate to return to bed, having woken with a sore throat and chills.

* * * *

Five hours later, Brent's condition had hardly improved. If anything, he felt worse. He could barely lift himself from bed, and doing so left him dizzy and nauseous. He entered the bathroom to splash water on his face, hoping to lessen the caul of weariness. Toweling himself dry, he heard the front door open.

As he stepped into the living room, he found Sam resting against the entryway. Her eyes were glassy and expressionless. "You're home early," he said.

Sam shivered, as though experiencing a chill. "It just kind of hit me. One moment I was feeling fine, the next…this." She raised her arms dramatically, as though her whole body were diseased. "I just had to leave.

I couldn't stand it any longer." She approached, hunched and coughing, to offer a weak hug. "You don't look so great yourself."

Brent cleared his throat. "I'll be all right." He helped Sam out of her jacket, placing it and her handbag on the kitchen counter before leading her to the sofa.

"Well, I feel absolutely horrid. I'm surprised I had the energy to lug myself home, actually." Sam managed a painful-looking smile and with some effort removed her shoes. She sank further into the sofa. "Aren't we the pair. Mind getting me some pills?"

Brent wanted to ask her about the construction, but decided it could wait. He stepped into the kitchen and began rummaging through the medicine cabinet. Eventually he located the appropriate pack, though struggled to uncouple two tablets from the plastic molding. He filled a glass with water and returned to the sofa.

Sam was already asleep. Sitting next to her, Brent placed the meds and water on the coffee table and then reached for the remote. As he flipped through channels, he found it difficult to focus on any single program. His attention kept shifting to that other screen, the one whose static display of a mysterious new edifice both fascinated and chilled him to the core.

He tucked in closer to Sam, his eyes growing weary.

* * * *

"—construction of the church is nearly complete, and even though its services are limited at this point, patrons are encouraged to—"

Brent recognized the voice, and he squinted in a half-awakened state to discover its source. The radiance from the television was excruciating, leaving him momentarily confused as to his whereabouts. Sam was still at his side, lightly snoring. The apartment was dark, as was the city beyond the window.

Onscreen a local reporter was staring directly at Brent, as though waiting for him to respond to her spoken message. She was frozen in a nimbus of light, standing in front of a familiar-looking building. Next to her was a doctored-looking individual whose sleek suit and tie seemed interchangeable from the structure itself. His self-assured stance had Brent recalling certain department store mannikins.

The bulk of the news story had run its course, and the reporter was presently signing off. Her appearance startled Brent. It was hard to believe, aside from the voice, that this was the same individual he had grown so accustomed to over the years. Darkness rimmed her eyes, and she appeared to have aged two decades. Her final words were indecipherable whispers.

Brent pushed himself from the sofa, stumbling lightheaded to the windowsill. Sure enough, there was the news van. The reporter, however, was gone. Most of the "church" was shrouded in darkness, but Brent thought he detected movement in the periphery of his vision. A construction crew would not be operating at such an hour without spotlights, yet all he could imagine was thousands of worker ants scuttling over a nighttime mound.

A crippling cough broke Brent's reverie, and he turned to find Sam gazing curiously in his direction. "What are you looking at?" Her voice was muted and she appeared on the verge of reentering sleep.

"A church," Brent said, relieved to have finally broached the topic. "They're building some kind of church."

Sam started coughing again. "I'm sorry, what was that?"

"The construction that's been going on," Brent said, not hiding his irritation. "Don't tell me you haven't noticed."

Sam wiped distractedly at her nose, looking at Brent as though trying to recall what he had just asked. "Help me to bed. I don't know what this thing is, but it's getting worse."

Without hesitation, Brent helped Sam to the bedroom. She remained silent all the while, seeming to concentrate solely on her mobility. For a terrifying instant, Brent envisioned them as obliging companions fifty years hence.

Was this truly what old age felt like?

* * * *

The phone was ringing.

Brent stumbled from bed, shielding his eyes from the morning light. By the time he pulled the receiver to his ear and grumpily engaged the caller, the dial tone had already commenced. He wondered why anyone would be calling so early, but the phone's digital display quickly answered that question. It was a quarter past noon. Consulting the caller-id, Brent recognized the number and the reason for the call.

Returning to the bedroom, he found Sam sprawled facedown, covers bunched over her ankles and one arm stretched outward as though she had been seeking his comfort. He sat on the edge of the bed, slowly summoning her into an upright position. Matted black hair eclipsed much of her face, leaving a single ear visible. Brent whispered the news regarding the call, and a moment later Sam parted the veil, swaying and frail as a reed. Her eyes were bloodshot, her lips parched, and she was already cursing her lot in life. She reached unsuccessfully for the phone.

"You need to rest," Brent said, holding the receiver behind his back. "I'll return the call, then head over to the pharmacy. Try not to worry.

Everything's going to be okay." Even as he said this, he had a sudden premonition that the illness, whatever the hell it was, would remain a permanent fixture in their lives, and that the only thing left to do was adapt.

* * * *

Arriving at the first intersection, Brent waited with other pedestrians for the light to change. He placed a hand on the traffic-pole for support, glancing back at the building which he still had a hard time referring to as a church. As of yet there was no indication of a cross, or any other outward sign, and if the news had not reported it as such, he would never have taken it for anything but a financial center.

The light switched to green and a mass of the city workforce shambled across the street. Brent studied a lethargic few, surprised to find that their complexions closely resembled his own. Hardly any of them looked the picture of health, what with their shirts improperly buttoned and hairstyles comically askew.

When he arrived at the pharmacy, Brent drifted past a line of people vying to get inside. He cupped his hands and peered through the storefront window. The interior was packed with customers whose blank expressions and slumped shoulders suggested they had all the time in the world. No pharmacists were in sight. Had the horrific implications of their growing customer base been too much to bear?

Repelled and somehow humored by the throng of humanity crammed within, Brent turned and started for home. The queue of customers desiring to visit the pharmacy now stretched around the corner for as far as he could see.

* * * *

Nearing his apartment, Brent noticed a group of individuals exiting the expansive glass doors of the church. Their unmistakable joie de vivre had him feeling uncomfortable for reasons he could not explain. He considered crossing the street, but instead followed his anxiety back to his apartment, where it became flesh in the long foyer mirror leading to the stairs. Brent raised his arms in defense against the menacing figure already on the verge of attack.

Pale and wizened flesh, dark circles about the eyes: the wreckage of his illness was finally perceived.

Turning from—and thus into—his diseased self, Brent began an exhausting ascent of the stairwell. When he arrived at his apartment, he slipped inside as quietly as possible, not wishing to disturb Sam. He found her on the sofa, wrapped in a comforter and staring at the television.

"Something's wrong with it," she whispered hoarsely. The way the comforter had molded to her body suggested nothing less than a fully-developed cocoon. Brent hoped that a transformation was taking place within, that a healthy Sam was on the verge of breaking free.

Another news reporter was onscreen, appearing as ill as the colleague she was no doubt meant to replace. Her mouth was moving, yet nothing emerged from the emaciated lips. Brent asked Sam to increase the volume. Instead, she began flipping through a seemingly endless supply of static-filled stations. In time, she came full circle to the mute reporter. "Like I said, something's wrong."

Brent grabbed the remote, more forceful than he had intended, and pressed the on/off button. He waited impatiently for the flashing diodes to darken before powering it all up again. The reporter's resurrection, when it came, remained without sound.

"Did you make it to the pharmacy?"

Brent continued tinkering with the remote.

"Please tell me you found something." A fissure opened in Sam's shell and an appendage vaguely resembling a human hand wiped her nose.

Before Brent could reply, he heard a disturbance at the door. It sounded as though an object was being pushed beneath the jamb. When he turned to investigate, a shimmering pamphlet awaited. He bent to retrieve it, embarrassed by how much energy it took to do so.

"Some reading material," he said, tossing the item next to Sam. "Listen, I need to lay down for awhile." But Sam had already gone back to staring intently at the television, oblivious of his statement or the pamphlet at her side.

* * * *

When he woke, Brent took in only a fraction of the available light. He made a cursory attempt to loosen the sleep from his eyes, then turned to nuzzle Sam. His hand fell on empty sheets, and with that he experienced a wave of confusion and sadness, leaving him to believe (if only momentarily) that they had gone their separate ways.

Trudging into the bathroom, Brent stooped over the wash basin and began to flush out his eyes. He flicked on the lights and stared aloofly at his reflection. The shadows encircling his eyes were more prevalent under the fluorescents, and his lips, once so full, were practically nonexistent, as if they had receded into his gum-line. When he smiled, a set of rotting teeth grinned back.

Concern for his well-being shifted to Sam. He staggered to the living room, fearful of finding her on the brink of death. There was the cocoon, split down the center, its occupant gone. Feeling lightheaded, Brent retreated to the window and, by some impossible projection of his emotions, glimpsed Sam's pre-illness double standing directly across the street. She was mingling with a group of smartly-dressed individuals.

Brent knocked on the window. Sam couldn't possibly have heard from such a distance, yet her focus shifted and she began to wave. The greeting turned into a summons, beckoning him outside. Leaning forward, Brent mashed his nose against the glass, trying for comedy to convey his condition.

Not long after, he turned from the scene, certain that it was nothing more than an illness-induced delusion, and eased himself onto the sofa. He considered turning on the television, but instead began a cursory inspection of the pamphlet. It reminded him of the glossy handouts offered to prospective car buyers. In this case, however, the contents were devoted to interior and exterior images of the church, as well as numerous embedded articles. He started reading one such entry (entitled "Diary of an Illness"), but was interrupted when the front door sprang open.

By the time Brent's eyes lifted from the text, Sam was already at his side humming a familiar, upbeat tune. Hearing it brought back all the joyous moments in their relationship. Brent attempted to replicate her smile with his own defective lips, but failed miserably.

"You look...better." He couldn't think of anything else to say.

Sam was staring reverently at the pamphlet in his hand.

"Have you read it yet?" she asked brightly, and then, before he could answer, "I'd like to take you there. And the sooner the better. They call it a church, but it's something so much more. They even have a cafe."

"You went *inside*?" Brent was surprised by his slightly accusatory tone.

"Course I did. After reading that, who wouldn't want to? Really, we must go. Here, I'll help you." Sam shifted closer, as though ready to carry him if necessary. She certainly appeared robust enough to do so.

Brent stilled her advance. "I'm in no condition to go anywhere."

Sam tapped the pamphlet before striding effortlessly to the window. "It's an extraordinary achievement, isn't it?" Her tone of reverie frightened Brent. He stared at her dignified silhouette until the surrounding light was too much to bear.

"Well, it's there for you when you're ready. But don't wait too long, mister." Sam was now standing at the open front door. "Important things are happening."

Brent tried to speak, but by the time he uttered his first syllable, Sam was gone. The silence which followed was unnerving, and all he could think to do was reopen the pamphlet and continue reading "Diary of an Illness."

He perused the first line—*It was only after I walked through these hallowed doors that my true recovery began*—and immediately tossed the pamphlet aside, his irritation resonating like a force that projected him to the window. The polished surface of the church astounded him as if for the first time. No machinery or workers were present, not a single speck of debris left behind.

While many patrons appeared healthy and hale, another set wandered clumsily about, clearly not in command of their faculties. What disturbed Brent the most, however, was that none of the thriving ones made any effort to assist the ill, even if this merely involved something as simple as crossing the street.

Brent shifted his attention to a solitary figure standing on the sidewalk a block away. The man seemed oblivious to his surroundings, his sole focus upon a manhole cover. He was holding what looked like a crowbar, though it might very well have been a piece of scaffolding from the corner building.

The man wedged the implement between the cover and its rim, yanking until it popped free. He then crouched and began inserting himself into the hole. In the time it took Brent to wipe his burning eyes and refocus on the scene, the man was gone.

Feeling faint, Brent stumbled to the sofa and collapsed.

* * * *

When he regained consciousness, it was night.

He called for Sam, or at least made the attempt. What slithered from his ruined mouth was a kind of grotesque moan. His throat felt raw, and the effort of uttering further syllables left him gagging for breath. He staggered toward the kitchen, stopping nearby to examine the portrait of an old man hanging on the wall. It was only when this figure moved that Brent realized it was his own reflection. He and Sam had purchased the mirror at an antique store just last week.

Entering the kitchen, he reached for the phone but inadvertently knocked it to the floor. He dropped to his knees, cupping the device as if it were a stunned bird, his only remaining connection to the outside world. He dialed emergency services and was surprised at how promptly a voice answered. Strangely, the individual sounded exactly like the reporter who had covered the story about the church.

The recorded message spoke of the regenerative nature of the facility and asked, at its conclusion, if the caller wished to be visited by a representative. Brent's only requirement was to utter an affirmative and someone would be dispatched. He attempted to respond, but his voice betrayed him. A few seconds later, the woman began a detailed account of her own brush with illness. Her calm and even tone, along with the knowledge of Sam's abandonment, enraged Brent enough to slam the phone against the floor.

He needed to get out of this coffin, needed to find Sam. How much longer did he have before his senses shut down for good? He returned briefly to the living room window, longing to see the city restored to his remembrance of it before the illness, before the new structure had risen. Instead, he glimpsed hordes of citizens, their numbers so dense as to eclipse sidewalk and street. Brent reeled from the window and stumbled to the front entry, wheezing all the while.

He stepped outside, into a world that seemed bent on separating him from Sam. His every remaining breath would go toward seeing them reunited.

* * * *

Pushing his way through the sickly crowds, he stopped at the end of the first block to regard the church. He shielded his eyes from the glare, but the sensation of burning continued far longer than it should have. No other structure was lit up at this hour, as though the church itself had absorbed every ounce of the city's cold fire. Brent peered into the distance a final time, capturing the image of a vibrant crowd mingling beyond the windows.

He continued down the street, past the darkened pharmacy, glancing only sporadically at the faces surrounding him. During these instances, it felt as though he were looking into a funhouse mirror at multiple representations of himself, so ingrained was the illness among the populace.

Blocks later, he arrived at the end of a structured line of people. This heartened him to a degree because it meant that someone amid all this chaos was attempting to organize and perhaps resolve the matter. He stood in line for a few minutes before he felt compelled to wander ahead, merely to glimpse the spectacle that lay in wait. Maybe another pharmacy had opened its doors; or better yet, a makeshift medical facility.

Filled with a modicum of hope, Brent quickened his pace.

When he arrived at the next block, however, the reality of the situation stopped him cold. Feeling faint, he reached out to the glass wall of a department store, smiling at the individuals in the display window before realizing they were mannikins. He turned from the pale figures and stared in disbelief at the ritual now taking place before him.

A representative of the church, similar to the one Brent had seen on television, stood on the opposite side of an open manhole, gesturing to the supplicant across the divide. Words were uttered, and in the next unbelievable moment the recipient of the benediction bent and scuttled gratefully into the hole.

Words rang out to the next in line:

"A new life awaits. A new light. May peace descend upon you."

Brent closed his eyes, imagining Sam uttering similar words from the rim of another city void. If anyone should baptize him into oblivion, it had to be her. He pushed on, growing wearier by the step.

Teatime With Mrs. Monster

by James Aquilone

Inside my brain I'm saying, "Don't move, Kylie. Don't breathe. Don't make a noise. He'll hear you."

It's warm and icky under the porch. There are spiderwebs in my mouth and bugs crawling on my legs. Maybe it's my 'magination. I don't know. But it's safe here. Daddy doesn't know 'bout my hiding place.

I hear him above me in the house. He's cussing and stomping like crazy. The floorboards groan like in the haunted houses in those scary movies I used to watch with Mama. Daddy is saying he'll find me when he gets back, he'll find me and then he'll take care of me and then I'll learn, I won't be bad no more. I knew that's what he'd say. So when the Bad Thing happened I runned straight out of my room and hid here. Daddy said, "Where'd you think you're going?" But I was past him and out the front door already. It was only a matter of time before he goed upstairs.

He's screaming now, "This is your fault, Kylie! You little brat! No more friends in the house! No more tea parties! Not ever again! What a mess! What a damn mess!"

I put my hand over my mouth so he can't hear me breathing. I seened that in those scary movies too, when the monster comes looking for the little girl and she's hiding in the dark. But I'm not scared of monsters. Monsters never hurted me.

I'm lying on my tummy near the porch steps and I see Daddy's big dirty boots as he booms down. I can see the boards bending. I think maybe they'll break and he'll see me. Then he'll drag me out and take care of me. Mama used to say she'd take care of me when she was alive. But she meant it different.

I see him crossing the lawn. I see he's carrying something in his arms. It looks like a bag of garbage. He throws it in the back of the truck, gets in and drives away.

But it wasn't my fault. It was Amy. She made Mrs. Monster mad. I told her to shut her stupid mouth but she wouldn't listen. Daddy doesn't think Mrs. Monster is real just 'cause he can't see her. But Mrs. Monster says he can't see because he doesn't wanna. People, growned-ups 'specially, don't want to see monsters, they don't want to believe they're real. That's why I thought Amy would see Mrs. Monster. She's eight like me. But Amy is stupid. I hate her and I don't care if I never see her again.

Me and Mama used to have tea parties all the time. She'd make up stories and we'd pretend. She said I was good at it. She'd say, "What a livid 'magination you have." After Mama died, I asked Daddy if he'd have tea parties with me. But he said no. He don't have time.

So I have tea parties without him. I don't need him. I have Mrs. Monster now.

Daddy says I should play with the kids in the neighborhood instead of staying in my room all day. I say the kids are stupid, I don't want to play with them. When Amy came over today I seened his eyes were happy. Most times they're sad.

Amy is taller than me. She has red hair and freckles. She talks with a lisp and spit gathers in the corners of her mouth when she talks too much. Which is all the time. Sometimes I make fun of her but she's the only kid that comes to my house. I never invite her, she just rings my doorbell. Most times I don't answer. Today I did.

Daddy said, "Why don't you go outside and ride bikes or something." He didn't want to hear no racket. I ignored him and took Amy by the hand and goed upstairs.

In my room there is a small round table with small chairs too. The teacups were already out, the kettle in the center. There was one for me and one for Mrs. Monster. There wasn't one for Amy. I didn't know she was coming.

I searched in the toy chest against the wall. At the bottom was a cup with flowers on it. The flowers were red like old blood. The handle had broken off but it was OK.

Amy said, "Don't you have any dolls? I want to play dolls." She said it *doll-shhs*.

I put Amy's cup on the table. "Dolls are stupid," I said. "We're going to have a tea party."

"But shouldn't you have dolls around the table? Or is it just going to be me and you?"

"No, silly. Don't you see the other teacup?"

We sat and I poured Amy's tea. "I hope you like black tea."

"I prefer Earl Grey," she said trying to sound like a big girl but her lisp made her sound like a dumb baby.

"Black tea is all we ever have. So you'll have to like it. Mrs. Monster only drinks black tea. She says it's the best one."

"Who's Mrs. Monster?"

"She's sitting next to you, silly."

"Oh," Amy said and made an ugly scrunchy face like she smelled something bad. "I don't like monsters."

I could tell Mrs. Monster didn't like Amy. Nobody likes Amy. That's why she plays with me.

"Mrs. Monster said hello," I said.

"That's a weird name."

"That's what she's called."

"No princesses? I'd rather have tea with princesses."

"Princesses are stupid."

"You're a loon, you know that?"

"Take that back!"

"No," she said and took a sip of her tea, all dainty-like, with her pinky up in the air.

"You made Mrs. Monster mad," I said.

"She doesn't look mad to me. Actually she don't look like nothing, 'cause she's not here. She's imaginary. Crazy people have imaginary friends, you know? Wasn't your mother crazy? That's what mine says. I think you're a loon too."

Daddy called Mama crazy once. I remember in my brain. I was so mad at Amy. Mad like when Daddy gets and I have to hide under the porch. Then Amy started singing "loon loon loon." I didn't want to see Amy's stupid ugly face so I shutted my eyes so tight I seened fire in my brain. That was when the Bad Thing happened. I don't remember what went on but Amy screamed. I heard other sounds too. Bad sounds. Monster sounds. I was too scared to open my eyes. I runned, my heart going thrum-thrum-thrum. "Go to your safe place," I said inside my brain, just like Mama used to tell me when Daddy's eyes got mad and his face turned red like burning.

I could stay under the porch. Daddy will never find me. He's never found me before. Once I stayed under here the whole day and it got dark and I only came back home because something bit me—I think it was a rat—and besides I was hungry. Daddy was real mad that time. He hurted me. I know he's madder than ever now 'cause of the Bad Thing and when he gets back he's gonna be worse than any monster I ever seened in the movies. I think then in my brain about Mama and our tea parties. She'd say, "Do you see that monster sitting next to you?" And I'd laugh. Mama'd say, "Aren't you afraid?" I'd say no. "That's right, baby," she'd say. "People are worse than any make-believe monster. Don't you never forget that."

Daddy isn't a monster, he's my Daddy. But I see his eyes in my brain and I'm so scared I'm shaking. Then in my brain I hear Mrs. Monster say, "Don't worry, baby, I'll take care of you but first let's take care of Daddy." I turn around and crawl farther under the house, dirt getting in my mouth and nose, until I come out in the backyard. The toolshed is open. Stupid daddy.

Train to Nowhere

From the files of Nick Nightmare
by Adrian Cole

It was a grimy kind of day, if you know what I mean: grey skies, grey buildings still damp with the night's downpour, grubby streets, and curling clouds of smog—you get the picture. Was there a man dismayed? Yeah, I daresay there were plenty, but not this one, no sir. Today I was bright-eyed and bushy-tailed, bouncing along the backstreets of Manhattan on my way to a rendezvous with the unique and invaluable Artavian Wormdark, the Main Man when it came to hunting down book treasures that no one else could unearth. I always enjoyed a trip to his private shrine, but today was a special day. He had something for me. Something I had been trying to nail for a long time.

A first (and only) edition of a forgotten pulp entitled *The High-Heeled Hangman*.

I've said before I have a predilection for private eye pulp and it's no big secret that my hero is the incorrigible Ned Killigan, the blast 'em first and question 'em later tough guy, who shoots, punches, kicks and generally clobbers his way through a hefty stack of pulp adventures. Well, *The High-Heeled Hangman* is not one of Ned's—it's a stand-alone—but it comes very close to the quality of the master's. And it's damned elusive these days.

Wormdark answered the door, bowing down politely, his ancient face cracking up into a grin of a thousand wrinkles. He waved me into his den. In recognition of the magnitude of his find, I was to be admitted to the holy of holies, his private study, which was embedded deep down in the bowels of his brownstone. Three stairs led that way and it took several keys to unlock the door to this most hallowed of crypts. It was not unlike entering the guts of a pyramid. There were so many books lining the walls that they looked like they were holding the whole place up.

My host dropped into a big fat armchair and I sat in a slightly less weighty seat, trying to feign patience, though I was clutching my hat so tightly I was in danger of crushing it into a shapeless wad of material.

"So how are things?" said Wormdark. He was wizened as a Brazil nut, a half-pint little guy but with a heart twice as big as most others.

There was a twinkle in his eye that suggested he was having some fun with my eagerness.

"Busy, busy," I grunted. "The Devil never sleeps."

His little body shook to silent laughter. "I have heard," he said with that crooked smile. "You do good work, sir."

"Someone has to try and keep the streets clean."

He turned, to where one of many shelves butted out, a score of booklets, magazines and thin books cramming its length, and slid one out, handling it like it was made of thin glass. He gently gave it to me and I took it carefully. It had a lurid, paper cover, one I recognised at once— a partially dressed dame, crouched down in the shadow of a dangling corpse, the title scrawled in blood-red letters. Oh yeah, this was *The High-Heeled Hangman.* The hunter had brought home the bacon. I gently flicked it open to the title page and nodded, supremely delighted.

Wormdark watched me. My guess was he took as much pleasure from seeing my reaction as I did from receiving the prize. "I've not read it myself, but it's said to be a classic," he said.

I put the book down and pulled a wad of greenbacks from inside my jacket. "Five hundred," I said, happily handing them over. I'd have paid him a whole lot more, but it had been tough enough to get him to agree to this figure. He was generous with his some of his clients and I guess he knew he could rely on me if he needed my own kind of expertise at any time. He slipped the money into a drawer, almost embarrassed to accept it.

I picked the book up again, loving the feel of the old pulp, with its uneven pages and unique papery smell. As I flicked through, something fell out and dropped on the table. It was a sealed envelope. Wormdark and I both stared at it, momentarily frozen like a couple of guilty kids. I could see by his face that he hadn't known about it. Most dealers would have swooped on it and tried to bluff their way into saying it wasn't part of the deal and all that crap before grabbing it back.

Not Wormdark. He gestured for me to pick it up. "I hadn't seen that," he said. "Whatever it is, it's yours. Please, take it and consider it a bonus."

"Hell, Artavian, I've got what I want. You have the envelope. I've read *Casting the Runes.*"

He scowled uncomfortably at the reference and sat back. "Good grief! In which case the envelope is definitely yours. Take it, take it."

I grinned and picked it up. "Let's at least see what's here. Probably a laundry bill or a—" My words were cut off as I slit the envelope and slid out its contents—a single card, neatly inscribed, with a golden border.

Dear Reader,

*Love the world of THE HIGH-HEELED HANGMAN?
Then I would be honoured if you would join me and
my company of friends on our thrilling journey to the
Dance of a Lifetime, where we will be celebrating this
classic pulp novel in a splendid pageant. Please wear
fancy dress accordingly. A very special locomotive
will be leaving for our secret rendezvous. You will find
dates, time and precise instructions on the reverse of
this card. It would be a joy to welcome you, along with
many other aficionados, to the revels.*

Carmella Cadenza

Something about the lady's name rang a bell. I picked up the book
and turned it over, reading through the blurb on the back cover. That's
where I'd seen the name—the villain of the piece was called Carmella.
I hadn't read the book, although I knew a few things about the plot. A
down at heel private dick, not quite in the same class as Ned Killigan,
locks horns with the aforementioned dangerous *femme fatale* and thwarts
her evil plans, but at a price. I'm a sucker for the emotionally damaged
hero.

I read the invitation out to Wormdark. "So who is Carmella? I mean,
really?"

He threw up his arms in a gesture of bafflement. "A *nom-de-plume*,
perhaps. This Dance of a Lifetime event would be the key to that. One
way to find out. What are the instructions?"

I flipped the card—this event was taking place three days from now.
The instructions were detailed but in general referred to an old railway
yard that I knew about, but had never had cause to visit: a spur that had
been shut down for many years, previously used for freight and switch-
ing. Looked like someone had cleaned the place up and was hiring it out
for private functions, with their own locomotive to boot. I have to admit
I was intrigued.

"So are you going?" said Wormdark.

"Hell, I don't have a thing to wear."

* * * *

So there I was, three nights later, standing on an abandoned dock
in the blurred moonlight, looking west across the Hudson to a far shore
where there were as many shadows as lit-up areas. I'd arrived here at

the appointed hour, following the instructions, so I had a carry-all with a change of clothes—my concession to fancy dress—and my two Berettas tucked firmly in my belt out of sight. Without them I'd be going blindfold into a minefield.

Someone called to me from out of a chunk of darkness down on the water along the dock and I saw a shape drifting across the murk, some kind of low, canoe-like craft, being rowed by a single, hunched figure. I would have thought it bizarre, but I'd met this character before. Come to think of it, it was still more than a bit weird. I remembered he called himself Fred the Ferryman. He'd proved a friend in the past, so I was okay with him. He turned a wide, grinning face up to beam at me.

"Right on time, Mr Stone. You all set? Climb aboard." His neckless blob of a head was split almost in two by that grin. This guy gave new meaning to the expression, happy in his work.

There was a set of narrow, slimy steps dropping to the water and I gingerly made my way down to the canoe-thing. Fred got hold of an iron ring in the stonework and held his craft as steady as he could while I embarked. As I sat there and let him row me out over the river, I wondered where, exactly, we were headed. This guy slipped to and fro along the weirdest route, so I couldn't be sure that I was going to disembark in the same New York I lived in. I reminded myself that, as far as I knew, Fred was an ally, or at least neutral in the grand scheme of things.

"So what's this all about?" I asked him.

His grin widened, if that was possible. "I'm just the man who rows the boat, Mr Stone. I've been paid to get some of tonight's guests to the party. Sounds like it's gonna be fun. You read that book? You ready to meet the High-Heeled Hangman?"

I had read the pulp over the last day or two. Classic cop pulp. I liked the hero, whose moniker was simply O'Reilly. He was a slob, his entire attention focussed on bringing down the notorious Carmella, the High-Heeled Hangman of the title, as it turns out. She's a crime queen, responsible for executing—hanging—anyone who stands in her way, including cops and their families. She makes the mistake of holding a neck-tie party for a big buddy of O'Reilly, and he sets out to bring her down. He doesn't know the Hangman is a woman until near the finale, but it doesn't stop him from wreaking havoc and nailing her. The language isn't Shakespeare, but my guess is, the Bard would have loved—and probably pilfered—the plot.

"So who you gonna be tonight?" said Fred. "Got to be O'Reilly, right?"

I gave him my best mysterious smile. "Nope. Too obvious. So what do you know about the hostess?"

He laughed fit to make a demon squirm. "She'll be playing the part of Carmella, for sure. But as for who she is, who knows?"

That was about it for conversation and when I got out of the craft and went up the steps to the quay the other side of the Hudson, I was none the wiser. What did rattle me was how that invitation card had got into the book I bought off Wormdark. I knew he'd been genuinely surprised to see it. I gave Fred a cheery wave and turned to wander across the deserted expanse of concrete before me. There were marshalling yards and platforms somewhere near here—Weehawken station—but this part of the place was run down and abandoned. For all I knew, I'd crossed over more than just the Hudson. This could easily be the Pulpworld, that bizarre, parallel domain I sometimes entered.

I was beginning to wonder if maybe the whole shebang had been cancelled when another figure emerged out of the cement surroundings. I knew I was on the right track when I saw him: he was dressed in smart livery, a burgundy jacket with gold-coloured buttons, sharply creased black trousers with a burgundy stripe down each outer leg and black shoes that had been polished enough to dazzle. He also wore a cap with the motif CARMELLA'S EXPRESS around the rim.

He bowed. "Good evening, sir. I am Maurice, your tour guide for this evening. Do you have your ticket?"

I handed it to him and he perused it, smiling beatifically, and handed it back. "Please keep it with you at all times. Would you like to come this way? There is a changing room set aside for guests. The train will be arriving shortly and departs at 11.04 precisely."

I nodded, tempted to ask the significance of the "0.4" but I let it pass. Instead I went with him along the dusty platform to what looked like an old waiting room. It had evidently been dolled up for the occasion—fresh paint gleamed and its smell still clung to the air. The same burgundy and gold colour scheme had been used and it had something of a circus feel to it. Inside the room there were several benches against its walls and plenty of coat hooks. If anyone else had used it tonight, they hadn't left anything in here.

Maurice left me to change and I did so quickly. I'd brought a long priest's habit, with a cowl. Experience had taught me that a cowl was always handy, particularly if you weren't expected to be wearing a mask. I put my working coat in the carry-all and just slipped on the habit, tying up its cord belt in a way that would make it easy to open it and pull out a gun or two if I needed to. Or one of the several knives I had hidden about me. Okay, I was a bit edgy. A man has enemies, right? You don't take chances. Assume they're waiting. Be prepared, and all that sensible stuff.

When I came out of the changing room, Maurice eyed me up and down fussily, nodding as if he was satisfied I met the necessary standards. "Ah, the priest, Father Burracunda," he said, referring to the character in *The High-Heeled Hangman* I'd selected. "You'll be the third, but that's fine. We have at least two dozen O'Reilly's so far. People can be so unimaginative."

"Glad you like it, Maurice."

He bowed again and led me to the platform. I saw now that a small crowd had gathered and I recognised most of the characters on display, some of them, as Maurice had intimated, here in numbers. The only one missing was Carmella, so I surmised the ladies had been warned off that one. My guess was it would be the exclusive province of our hostess. Joining the crowd—I reckoned on there being at least a hundred people in all—I exchanged nods and smiles, most of them nervous. I didn't see anyone I recognised through the costumes or the make-up, which suited me fine. I had my cowl down at this point and I didn't think anyone here would recognise a low-key private eye from the darker corners of the city.

The appointed hour drew near and we heard the coming of the metal beast that was to whisk us away on our journey. It burst out of a cloud of boiling steam alongside the platform, a fabulous steam engine, something out of the last century, immaculately preserved, gleaming and sparkling like new, pistons pumping, wheels rolling, steam billowing out like a charging dragon. Its ornate nameplate proclaimed it to be **Smokestack Lightning**, and I have to say, that huge smokestack was magnificent! I'm no expert in these things, but I have to admit I was pretty knocked out by it and as it shuddered to a halt I understood perfectly what it was that fired up the fans of these monsters.

The crowd was cheering loudly and I realized that I'd joined in. Hell, this was supposed to be a fun night, so why not? I could see Maurice and several other tour guides in uniform all beaming at the train, already opening doors to its numerous carriages. And what carriages! No expense had been spared in dressing them up. They were like new. Best possible livery, everything polished and gleaming—period fittings—hell, it was like we really had stepped back over a hundred years. I got into one of the carriages, gently ushered in by Maurice, and found a seat by a window. The carriage quickly filled up.

It didn't take long to get the crowd on board. We were all like kids, excited, over-eager and revved up to high speed. I let the madness sweep me along. This could be fun, after all. My natural suspicions began to subside a little. Not completely: I've had my butt kicked too many times to let my guard down to that extent, but at this point it did seem like a good time was about to be had by all. Anyhow, it was too late to back down. The train whistled noisily, steam wrapping around us like cloudy thunderheads and we were off, gathering speed in no time. There was nothing to see outside the windows, just an impenetrable wall of darkness and not a single city light to break its monotony.

Maurice stood at the end of the carriage and called patiently for silence. Once he'd quelled the excited mob, he turned on the charm again. "Ladies and gentlemen, on behalf of your hostess, Carmella Cadenza, may I welcome you to our little jaunt, which will end in approximately one hour's time at our destination, where you will be able to participate in the Dance of a Lifetime. It will be a celebration of the popular modern classic you all know and love, *The High-Heeled Hangman*. There will be food, drink and all manner of games and entertainments. Carmella herself will preside and we promise you an abundance of merriment, the thrill indeed of a lifetime! My colleagues will shortly be serving the very best wine to you all, or if you prefer something less heady, that too. In the meantime, relax and enjoy the company. You may smoke if you wish to, and indeed, take what pleasures you will. Tonight is about enjoyment!"

There were more cheers. I was wondering about payment. I mean, this trip was fine and promised to end up in a party to end all parties. So what was the price? Maybe the lady in charge was a big, big fan of the book and just liked to gather as many fellow fans as she could for a good time, at her own expense. Wacky but not that unusual. I'd enough experience of the wealthy members of my world to know they were happy enough to toss their dough about like confetti at a wedding. Even so, part of me remained cautious. I didn't want to find myself in debt to anyone, least of all some hedonistic eccentric.

A smallish guy dressed up as a newspaper seller (a minor character from the book) asked if the seat next to me was spare and I waved him to it. He took off his hat and ran his fingers back through his thinning hair and peered at me over his spectacles. "Pleased to meet you," he said. "I'm Hal Drewster."

"Hi. I'm Nick Stone. Or Father Burracunda, if it isn't obvious."

He smiled and we shook hands warmly. He seemed like an okay guy, a bit on edge, but in this bizarre company it was hardly surprising.

"What's your line, Hal?" I asked him. "I mean outside this party."

"I'm an artist. You might recognise some of my stuff. I did the cover for *The High-Heeled Hangman*. Only I use a pseudonym. Japetus."

"Japetus?" I repeated, impressed. "No kidding? You're Japetus? My hero." I meant it. It was a real gas to meet such a talented guy.

He looked slightly embarrassed. "That's very kind of you, Nick. I did a lot of pulp cover work in my early days. Pretty lurid, eh? Man's got to earn a crust. These days I do mostly private stuff. Can't complain at the benefits."

"I love those old covers. I've hoarded a pile of 'em. So you got an invite. Know anything about our hostess, this Carmella dame?"

I thought a shadow crossed his face for a moment, but maybe it was just the movement of the express. He shook his head. "It's all kinda mysterious. Rumour has it she's the granddaughter of Luke Dane, the guy who wrote *The High-Heeled Hangman.* It was his only success, although a modest one. If you've read any of his others, you'll know what I mean. He was too fond of the booze to stick at it and died without a *sou* to his name. Maybe Carmella is making up for it."

The wine arrived and we both took a glass of what turned out to be very superior stuff. I'm not big on vino, but it was okay. Even so, I sipped it cautiously. I wasn't going to let my hair down until I knew a mite more about what was going on. Hal took the same view.

By the time the train started to slow down, then break, crawling noisily into our destination, it was close on midnight, and as we stepped out on to the platform, the big station clock overhead, as much an antique from the steam age as the locomotive, indicated it was dead on the witching hour. Nice timing, and it explained why we'd left dead on 11.04 pm. The section of the station we were using had been painted and decorated in the familiar Carmella livery, and there were flags and bunting draped around its high beams and low doorways. We moved en masse through the reception area, more than a few of the crowd already a little worse for the vino, and found a fleet of horse-drawn vehicles waiting to whisk us away further into the night.

Hal and I kept together, studying the small township we seemed to have ended up in as its ancient buildings sped by. It looked like we'd slipped back in time to some old frontier town at the back of nowhere and I was expecting to see a cow hand or gunslinger lurch from the buildings, just for effect. There were a few lights on here and there, old gas affairs, but maybe everyone was asleep. No late night drinking for whoever inhabited this broken-down backwater. Maybe they were all Methodists.

The fleet pulled up in front of one towering pile, an untypically large wooden building that was so covered in neon it would have stood out on Madison Avenue on New Year. A huge banner was draped across its higher ramparts, proclaiming THE DANCE OF A LIFETIME. The wide steps leading up to it were lined with more of our guides, all dressed in their uniforms, their faces pasted with smiles like toy soldiers. People were heading for the tall doors, eager to get inside and start the next phase of the party. Obviously no one apart from me and Hal had any reservations about how this might end. I got the feeling there was something my artistic friend hadn't told me.

Inside, once we'd got past the brilliantly lit foyer with its dangling chandeliers and potted palm trees (the genuine article) and been given yet another glass of vino, we made it through to the ballroom, a huge cavern more modern day than the stage sets we'd seen so far. A full-blown orchestra was earning its corn and I admit it was a classy outfit, pumping out a selection of classic swing pieces so that several couples got straight down to it and danced across the floor like old pros. There were three bars and there was a side room where there was a spread of food that would have fed a couple of small towns. Everything here was lavish.

Two very exquisite young things, dressed in jewels and feathers, popped up in front of me and Hal, smiling their most seductive smiles—about ten on the Richter scale—and asked us if we'd like the pleasure. Hal was too embarrassed to accept, and I wanted to check out the scene before I dropped my guard, so I politely declined the offer on our behalf. The girls didn't take long to find two other gents who were more than willing to be whisked out on to the floor.

"What I really want," said Hal, leaning closer so I could hear him above the excited din, "is to get a real good look at our hostess. I want to see her face."

"Yeah, that would be cool," I agreed. We'd squeezed our way through the mob, which somehow seemed to have quadrupled in size—maybe more locomotives had pulled in. We got close to one bar and used it to prop ourselves up where we could see across what was now a sea of heads. Beside the raised area where the band was performing, there was another dais, I guessed for a singer. However, when the vivid burgundy curtains behind it swished open, the woman who emerged was no songbird.

Dressed from head to foot in a shimmering green dress that dazzled the eye and spread light like one of the overhead glitter balls, and wearing enough jewellery to embarrass a queen, she was tall, curvaceous and definitely Hollywood A-list material. She was wearing stilettos that could have doubled for a small set of steps they were that high and the twin slits in the sides of her dress revealed impossibly long, shapely legs. Don't get me wrong—I wouldn't have swapped her for FiFi Cherie, my own particular favourite night club singer, for a moment—but I was impressed. The audience howled with delight, cheering and clapping as the incarnation of Carmella raised her lithe arms, golden bangles and all, and gestured for silence.

She got it and the place held its breath. Hal wasn't going to get his wish, not yet anyway—she was wearing a mask. It was a delicate thing and hid her eyes and nose, but her mouth was visible, the thickly rouged lips, gleaming seductively, slightly curved in a smile calculated to raise the temperature of human blood a few degrees.

"Welcome!" she called in husky tones and the response was deafening. "It is *such* a pleasure to see so many fans of the Hangman. This will be our third year of revels in celebration and there is *so* much fun to be had tonight. Eat and drink your fill, you gorgeous people! We have *wonderful* music from the incomparable Sergio Bambosa and his Big Band and only the finest singers to stroke your heart-strings. Later, we will have our annual ceremony, when we will be executing all the usual suspects."

This met with a huge roar of delight and I glanced askance at Hal. I had to wait for our hostess to finish her patter and for all the subsequence howls and cheers to die down before I got an explanation. Apparently Hal knew the ropes at this bash.

"It's a crazy gimmick in honour of the book. You know that the 'mysterious' hangman knocks off a dozen victims before finally getting herself nailed by O'Reilly. Well, our hostess selects the best of the company dressed as the victims. There's always plenty of them. The world is full of exhibitionists, right? Then they get to be strung up." He grinned at my expression. "Hell, not for real, Nick. It's a ritual. At the end, Carmella escapes the clutches of O'Reilly and, unlike in the book, lives to fight another day. That'll be next year's party."

I got to admit, the idea made me feel uncomfortable. Mock hangings? Hell, it was okay reading good—even gory—pulp, but this seemed a mite kinky. Mind you, I guess a lot of people enjoyed mayhem in the movies.

I studied Hal for a moment. His outfit was simple enough, a crumpled suit, old shirt, scruffy shoes. He was a newspaper seller in the book, Little Louis, who passes in information and tips to O'Reilly and earns the wrath of the villain. He gets strung up for his pains. "You realise, Hal, that you're in line for one of the parts in that ceremony?"

He grinned, but not that convincingly. "Me? Heck, no. My costume is a bit cheap, even for my part. There'll be others here who'll l be picked way ahead of me. That's why they come, to get selected for the hanging. It's that kind of gang."

I shook my head. "Whatever," I said, sipping my wine. I preferred whiskey, but I'd had too much wine to swap now. I wanted to keep a clear head.

Hal and I sampled the food, which was about as good as it gets, and I noticed he was taking it very easy on the wine, as though something was bothering him and he wasn't going to let himself go, unlike the rest of the crowd. Whatever was bugging him, he kept to himself, but I had a feeling he would clue me in, given time. Whatever it was, it kept me sober and alert.

It was close on two am when Hal and I were singled out by a bunch of the tour guides in their slick livery, only these weren't the sleek and slender versions. Half a dozen of them—all big lugs with the mashed faces of boxers to go with the build—gathered around us. My guess was their politeness was forced and would end the moment we raised a finger to argue with whatever it was they wanted. It was Hal. Big Ugly Number One tapped him lightly on the chest.

"Congratulations, bub," the monster growled. "You made it to the selection for Little Louis, the newspaper seller."

"I did?" said Hal, but I knew his pleasure was feigned. "But my outfit is so cheap."

"Well, you caught the boss's eye, pal. Don't worry none. All in good fun. Come with us."

The six thugs all eyed me quietly, but their expressions made it clear that I wasn't invited to this particular party. Hal shrugged and made to go. I didn't like it. Not one bit. Okay, there were a lot of people here going through this routine, and a final line-up would be made, but I smelled a rat or two. A nest of them, in fact. Added to that, I could smell Hal's fear. He was not happy, no sir-ee.

I waved him away as if I'd succumbed to the drink, and leaned indifferently on the bar, now conveniently ignored but watching as Hal was gently prodded through the crowd. People cheerfully clapped his passage, presumably envious that he had made the final cut. I waited until I felt I wasn't being watched and slipped away through the crowd at a tangent to the heavies taking Hal to wherever. I wanted to be in on the selection process, though not openly.

They bundled him through a door which had two more big lugs covering it, so I had to take a chance on the next door along. It took me into a corridor and it looked like it may run parallel to the one beyond the other door. Its walls were thin, so I pressed my ear to the wallpaper and I could hear the muted passing of Hal and his new pals the other side. I went up my corridor, half listening out for anyone joining me. There were a couple of washrooms in this corridor, so I had an excuse to be here if I got seen. There was also a light switch, so I doused the lights, the total darkness suiting me.

I got lucky. Hal had been taken somewhere beyond—a room I guessed—and I heard its door close. I couldn't hear the voices clearly. After a few minutes they stopped. I took out one of my smaller knives and cut into the wallpaper, peeling it back from the slit. It revealed wood panelling, cheap stuff, probably temporarily run up just for the night's entertainment. It was easy to prize two panels slightly open and cut an eye-hole. Light beamed in from the room beyond. I got lucky again—I'd made enough of a hole to get a good view of the room, which wasn't much of a size. Hal was sitting on a low bench, looking pretty glum, but he'd been left on his own, at least for a time. I decided to be the action man and was about to tap on the panel, when his head jerked up and the door to the room re-opened.

The two plug-uglies who came in looked like bull gorillas on steroids and Hal leaned as far back on his bench as he could. A third figure entered. Carmella Cadenza, in all her finery, now a superb scarlet and orange dress that looked like it was ablaze. Those high heels certainly made her tall. I saw the masked face and from this close, the eyes, which were a curious yellow-green. They fixed Hal the way a snake must fix its next meal.

"Well, well," she purred. Not a snake, then. A big cat. Probably as bad, if not worse. From Hal's expression, he sure felt that way. "The celebrated artist, Hal Drewster. Nice of you to accept the invitation to join my little *soiree*." I could see that her steely voice was grating along Hal's nerves like a stiletto along a piano wire.

"My pleasure," he said, though he didn't get up. "I wasn't expecting special treatment, though."

"Oh, yes," said Carmella, her long, pink tongue licking her lips so that I could see a fine set of teeth, partially coated in lipstick that looked disturbingly like blood. "The very *best* treatment, Hal. Or should I say, Japetus? You've been a very naughty boy."

"I think you're getting me confused with someone else. I'm just a crummy artist, ma'am—"

"You're far too modest. There's nothing crummy about your work. Your early work—all those *lovely* pulp covers—was one thing. But your new career, ah, that's an altogether different proposition, wouldn't you say?"

Hal was about to protest, but Carmella's voice changed, hardening and hitting him like a slap. "Don't waste any more of my time! *I know what you are*. I know what you do, Japetus. You paint demons and trap them in your accursed paintings! Among your victims are more than a few of my *friends*. I may not be able to release them, but at least I can put a stop to your infernal meddling in our affairs. Don't deny that you are here for one reason—to get a good look at my face so that you can scuttle away to your grubby little retreat and reproduce my exact likeness. You do have that skill. And in painting me, you would render my powers impotent!"

Hal shrugged. There didn't seem a whole lot of point arguing. It explained a lot to me. I had known all along there was something bothering the little guy.

"Well, your number's up," Carmella went on. "You can stew on this for a while—tonight, at the grand lynching ceremony, you'll be our Little Louis, the newspaper seller. You'll be hung like all the other victims of the High-Heeled Hangman. Only in your case, it'll be for real. An accident, a *ghastly* mistake. There'll be a few legal recriminations, but I'll take care of that."

Hal tried to look calm, but he wasn't doing a very good job of it. "Don't suppose you'd grant the condemned man a last request?"

She bristled, but then relaxed. "I'm not inclined to generosity. Especially with someone like you, who has been responsible for some intolerable *interference*."

"It's a very simple request, ma'am."

"What is it?" she said through gritted teeth. I could feel my watching eye filling up with water, it had become that cold.

"Let me see the face I would have painted. Let me look upon beauty—real beauty—one last time."

Her lips curved in a smile. "For goodness' sake, Drewster, you don't think you're going to escape from this mess, do you? You're not harbouring some *ludicrous* plan to evade your fate and wriggle off into the desert, are you? Even if you did, there's nothing out there. Nowhere to go."

"No, of course not. I understand the hopelessness of my situation. Which is why I'd like to see you. What better final image for me to take to my grave?"

"Is this how you charm all your female victims? Very well." Carmella turned to her two henchmen. "Turn to face the wall," she told them. "And you, Drewster, don't try anything funny. We can always snap your arms and legs right now."

The thugs did as asked and Carmella slowly undid the strings holding her mask in place. I have to say, her face was amazing, exquisitely beautiful, classic, perfect skin, proportions and so on and so on. This was a world class face, which belonged on the covers of all the top magazines, in movies, you name it. I drew back, slightly stunned.

When I looked again, Carmella had put her mask back in place. Hal was nodding. "Thank you," he said. "You are indeed the fairest of them all. Snow White wouldn't get a look in."

"I'm glad you've retained your sense of humour. I'll leave you now. Make your peace with the world. My colleagues will be back to prepare you before you know it." At that she left, taking the two monsters with her and Hal slumped back on to his bench. Clearly, he didn't have an escape plan.

I, on the other hand, did. This time I did tap on the panelling. At first Hal didn't respond. Then he looked up, realised someone was tapping, and came over. When he was close to where I was, I spoke to him.

"It's me—Nick. You look like you need a hand."

"Things just got bad," he said. "Those bozos will be back very soon. You better scram, Nick. If they get hold of you, they'll string you up for real as well as me."

"To hell with that, buddy. Step back a few paces. This wall may look solid, but it's as thin as paper. I'll make this quick."

He did as I asked and I put my shoulder to the wall. It disintegrated and I almost tumbled into the room. The panelling hadn't been designed to take an onslaught from me in rhino mode. Hal grinned at me as I dusted myself down. I shoved him through the hole I'd made, not bothering to try and affect any repairs that might have disguised our exit.

Back in the corridor, on my side, we went further into the building. I didn't think it would be the smartest of moves to go back to the bar and the dance hall. I flicked on another light switch and we were in a small maze of corridors—nothing for it but to chance our arm and try one of them. A few doors ran off it, mostly cupboards, empty spaces, but one led to the outside. There was a yard, with a wooden gate at its far end.

We slipped across in the darkness. The gate had a lock, but it was easy enough to rip a couple of the gate slats apart and pull the door open. Outside we skirted the buildings, still in almost complete darkness. We found a lean-to that looked like it would be an okay place to hole up briefly while we figured out our next move, so we crowded in and pulled the door to.

"We won't have much time," Hal said. "Once they know I'm free they'll set the whole pack of hounds to hunting me down."

"That was a smart move," I said. "Last request. So now you can paint Carmella, accurately, and presto, she's lost her powers."

"Yeah. I have a photographic memory. I have every last inch of that face locked in here." He tapped his head.

"Well, buddy, if you get forgetful, don't worry. It's not a face *I'm* gonna forget for a long time. Who the hell is she?"

"She has some very dark powers, like she's some kind of demon. I didn't know such things existed, until I was recruited by a certain group dedicated to fighting them. There are different ways to neutralise them. I paint them and it seems to do the trick."

"Glad to hear it. If Carmella gets a hold of us now, we'll be dangling at the end of a rope, side by side. I don't think there's any point making a run for the desert. My guess is, there's nothing out there—limbo. The only way out of this mess is to get back on that train and somehow lie low until it pulls out in the morning."

"I agree. There is one problem, though, Nick."

I couldn't see his face clearly in the darkness, but my guess was that if I had it would have looked pained. "Do I want to know this?"

"I can go back to my studio and paint her, no problem. But I have to use a special type of paint to do it. I use all kinds of ingredients, mostly organic. It's a very old process. I have all those ingredients. Except one."

I could have taken a good guess what it was.

"Her blood, Nick. I need at least a phial of her blood."

* * * *

I knew there was no point in trying to find our way back home unless we had Hal's pound of flesh with us, metaphorically speaking. Without it we'd be tracked down for certain and cornered like rats in a trap. Our one hope was that Carmella and her cronies didn't know Hal had had help breaking out. So I told him he needed to become invisible and leave the dirty work to me. Not that I was bristling with confidence. I didn't rate my chances highly, though I didn't say so. Instead I left him to search out someplace where he might just avoid detection for the rest of the night, preferably somewhere near the loco and went looking for our hostess. Hal gave me a small phial, in the hope that I would fill it with the necessary blood.

I looked at my watch: just after 2.30 am. With any luck the massed guests would be crammed into the main dance hall, eagerly awaiting the culmination of the ceremonies. I figured they couldn't start without Hal, so I was going to have to make good use of the time. I didn't have much of a plan, seeing how this had all been dumped on me out of the blue. There was no time to grumble about it. I checked the buildings in the darkness and saw a way back in, high at the top of a rusted iron fire escape—a window that looked like a firm elbow would open it.

I went up to a precarious landing and used my thick robe to cover the window panes as I cracked them, making as little noise as possible. Once I was inside, I had to move around by feeling my way. I was in an empty room and it was easy enough to find its door. It wasn't locked, so I edged it open. There was a faint glow in the corridor beyond, so mercifully I could see my way around. Faint strains of music came up from somewhere below. I took out a gun and nosed forward like a cat on its night rounds. At the end of a landing there were stairs winding down, so I pushed on, the light growing.

This seemed to be a part of the huge building complex that hadn't been used in a long time, dusty and web-strewn. I wasn't expecting to find Carmella here, so I kept going down the various old flights of stairs. They seemed endless and I was getting concerned that I might end up going round in circles, like I was trapped in a goddam maze, when I had another stroke of luck. There was a wider landing below me, with a balcony that was high up over the ballroom. A loud babble of noise rose from the depths as the crowd waited for some action down there.

On the landing I could see a solitary guard, dressed in the ubiquitous burgundy livery, standing outside a door, arms folded, face a bored mask. It was tip-toe time. My guess was, the boss lady was beyond that door, waiting for news of Hal's inevitable capture. I slid along the wall, an invisible shadow. The guard yawned once or twice. It must have been long past his bed time. When I reached him and jammed the Beretta into his ribs, he gasped like he'd been ducked in cold water, but one look into my eyes and he knew to keep his mouth shut.

"Where's Carmella?" I whispered.

"What are you, some kind of maniac?" he said, just as quietly, acutely conscious of the gun in his ribs. I jabbed a bit harder. "She's in there, but—"

"Who else?"

"Some of the guys. Three of 'em."

"Open the door, nice and slow. I'm not fussy about whose head I blow off," I told him, favouring him with the kind of glare that would have scattered a field of crows.

He didn't have the stomach for a philosophical debate and did as I asked, pushing the door open slowly. I nudged him in, keeping his body as a shield—he was a big guy, so I was mostly hidden behind him as I pulled the door shut.

"I told you I was *not* to be disturbed!" said Carmella, her voice a lash. She was still dressed in her figure-hugging scarlet and orange dress, and wore the mask that covered her upper face.

I peeped out from behind my human shield. "I didn't get that message," I said, pointing the gun directly at her.

The three tough guys who were with her—more of the burgundy brigade—all went for their own guns like fired up gunslingers. I didn't think this was a time for niceties, so I let them all have it, dropping the three of them like sacks. I consoled myself in the knowledge that they all died quickly.

Carmella gaped, her mouth a wide 'o' under her mask. I felt the guard in front of me tense, so I gave him a neat clip on the temple that put him out double fast. He sank down and decorated the carpet in one flowing movement. I walked forward towards Carmella.

She was glaring at me as though her eyes would reduce me to a pile of ashes, and maybe if I'd let her carry on they would have done. I stepped closer and she drew back towards a table behind her, one hand reaching out towards what I guessed must be a button or an alarm. I fired off another round and it shattered the tall table lamp behind her arm, pretty green glass spraying in all directions.

"Damn you!" she snarled, snatching her arm back and shaking it as if it had been burned by oil from the lamp. She pulled back a sleeve, revealing one long, slender arm and I saw what had happened—some of the glass had ripped her flesh. And—hey, this was handy—it had drawn blood. Someone was watching over me tonight.

"I normally draw the line at brainless goons when I'm shooting people," I told her. "But tonight I'm in a mood, lady. You do what I tell you, or the next bullet will be all yours."

"Who are you? What do you want?"

"Me? I'm a vampire, ma'am. All I want is a little blood."

She may have been wearing a mask, but she knew exactly what it would mean if she gave me what I wanted. It would be like handing over her soul, assuming she possessed such a thing.

I took out Hal's phial. "Here, fill this. If you do, I'll think about letting you keep that pretty head on your shoulders. No tricks, lady. I can just as easily drop you and collect the blood while it's still warm."

"Whoever's paying you can't give you what I can. Screw them and work for me. You have no *idea* what that would mean, believe me."

"Oh, I have a real good imagination. Come on, let's do this." I tossed her the phial and she almost caught it, deliberately letting it slip so that it bounced on the carpet. She bent down, trying to play things casually and I was ready to put a bullet in her—not to kill her, I really didn't like shooting dames, even the really nasty ones, just to wing her to show I meant business—but she was a crafty one. She must have hit something because I felt the floor heave under me. I lurched forward as the carpet gave way and I fired up at the ceiling. I was only a foot or two from her, but I was going to fall. I made a grab for her as she laughed. My fingers caught at her sleeve and I felt it tear, ripping away a chunk of orange material as I fell.

I landed hard, maybe six feet below, in another room. Before I could fire a further shot up at Carmella's snarling face, the trap she had opened closed again. I was in darkness. Instinctively I rolled up the material I'd grabbed and stuffed it in my pocket. I groped around for a door, found one, and opened it slowly. I was on another balcony, just under the main one overhead and the orchestra was somewhere below. Quickly I made a break for it, unnoticed by the guests. They were getting pretty rowdy now. I guessed the proceedings were behind schedule and folks were getting impatient.

As I left the balcony, I heard a shriek from above me. Carmella was rallying the troops and I was a hunted man. Every servant she had would be after me now. I decided I'd stand a better chance of getting away, at least for a time, if I headed back up for the roofs. The whole building down below would be seething with people eager to join in the ruckus and once the guests all got the scent of blood, there'd be no holding them.

Back outside in near total darkness—the clouds had piled in—I scrambled across the roofs until I found another fire escape and went down it as fast as I could without slipping and falling to an early grave. I wove my way through a few sheds and across railroad tracks and fetched up beside a bigger wooden shed that looked like it might be the terminus for the locomotive. From my hiding place I was able to look back at the main buildings. Light was streaming from a score of windows on all levels and I could hear shouts, screams and general hubbub.

I edged along the outer wall of the big shed until I reached its open doors. The loco that had brought us here, *Smokestack Lightning*, had been uncoupled and put inside. It was silent now, its furnace damped down, a few faint wisps of steam drifting around wheels that were above head-height. Its carriages stretched away along the track into the darkness, unlit and silent, although I could hear something right down at their end, voices and the clank of steel tools.

"Nick," said a voice behind me and I swung round, Beretta ready to blow the first assailant into the Great Beyond. It was Hal.

"We got a problem," I told him. "The loco isn't ready to haul us out of here. We've got no more than a few minutes before Carmella's goons figure we're not in the building. This is the next place they'll look."

"It's okay. There's another loco at the other end, facing home. All we got to do is hijack it."

I looked at him. "Is that all? You know how to drive one of these things?"

"No. I was thinking we could persuade the engineer to do that for us. That is, you could, with one of your irons. Did you get the phial?"

"I dropped it." Even in the poor light I could see the look of horror on his face.

"You what! Hell, without it, we're sunk. Carmella will find us and we'll be like two fish in a barrel."

"This any good?" I said, pulling out the ripped sleeve of Carmella's dress. I gave it to him.

"It'll help. Not the same as—but it's soaking."

"It's her blood. I nicked her and she used her sleeve to mop it up."

"Yes!" he said, his eyes widening. "Even if it dries out by the time we're home, it will be perfect." Obviously I'd made his night.

"Move your ass, then." I used the darkness again to shield us as we headed on down to the front loco. We ducked back as a mechanic suddenly appeared, but then headed across the tracks to another small shed, whistling casually, so I knew we hadn't been seen. The other guy was up in the driver's cab and we heard the unmistakable sound of him shovelling coal. Lamplight shone down from above. I whispered instructions to Hal and slid between the loco and the first carriage to the other side. I noticed that the carriages hadn't been coupled yet, which suited me fine.

I'd told Hal to shin up the steel ladder to the cab and grab the driver's attention. In the meantime, I went up the ladder on the other side. I heard voices arguing as I swung into the cab. The driver turned to face me, eyes bulging as he saw the Beretta directed at his chest.

"What in tarnation is going on?" he snarled, both hands clutching a long shovel as if he would use it to scythe me and Hal in half. His sleeves were rolled up, his arms gleaming with bunched muscles that would have put Mr Universe to shame.

"The next train will be leaving immediately," I told him, waving the gun.

"You kill me, mister, and you won't be taking this train anywhere."

"I wasn't thinking of killing you, pal. I thought maybe a shattered elbow, or a kneecap, or maybe I could just blow one of your feet off." I directed the gun downward. "So let's get this show on the road."

He nodded towards the boiler. I could see that the furnace was lit, coals glowing, but it didn't have a lot of strength. "You'll need to load up with plenty of coal before we can get moving."

"So get loading. Hal, there's a spare shovel. Give him a hand."

Hal grimaced, but set to. I kept one eye on the two of them as they shovelled more and more coal into the boiler and I kept the other eye on the depot around us. There was still no sign of pursuit, but the second mechanic was coming back, wielding a spanner the size of a sledgehammer. He seemed to be preoccupied with another part of the loco, so I let him get on with it.

When I heard what sounded like a mob finally coming across the yard, I guessed it was time to make the break for it. "Okay, let's move."

"I need the pressure up," said the driver, squinting at the gauge.

I put my gun close to his temple. "How much pressure do you need, pal? Get going," I shouted. The boiler was roaring by now, the heat almost overpowering. I waved the gun again and the driver threw down his shovel, swore a few times and started to pull levers and lift handles. Hal sat down on the heap of coal in the tender, face blackened, sweat dripping off him.

The loco shuddered and came to life. There were instant shouts from below, but we began to move. It wasn't long before the huge beast gathered some momentum. My guess was, without having to haul all those carriages it would accelerate quickly. I was right. In no time we'd left the siding and the howling pursuit and were starting to pick up real pace.

"She'll follow us," Hal shouted to me above the roar.

"How long before the other loco can be ready to follow?" I called to the driver.

He was scowling. "She won't catch us. But Carmella will. You think this is the only way she can travel? Mister, you screwed up real bad when you hijacked this baby. I'll keep her running at full speed for you, but we'll be caught long before we get back to the city. And you won't live to see the dawn."

"You just do your job," I growled, playing it as tough as I could. I turned to Hal and spoke to him quietly. "So if Carmella does catch us up, do you have a plan to keep her off our back until we get home?"

He looked dead beat, panting for breath. The effort of shovelling all that coal had near given him a heart attack. "Sort of. I could use the material. If I burn it and her blood with it, it would cripple her. Enough to hold her up, though she'd recover in time. I reckon she'd forget about subtlety and just come looking for me. Probably have my studio flattened and me with it."

The loco was now moving at top speed, roaring down the straight track like a missile. The driver had made no attempt to screw up our flight, which meant he was confident that it would do us no good. In fact he was grinning, wild eyes facing front. I gave Hal my Beretta, took off my priest's garb and tossed it away. I picked up the spare shovel and began using it, knowing that if I didn't, we'd lose speed.

My muscles were aching and my spine was on the point of cracking when I realised that the driver had been right about Carmella. Eschewing the use of the second loco, she had employed other agents to follow us. I don't know what they were, but they came in fresh clouds of darkness, howling overhead and on either side of us like a storm wind. Faces leered at us from that pitch fog of night, and claws writhed like solid smoke as the demonic minions began to close in. Our driver's grin had widened, as if a bunch of his pals had showed up. Then I got it—he was one of them.

"Hal, you better work your magic," I shouted at him. "They're going to wrap around us and rip us off the rails."

He nodded, dragging the scrap of material from his pocket and holding it up to the skies in his right fist. In his other hand he held a Zippo and he flicked it on, bringing the wavering flame close to the material. Demon eyes, blazing like coals out in the night, fixed on that flame and there were horrific screams and shrieks, as if a whole posse of souls were being mangled and torn. And I saw Carmella's face out there, no longer masked, but no longer beautiful either—it was contorted into a hideous parody of a face, all teeth and snarling lips, the eyes insane with fury.

Hal's mummery was working, though. The black clouds were easing back, taking Carmella's visage with them. They hovered, but no longer threatened to embroil us. Carmella didn't want that blood burned up. So we were in a stalemate, except that the loco kept on roaring ahead. At this rate we would be back in the city long before dawn. Inspired, I found fresh reserves of energy and heaped more coal on the furnace. Hell, and guys did this for a living at one time? I had a new respect for them.

The stand-off held good for the rest of the run, although the black clouds fumed and boiled around us, threatening to close in the moment Hal and I faltered. Hal didn't show any signs of that, though. He just gritted his teeth. When the loco started to slow, I looked through the narrow side window and I could make out the shadowy first buildings of the city up ahead. Our demon driver's grin remained fixed as he pulled his levers and switches. I heard the wheels screeching under us as we got slower and slower. After a while we were coming in under a huge roof, rattling beside a wide, empty platform, one of several. There were a few lights on, but no sign of anyone.

When the train halted, steam hissing noisily from every joint, the driver folded those huge arms and turned his wild grin on us. "That's it, people. Terminus. Time to disembark."

I'd collected my gun and Hal still had a grip on the Zippo and material, but the driver didn't seem inclined to bother us. He just watched as we clambered down on to the deserted platform. As I looked this way and that for some kind of unpleasant reception committee, the loco shuddered into life and started reversing. Minutes later it had become no more than a steam-shrouded blot in the distance. Hal and I were ostensibly alone.

"Let's get outta here," he said.

"I don't think it's going to be that simple," I told him. "She quit too easily. The delectable Carmella isn't going to take this lying down."

We moved on down the platform, weaving in and out of the columns that supported the ancient roof canopy. There seemed to me to be a whole lot more dust and rubble here this time, like this was an *older* version of the place we'd left earlier. I was beginning to smell that familiar stench of rat.

Hal ducked as if something had swooped above him. I looked up to see a few scrawny pigeons in the rafters, but I could hear scratching on the outside of the roof. Lots of it. Carmella's horde had followed us for sure and that's where they'd gathered, maybe for one last attempt to foil our efforts to get home.

"I have a bad feeling about this place," said Hal. "It's not our city. We haven't crossed back at all. She's tricked us. We're trapped. Cut off."

"I get the picture, Hal."

"Time's with her," he said, looking about as glum as it gets. "She can surround us and sit pretty, starve us out. Or wait till we're asleep. All it would take—"

"Give me a break, Hal. I know the score." I wasn't going to stand and wait for the world to end, so I had a look around. The platform opened out on to a wide area, which I took to be dockside. It was partly obscured by fog. We headed for it and realised just how wide—and ex-posed—it was. Sure enough the air—of the foul and filthy kind—buzzed and hummed with Carmella's flying mob and at once the creatures were dive bombing us like demented seagulls. We could feel the slash of their talons mere inches from our heads.

I would have fired a few rounds at them, but I guessed it would be a waste of ammo. Instead I pushed Hal forward and we kept going to-wards the edge of the docks. The fog shifted briefly and we realised we'd gambled recklessly: we were exposed out here on an entirely flat area, wide enough to land a bomber. Several times we had to duck down to avoid more rushes from the aerial creatures, now shrieking and scream-ing, fuelled no doubt by Carmella's indignation.

"Get that piece of dress out!" I shouted to Hal above the din. He did it with shaking hands and flicked on his lighter. That flame seemed very small, fading like a spent match.

We heard things landing in the fog all around us on three sides. Again the murk cleared and exposed a mass of clutching, clawing horrors, tooth and claw, closing in. This time I did loose off a round: it tore ineffectively through the ranks of Carmella's demonic thugs. They'd not taken on solid form—yet. My guess was, we were safe until they did—up to a point.

"Maybe this will repel them," said Hal, tugging something out of his coat and passing it over. It was a crucifix, more brass than silver. I don't have much faith in such things, but I held it up and snarled my best snarl. Something swooped down and I felt the crucifix snatched from my grip. Three aerial demons had a hold of it and began attacking it with fang and claw. In no time they had reduced it to a tangled mess and flung it aside, where it melted into a thick, bubbling globule.

"That could have gone better," I said to Hal. By now we'd backed up right to the river side. Looking across that version of the Hudson, its surface writhing with more pale fog, I could barely make out a city skyline on the far shore, but there were no lights there, as if the place was as abandoned as this crumbling station. Carmella's rabble closed in, on the ground and above us, like vultures around a dying victim—or two. If there was a gate back to our own version of New York, I had no idea where it was, nor did I have a key.

All we had left to try for was a plunge into those repellent waters. As I looked, they rippled. Whatever swam beneath the surface was not a draught of salmon, that was for sure. The closing nightmares made up our minds for us—we were going to have to jump. Hal's face was aghast. On another day I might have laughed.

"Ahoy there!" A faint voice drifted out from across the river. Something emerged from the fog.

"Now there's a thing," I breathed, relieved. "I do believe it's Friendly Fred."

I was right—the Ferryman was rowing steadily towards the quay in his familiar, low craft. Presently he roped it up to an iron ring at the foot of a set of stone steps I'd not noticed—and grinned up at us, his face clearly not that of a demon. A flaming brand at the stern threw him into brilliant relief—relief being the operative word.

"Took me a while to find you guys," he said. "You must've slipped a few tracks. What happened? "

"Yeah," I said, waving Hal down the steps ahead of me. I could hear various uncouth noises behind us as the demonic swarm cottoned on. Darkness threatened to surge in over us in a wave. Hal and I tumbled into the craft. Fred got the picture and stepped lively, to use a nautical term, rowing like blazes so we were out on the water in no time.

Once again, Hal held aloft the piece of Carmella's torn dress and the Zippo, which did the trick in holding back the swirling fog, now choked with snarling faces and slashing talons. The worst of them had solidified, so I wasted no time in spraying lead, bringing down several. They smashed into the water and at once were embroiled in chaos, like a score of crocodiles had come to join the fun. I thought I could hear thunder somewhere and the wind was getting up, rippling the water around us. If Hal and I had gone into it off the dockside, whatever was in there would right now be inflicting some very nasty things upon our hapless carcasses.

I heard one God-awful shriek, long and tormented. That, I told myself, had the ring of a woman seriously scorned.

Fred, undeterred, took us across the river like this was a sunny afternoon in Central Park. As we moved, the mist wrapped us, cold but for once welcome, shutting off the unspeakable things we'd left behind. Presently the way ahead lightened and the night cityscape became brighter. We'd crossed. That was *our* New York. Hal sank down, completely drained. I admit I was pretty done in myself.

"So—was it a good party?" said Fred.

"Sure—the dance of a lifetime."

* * * *

"What d'ya think?"

Hal stepped back from the painting. We were in his private retreat, an underground apartment converted from a section of a disused Metro station. One side of the high, curving wall was a long frieze, dozens of brightly coloured figures, full-on portraits. The latest addition to this dazzling display was that of Carmella Cadenza, *sans* mask. Hal had reproduced her face superbly. He really did have a photographic memory. He'd caught every detail. And, yeah, it was beautiful. Those eyes—man, they were alive! Boring into us with frustration and fury.

"I have to hand it to you, pal," I said. "You've captured her—literally."

He'd wasted no time when we got back to his place, mixing a whole lot of ingredients to form his paints and pigments, whatever. He'd soaked the material from the dress and squeezed every last drop of blood out of it. Weird, but it had done the trick.

"So all these figures were demons?" I said.

"Sure. Once they're done, their host bodies become plain old mortals again, without any power. Carmella will never forgive me, but she'll be okay. She'll just go back to the normal world. I'm sure she'll do fine. A woman with her looks. In time, these paintings will fade away to nothing. You can see that the first ones I did are almost gone. Like boxers, they don't come back."

"Well, that's heartening. What's less encouraging is there are still a few things about this whole business that puzzle me."

He started washing his brushes and whistling nonchalantly, apparently not listening.

"For instance," I went on, "I'm still mystified as to how I came to get a ticket to that party. It wasn't Carmella—she'd never heard of me before. It was you she was after. Somehow, I reckon the invite I got was meant for me and not just any sucker that opened that book. You wouldn't know anything about that?"

"Maybe it was destiny."

"Like hell it was. Listen, I like to be paid for my services."

He looked up at me, a hint of panic in his expression. "Yeah, seems fair."

"Here's the deal. You tell me the truth and that'll be enough. No recriminations."

He thought about it for a while, then shrugged. "Okay. Well, the fact is, Artavian got the book from me. I got it from a friend. I knew Artavian was after it and when I learned he wanted it for Nick Nightmare, Private Eye, Public Fist, I slipped that note into the book so's you'd find it. I figured you'd want to go to that party. I needed your help. And it worked out okay."

"I figured something like that. Why didn't you just call in at my office and come straight out with it?"

"You coulda said no. Hell, Nick, it was a pretty tough call, heading out there into limbo, looking to get hold of a phial of demon blood. The chances of pulling it off were not good. So—would you have refused?"

I looked up at the glaring features of Carmella Cadenza. Some guys would do anything for a woman like that. "We'll never know, pal. We'll never know."

A Cure for Unrequited Love
by Donald W. Schank

On a cushioned bed of furs—miniver and snow-leopard, ocelot and liger, and others more strange, with names known only to the savages that hunt them in faraway unnamed wildernesses of the empire's edges—the Crown Prince lies indolent, lost in reveries of mixed ennui and unrequited love. Unable—or unwilling—to move, to make the slightest of efforts on his own behalf, he vaguely allows the painted houris that anxiously attend him to look to his needs, only sighing in melancholia as they ply him with exotic morsels from foreign lands—sparrow's tongues honeyed and candied; the chopped livers of mythic beasts steeped in the phosphorescent wines of the far north and blended with the most delicate spices of the far southern seas; the vinegared loins of giraffe and triple-horned antelope; monkeys restrained, their skulls swan open and brains served living and blood-warm—and all go untasted. Carved crystal goblets—chilled with snow ice from far blue mountains, or warmed between slavegirls thighs, filled with golden mead made from the honey of queen bees, wines of all tastes and hues from blood-red to sea-green to sky-blue, the fermented milk of virgin priestesses—all are proffered and ignored with dispirited sighs and averted eyes.

The Empress, mother to the prince, sits in vain hope at his bedside, a mother's love tearful in her eyes, listens to his cherished whispered rantings, and understands all. Many a young man is a fool and bestows his love where there is no love to return, and the prince has fallen into that indiscretion. He loves a courtesan, a woman who plays him like a gold-thread-strung lute—each assignation carried with it a greater cost and a lesser fulfillment, plays on the frustrated infatuation of the prince. Coin and jewels, pearls and objects of superb workmanship, have flowed into her grasp, and with each passing assignation the payment is greater and the recompense lesser—and the pain of her son has grown greater with time and lessening resources.

She heard with love and compassion his murmured ramblings, always centered on "her eyes", the endless beauty of her eyes, lost voyagings into the depths of her eyes. And as the days passed and her son's fevered cries continued in torment she made up her mind and called to her most trusted servants and instructed them with a mother's love.

And her servants go forth to the gilded apartments of the courtesan, carrying with them in velvet cases spoons and knives of precious crystal, carven and diamond-dust-honed in their edges and curves to the sharpness of broken obsidian-glass, and they carry out their mission with all precision and exactness.

Within days they return, bringing with them two soft leather bags— each meticulously tanned with the nervous care of the artist who both prizes his work and dreads its commissioner.

With the delicacy and fervor of a mother's love the Empress presents to her sorrowing son the bags—barely the thickness of Egyptian linen, fashioned from the courtesan's severed breasts—each within its secret

depths held one of the courtesan's eyes, carefully crystallized and preserved like candied fruit.

The prince welcomed his present, awoke from his ennui, and ever
after looked into his beloved's eyes, held them in his hands whenever he
felt the need, and ruled well.

The Owl
by S. L. Edwards

Ebony darkness of nature puddled up in fog at the window,
The closeness of the muddled black madness silently sat low,
The melody of a thousand scraping branches screeched
Across the shadows of skeleton limbs that breeched
Upon the grey floor on which only coffin-dust sat
Pock-marked with the footprints of some hellish rat.

No stars made themselves apparent that dismal night
The moon, in ultimate cowardice, tucked away its light.
Only the faint illumination of some nightmare-yellow lamp
Painted the skies with clouds orange, putrid and damp.
I sat on my bed, bones too frail to shudder
But paralyzed with loneliness under my cover.

The sounds of some bleating monster honked and growled
Whilst little vampires in trash cans romped and yowled.
The bleating of some gigantic bat against the polluted sky
Heart beating, I felt that I soon would lie down to die.
I closed my eyes in these primordial fears
Crystallized in the excess of so many tears.

They told me this new world was a fortress temple.
Electric lights flickered, cackled, and wriggled
In knowledge that they were the harbingers of dawn,
That old, solemn night was no more, now not so long.
Their fizzing sputters were a million flutters
As old demons sat out along rusted gutters.

I was warm, that much I could safely agree
But my dear family had gone and left me.
And while I sat alone in that cursed house
All of my old horrors went darting about.
Things that could not be, heralds of old.
Eyes peering out of that closet hole.

The door was ajar as an unguarded gate,
That closet door which lay open to fate
The roof was against the attic, cold and dark realms
To which all vermin ascends and mold overwhelms.
The hole in the closet roof is a portal
Through which depart souls mortal.

The hole was black and hollow with unknown lights
The embodiment of nearly all my frights
Behind which sometimes a hand would move free
Causing grievance while my family would sooth me.
Eventually calm, I would succumb to slumbering,
Only to be awoken by some dead thing above me.

A clunk and shudder woke me from my night-day dreams,
As from behind the attic hole came terrible, tortured screams.
My neck cracked and shivered with popping alarms,
As I rose up in of bed to cross my old-withered arms
Against whatever creature might lurk around
In that attic's unholy, corpse catacomb ground.

There was the swift scraping of a curved reptilian claw,
A shadow darker yet passed in along attic's open maw.
Then came breathing, low, murky, heavy and grating
I closed my eyes, ready for whatever ghoul to take me.
Two orange-yellow orbs shined out,
My lungs expanded for one final shout.

...

All my sounds came out in one gasp and then after
Only a coughing, searing, clawing, painful laughter.
Where my nightmares once stalked
Only a fluffed-brown owl clumsily walked
Above my closet space he cooed
Asking meekly, "Who? Who?"

"Dear Owl," I replied, "I am but a meager old wretch
Surely not the mouse or rabbit you sought out to fetch.
If not for my severe age, I would give you bread
But, as you can see I am buried deep in this bed.
I apologize, dearest owl, do not be sad,
After all, life for an owl cannot be so bad."

The creature had a familiar air, like the owls of yesteryear,
From my childhood over there, a place far from here.
The owl shook his head as if to frankly disagree,
With a thunderous flutter he flew to my bed to see
If indeed I was the creature that he was here for.
Then, with a bone-rotting cry he turned to the closet door.

I covered my ears at its jubilation, and in a hot crying terror
I shouted that this hallucination was more than I cared for.
Wrenching my hand free from my ear, I grabbed a clock
Which I threw against the owl, hitting it with a loud knock.
The owl landed on the floor with a stupor
And I prayed the unseemly episode was done for.

And yet the screams were continual sounds,
And from the attic, those plutonian bounds
An answer came, lonely and distant at first
But as more replied, their crying got worse.
The eyes above my closet, doubled and grew
While across my room, more owls darted and flew.

The room smelt of animal carcass and decay
While the screams and coos slowly gave way.
The coos became chiming, as I heard a loud, churning bell.
And I knew then these creatures were heralds of hell.
I begged and I pleaded desperately for more time
And explained that I was not guilty of many a crime.

To my pleas the owls simply continued chiming
Turning their heads about in unsettling timing.
The room faded out as all death-harbingers took flight
And in the fluttering brown-blackness devoured all light.
I, for my part gave up my ceaseless screaming
And reluctantly set my mind to dreaming.

The darkness became light, all things made clear
My eyes were dry by then, without a single tear
All felt right, and as I spread my thought,
I comprehended what the owls had wrought.
I nodded and cooed, their beaks took me to the sky
As little by little, I accepted to die.

Then with a flutter I turned my new head about
And with a coo and a who, I saw my way out.
I took flight from my bed into the that lightened attic gate
To wait upon more souls to which to bring their fate.
With flaps and shudders one day I will come for you
To simply ask you only one question: "Who? Who?"

Bathory in Red

by Ashley Dioses

Her reddened fingertips embed
Themselves in flesh of dames.
Her reddened tongue has licked and bled
Dry nobles; doused like flames.

Her reddened lips have sucked and kissed
And tasted the life out
Of peasants not so sorely missed.
Their blood pours like a spout.

As pale as moons, her aging skin
Is reddened by slit throats
And gaping, ever gaping grins.
In baths of blood, she gloats.

Blood Siren's Alcove
by Ashley Dioses

The scarlet-painted scallops lined the walls
Anear dead sailors lured there by her calls.
The walls of bone and abalone formed
Her sunken alcove, whose dark chamber swarmed
With merfolk freshly killed, and human fools.
Their blood ensanguined angel-wings and jewels
From pearl-creating oysters, bits of shell.
When tides recede, her pool's a bloody well,
And she awaits the next providing wave
That brings new sailors near her song. They crave
The lovely courtship she implies, and yet
Their quick arrival they too soon regret.

Woodland Funeral
by K.A. Opperman

My love lay dead upon her marble bier,
Amid the autumn forest red and sere,
Through which a wind of whispering spirits roamed.
It seemed a mourning sprite it was that combed
The crimson bough above her raven mane,
All flowing wide like some dark queen's black train,
To rain upon her hair an autumn crown—
A diadem of almandines. Her gown
Glowed ghostly white beneath the Huntress Moon,
Which like a silver mirror shared the swoon
Of death upon her fair, pale face, and lent
The starry luster of the firmament
To her dead eyes, which seemed alive with light,
Although they stared from out the utter night.
And as I bent to kiss her purple lips—
Perchance to drown my grief in the eclipse
Of one last passion—all the woodland ghouls
Began to howl and mourn their queen, who rules
Forevermore in perfect, pallid death,
With perfumed whispers on corruptless breath.

The Lady in Scarlet

by K.A. Opperman

The Lady in Scarlet
That castle does haunt,
A raven-haired deviless fair,
Dressed red as a harlot,
Who often does flaunt
Her charms from a balcony there.

Her delicate cincture
With diamonds adorned
Her fingers are fain to untie....
Her silks of the tincture
Of blood are soon scorned,
To slip down white shoulder and thigh....

O look not upon her
Pale flesh, her fair form
That puts even Lilit to shame!—
Who looks is a goner,
Entranced as a swarm
Of rose-vines come slowly to claim.

The days are as hours
To those she enthralls,
Who sleepily reach for their queen....
Enfettered in flowers,
No skeleton falls,
Caught ever in crimson and green.

The Ghost Carriage
by K.A. Opperman

A ghostly carriage rides down lonely roads
On winter nights like these,
When whippoorwills and owls and witch's toads
Sing mournful symphonies.

A pair of sable stallions pulls the car,
But driver there is none,
And through the wine-red drapes that parted are,
There peers a skeleton.

O there is room for one more passenger
Upon this haunted ride—
So seems to say the grinning messenger
From out the carriage-side.

When you are weary, lost, and wandering
One twilight long from now,
Perchance again you will be pondering
That car, with sorrowed brow.

Hymn to Shub-Niggurath
by Darrell Schweitzer

Hail black goat of a thousand young!
Shub-Niggurath!
Great one from whom are nightmares sprung!
Shub-Niggurath!
Vile fruit of her cosmic womb,
wriggling as from out a tomb,
heralds of all mankind's doom!
Ia! Ia! Ia Shub-Niggurath!

Hail mother of madness and of death!
Shub-Niggurath!
We name you with our final breath!
Shub-Niggurath!
Scream for all our gibbering's worth!
Celebrate the noxious birth!
Countless spawn will claim the Earth!
Ia! Ia! Ia Shub-Niggurath!

—*Darrell Schweitzer*

(Melody: "Salve Regina" a.k.a. "Hail Holy Queen Enthroned Above")

For Clark Ashton Smith—

Noctuary of Sfatlicllp
by Frederick J. Mayer

"Chapter: Hieros Gamos"
(Translated by Chrisophe des Laurieres* & Transcribed by Frederick J. Mayer)

Les petites morts more
for La Femme Fatale
Madness of the Soul
sole deathly love shall
Entrall warp Rapture
capture passions all.
Cadavere females
assail this skin sense
Metempsychois
kiss so putrescence
Fall to necRomance
prance for your dance ball.
Pas de Duex eros
both insane profane
Marriage tandem fare
therein fleshy fane
Ball, egg, shell, Beastly
transmigration call.

Fin de siecle world
whorl alchemical
Metastaized bliss
this blood conjugal
Pall jouissance bled
bed cancer sex mall.
Un etre altere
where corrupt coitus
Massa damnata
a sin consumes us
Stall for human play
say goddess Nightfall.

*Note: This is the nomme de plume that Clark Ashton Smith used when he wrote poetry in French.

Sfatliclip's Ghoul*
by Frederick J. Mayer

Beyond a red vixen mask it
slips
open pachychilla
of nymphonecrotic nullipara
and erotical amatory,
amative plus amorous
amorphous Lady—
from Her nymphec came nugma.
This is the kiss,
the nyxis
of ghoulish succubus,
lips
upon a bed family casket.

*Clark Ashton Smith's unfinished tale "Offspring Of The Grave" is the source for this poem's inspiration, hence, this piece is also my small homage to C.A.S.

"In Memory of Clark Ashton Smith"

Nile Lamia Recalls*

by Frederick J. Mayer

"Old Egypt's gods…revealed were as the levin's fire and heat…sate the gods outcasts of time." THE RETRIBUTION, C.A. Smith

Cat house, House of Felines
Mistress of this mansion, Hathor;
lenocinant Sekhmet-Min
with rigor mortis erect phallus and flail,
invites all leonine lovers and lemans in
through supranatural supernatural
membrane door
portal cerulean
putrescent orfice:
Entrance guardian licentious Bes
draped in panther fur and skin
long and flowing tongue protruding
of this half-lion mask of a face living divine,
offers Sopdet's sahu in Akhu within
the pleasures of a sycamore bed
just a scent and a taste
of your pheromones
His asking price…
Outside evening Nuit's metaphonic blue
skin and supple heaving rhythm; inside
A dark-adapting eye of Ra
leans down seething corridor
to your lustful bone sarcophagus door
opening
Bastet with red cracked rubian
unbroken
cherry eyes await on mammaceous
hair lined cushions sublimate hideous
fears whirling
splurge bright goddess of Sun
and such at
night's nobleness
Ithyphallic Min hand of ejaculation
of cosmos Nun & Naunet crimson and primordial abyss
carotid, arteries, jugular miasma
Sates' inundation, flames hidden one
Bata

gender gentials sweating Amaunet
Hathor
as called by Greeks
Aphrodite
sexual acts Beset's rumped, thumped
seeping corrupt sensuous
sumptuous
flesh and more
theriomorphic-anthrapomorphic
and sinful you wrapped wound in sheets
of funeral drum parched skin beating
design
patterns, pestilence of souls blood
soaked linens, bloated under garmets
oblation
ignited carnage daisy-chain scorching
Sa Sa Sekhem Sahu, Sa Sa Sekhem
Sa Sa Sekhem Sahu
Sahuu
"I need not know your name,
as I know who I am, hmmm
'make you' human? Make you 'immortal'
feral one?"
felicitous bloody florid fire
witnesses
roar
Sa Sekhem Sahu, Sa
Sa Sekhem Sahu
degenerancy riparian mortal body
blow torched, spread, love is molten
limbs rent hot in susurration
in his, mankind's degenerary
stench, pyre, melting candle-fleshy
incense
surcease in pain seductive
desiccated, drippings droppings
dry ashen ashes Homo or lotus petals
on glutinous
dried
baked mud
and polished sand to glass, stained
reflections
darkly through the risen revealed
in orgy
Sa Sakhem Sahu!
Sekhmet!

* This is my homage to Clark Ashton Smith's extended prose poem/ tale SADASTOR & C.A.S. himself—originally thought of while I stayed in Egypt which Smith was never able to do himself.

Made in the USA
San Bernardino, CA
08 December 2016